PHILLY
BARKER
INVESTIGATES

Also by Joanne Tracey

JOANNE TRACEY

PHILLY BARKER INVESTIGATES

A PHILLY BARKER MYSTERY

First published in Australia in 2022

by Joanne Tracey

https://joannetracey.com

Copyright © Joanne Tracey 2022

Print ISBN 978-0-6450735-7-7

Epub ISBN 978-0-6450735-6-0

Cover design by Enni Tuomisalo of Yummy Book Covers

A catalogue record for this book is available from the National Library of Australia

For Mum –

this one's for you...

Chapter One

'My hammer's up …' Catherine Young, auctioneer and partner in Young and Johnson's of York, cast her practiced eye around the jam-packed room once more, received a nod from her assistant Becky who was monitoring internet bids, and struck her gavel against the rostrum with a resounding thud. 'Sold to Philomena Barker. The next item is lot 203 – a World War Two flight lieutenant's leather kit bag and suitcase. The suitcase has an embossed leather panel with the initials SJEC. I have some early interest in this one and can start the bidding at fifty pounds.'

The breath I'd been holding eased past my lips, my heart settling back into its usual rhythm. I wasn't sure whether it was the thrill of the chase, the burst of excitement at locating something rare and special, or the knowledge that I'd won it at a price low enough to guarantee some profit, but auctions never failed to get the blood racing through my veins. And this was an exceptional piece – a letterbox from a country estate. It didn't sound like much when you said it like that; after all, who gets excited about a letterbox?

This wasn't any old letterbox, though. It was a piece of social history masquerading as an oak box with gleaming brass hardware and a brass escutcheon hiding the keyhole into which, wonder of all wonders, fitted the original key.

Victorian and dating back to the late nineteenth century, it was from a time when the great estates of England hosted house parties that lasted for weeks at a time and when those guests would scribe letters with their fountain pens rather than tap out emails on laptops.

On each side of the box were two vertical pigeonholes, one of which would've held sheets of parchment with the insignia of the house embossed on it; the other would've held the envelopes. Carved wooden spindles separated the pigeonholes and the letterbox itself, with a narrow drawer at the base for telegrams.

If I closed my eyes, images of the ladies of the house, with bustled gowns and ornately decorated overskirts and trains, retiring to the drawing room after the men had left with the guns and the dogs were vivid. Some would read – perhaps *North and South* by Elizabeth Gaskell or even *Vanity Fair* by William Makepeace Thackeray. Some might pick up a novel by one of the Brontë sisters – Charlotte's *Jane Eyre* or Emily's *Wuthering Heights*. More shockingly one may have reached for Anne's *Tenant of Wildfell Hall*. Others would gossip – most probably about similar subjects that ladies today gossiped about – who's in, who's out, and who's sleeping with people they shouldn't be. They'd sew and drink tea, and do all those other things ladies of a certain class were bred to do in that era. They'd also write letters on the special stationery of the house and 'post' them through the brass encased slot on the top of the post box when finished, from whence they'd be collected by a butler entrusted with a key to the box and taken to the post office. The larger or more important the house, the more sought after would be a letter on the stationery from that house. There was no modern equivalent – perhaps a selfie with a celebrity?

That was what I loved best about being a dealer in antiques – the stories. A silver letter clip wasn't just a letter clip – over its lifetime, it had held business deals and long-awaited news from home, tales of love and loss, hellos and goodbyes. That brass Victorian skirt lifter I'd just missed out on purchasing had saved the hems of many a heavy skirt from the dust and mud – and its owner from the frowns that a mud-spattered gown could inspire. It also allowed its wearer the freedom to stride out and perhaps even to play a game of tennis or croquet. The Edwardian silver vesta case that was up next had been responsible for many a warming fire, and the nineteenth-century embroidery sampler I won earlier this afternoon had probably been part of a young girl's glory box and held all her hopes and fears for the future. Every piece that came into my stall was part of social history and told a story. And now this Victorian letterbox would join them.

Not that it was my stall exactly – I was, however, along with another five dealers, co-owner and stallholder in Chipwell Barn Antiques in the village of Chipwell, about twenty-five miles northeast of York. It was one of those villages with a village pub – The Chipwell Arms – a church, a dozen houses and not much else, but it was home to me and Balthazar, my blue roan cocker spaniel.

Gazing around the busy auction room I caught the eye of one of my colleagues, Eugene Ashton. He and his brother Ambrose specialised in military antiques and memorabilia – militaria, they referred to it – and lot 203 was their key drawcard in today's program. Always immaculately turned out, you'd never see one of the brothers dressed for auction day in anything less than a full tweed suit – including waistcoat. Today Ambrose was in a colour that would've allowed him to blend in with the autumnal tones of the moors, while Eugene's ensemble was in shades of pine green. Tomorrow, it could be the opposite. I would've suspected they shared a wardrobe except that Ambrose, who was, at seventy-five, the elder by two years, was portlier than his brother, the brown buttons of his moorland waistcoat straining to remain fastened.

Ambrose's face was set, his wire-rimmed glasses sitting low on his nose as if to peer over the top of them, attention focused on Catherine. As far as I could tell, he hadn't yet raised a finger, and the bidding was between a bearded man in jeans and a black puffa jacket at the back of the room and an older man sitting in the front row.

'Make no mistake, I'm selling at seventy-five pounds …'

said Catherine, and the man in the front row shook his head slightly, as did the man at the back. As she lowered the gavel to her bench, Ambrose lifted his finger.

'New bidder,' Catherine announced.

I ducked between the standing crowd at the back of the room and weaved through rows of chairs (apologising to those whose view I momentarily impeded) to where Eugene stood to watch the rest of the action.

'Sold!' yelled Catherine a couple of bids later, tapping her gavel on the bench and moving onto the next lot.

'A good buy,' I said to Eugene. 'What do you know about it?'

He flattened his grey hair in a gesture of self-satisfaction and said, 'The name and rank – and the fact that he was a Yorkshireman by the name of St John Cunningham.' He pronounced the name *Sin-gin*.

I gave a low whistle. That sort of provenance would add about twenty percent to the price they'd ask for it. 'How do you know that?'

'When we spotted it in the catalogue, Ambrose did some research. Thank goodness for military records,' Eugene said. 'And his son is a client of ours,' he added with the barest of smiles which, for the Ashton brothers, would be a wide beam from anyone else. 'Remember Sir Antony Cunningham? From Chipwell Hall? He comes in every so often to see what's new.'

The first time I met Sir Antony, he was dressed in

brown corduroy pants that looked as though they'd come straight off the (muddy) farm, boots that were in the same state and a flannel shirt where he'd done the buttons up crookedly. He'd popped his head into my stall looking for Ambrose, and we'd got talking about an oatcake drying rack that I'd had on display. When Ambrose walked in and addressed him as 'Your Lordship', I'd nearly choked on the tea I'd been drinking. When they were handing out the airs and graces, they'd skipped Sir Antony.

'Yes, I know him. He's the one you sold that caterpillar club brooch to.' The boys (even though they were both in their seventies, I still referred to them as 'the boys') had found the small gold brooch in a mixed lot box and had explained to me it had been awarded to someone who had been saved by the silk – meaning they'd been ejected from a falling plane and the parachute had saved them. If memory served me correctly, they'd paid ten quid for the box and made four hundred on the brooch.

'Aye, that's the one. That kit bag and suitcase we just bought belonged to his father. He came down in France sometime late in the piece. He left a pregnant wife at home, so young Antony never met his father.'

'How come the Ministry didn't return the bags to his widow?'

'That's where it gets murky. His bags and other belongings were returned to her, but she was consumed by grief –'

I almost laughed out loud at the deadpan expression on Eugene's face so completely at odds with the drama of his words.

'– that she left the management of everything to St John's younger brother, William, who inherited the estate when their father passed away not two years after St John was killed. According to Sir Antony, his uncle quickly got rid of everything that had belonged to St John.'

'Including the wife?' I asked, equally as deadpan.

'No, he married her,' said Ambrose matter-of-factly as he joined us.

A chuckle escaped from behind my hand.

'Well, might you laugh, lass, but William and the widow had no more children, so Sir Antony inherited – and he's been searching for information about his father for years. He'll be well chuffed with this, he will.'

As I always did, I smiled at Ambrose's use of the term 'lass' – particularly since I wasn't *that* much younger than them.

'Presumably chuffed enough to give you a premium price for it, I'm guessing.' I playfully nudged at Ambrose's tweed sleeve.

'Oh away with you, lass,' he said, opening his program. 'That was a nice wee box you bought. Got a buyer for it?'

'No,' I said. 'I'll pop it in the stall – although I love it so much, I might hang onto it. What else have you got your eye on?'

Ambrose tapped his program. 'This mixed lot. A few service badges, but a House of Parliament ashtray that's a nice thing.'

'Made from the remnants of the bombed buildings?' I guessed. When he nodded, I added, 'They always do well for you.'

'What else are you interested in?' Eugene asked me.

'Nothing much – just a nice little sampler and a sweet Edwardian silver stamp case I could imagine a fine lady taking from her purse or the drawer of her writing table. I saw a lovely pair of Regency pineapple bookends that I might have a go for, and in one of the final lots, there's a promising looking painting of Whitby included with a box of other odds and sods. I have no idea what else is in it, but if the picture's no good, the frame might be okay, and if the price is right …'

'And you do love a good rummage,' said Eugene, pulling on his flat Shelby-style cap, which was in herringbone rather than tweed. 'And that's what I love about general sales like this – you never know where the next bargain will be hidden. Right,' he said, buttoning his jacket, 'I'm off out for a brew. Ambrose?'

'Aye, ta,' said Ambrose.

'And you, lass?'

'No thanks. I'll grab one on my way out.' My phone vibrated in my jacket pocket. I pulled it out, checked the caller ID and scowled.

Ambrose chuckled and said, 'I'll leave you to it,' before

wandering back to his place against the side wall.

I waved him goodbye and answered the call. 'Hello, Stewart, what do you want?'

'Well, hello to you too, Philly. Where are you?'

'In York at an auction,' I replied. 'What do you want?' I asked again through clenched teeth.

'Who says I have to want something?'

I sighed, elbowed my way through the crowd near the door and pushed it open. Stepping outside, a blast of cold November wind sliced through me, and I balanced my phone against my ear while wrapping my scarf around my neck and zipping my jacket up. 'Because you usually do,' I said, shaking my head in resignation even though Stewart wasn't there to see it.

'I was wondering … we're in a bit of a spot … I wouldn't ask if …'

'No, Stewart, I'm not picking *your* children up from wherever you told your wife you'd collect them from.' I shook my head in exasperation.

'I wouldn't ask, except I'm stuck at work … you know how it is, Philly,' he wheedled.

'And what do you think I'm doing right now?'

'You said you were at an auction,' he said as if confused about the question.

'Yes, which, in case you'd forgotten, *is* my work. What's Alison doing? They're her kids, after all.'

'She's been caught up in Harrogate – something about

some curtains. You know how we're doing up the front room?'

'Why would I know that?' More to the point, why would I care?

'I told her I'd pick the kids up, but something's come up in a case, and I have to front a press conference. If you're in York, it's not far out of your way to get the kids and take them back to ours until one of us gets home. You wouldn't like to see Reuben and Misty stranded at the school gate, would you?'

'Given they're not my kids, I don't really care,' I said, although we both knew I did. 'Christ,' I finally said, 'you haven't changed, have you?'

'I'd be so grateful,' he said.

'I don't want your gratitude, Stewart; I'm doing this for your children and not for you or that child bride you left me for. Are we clear?'

'Alison isn't a child bride,' he protested.

'She's not that much older than our children,' I reminded him. 'Alright, what time do I need to be at the school?'

Stewart's sigh of relief came down the line. 'Three thirty.'

'I'll be there, but I'm not taking them back to yours. I have better things to do with what's left of my day than waiting around for you or Alison. I'll take them back to Chipwell with me, and you can collect them from there.'

'But —'

'I don't think you're in any position to negotiate, Stewart. Take it or leave it.' I looked at my watch; that mixed lot I was interested in would be coming up soon.

'I'll take it,' he ground out and hung up without saying goodbye.

I smiled briefly at the thought of Stewart sitting in his office, scowling at the phone, rubbing at his forehead in frustration. Stewart didn't like it when things didn't go his way – he never had. Not that it worried me one way or another what Stewart liked these days – he'd abdicated that privilege ten years ago when he left me for Alison, his personal assistant (oh, the cliché) and twenty years his junior. What did she see in him anyway? Fine, at fifty-nine, he was still good looking, his steel-grey hair making him look distinguished rather than old, and his daily six am run or cycle ensured his body was still in good shape. Maybe it was the power, or illusion of power, that came with his job? Whatever it was, Alison adored him – and Stewart did like to be adored.

Sliding the phone into the back pocket of my jeans, I made my way into the saleroom in time to hear Catherine announce, 'And now we come to lot 270, a mixed lot comprising a late nineteenth-century oil painting of Whitby harbour, artist unknown but of the British school, and sundry household items. Do I have any interest at fifty pounds? Forty? Who'll start me at twenty? Come on, the frame has to be worth more than that …'

Chapter Two

Half an hour later, I was out of the salesroom and heading north towards Easingwold in my battered but loved light green Landrover, Libby. Secured safely in the boot were my purchases – the country house oak letterbox, the pineapple bookends (that I was contemplating keeping rather than selling), the box of odds and sods I couldn't wait to rummage through when I got back to Chipwell Barn and a few other bits and pieces. After I'd paid Becky for the goods, I'd had a quick rifle through the box and felt that telltale ripple of excitement – the something indefinable that made my heart beat faster and the hairs spring to attention on the back of my neck when I inspected the painting. As I lugged the boxes to the car, I was already thinking of the art reference books I'd be consulting tonight – there was something about that painting that was worth more than the fifty pounds I'd secured the lot for, I was sure of it.

For now, though, I had Stewart's children to pick up from school.

While I'd never collected the children from school

before, Stewart and Alison had previously listed me (and my son Ryan and his husband Jordan) as an emergency contact, just in case. Luckily, I also had child car seats from occasionally looking after Ryan's four-year-old twins. I'd also attended enough family events for Reuben and Misty to know me well enough not to be phased when they saw me waiting for them at the gate.

'Philly!' Five-year-old Misty ran full pelt towards me, stopping only to throw her arms around my jean-clad legs. 'We get to ride in Libby!'

'You do,' I said, ruffling her chestnut pony-tailed hair.

Reuben, at eight, was more restrained but submitted happily to a solemn handshake and a kiss on the top of his head. 'Are you taking us home, Philly?'

'Better than that,' I said, opening the back door for Misty. 'I'm taking you to the barn! Mum or Dad will pick you up from there.'

'Yay,' sung Misty. 'Do we get to see Bally and Rochester?'

'You do,' I said, starting the engine after making sure both were strapped into their seats. Misty was possibly the only person in the world – other than his owners, Ambrose and Eugene – the cranky cat tolerated. Jet black, you could normally find Rochester sitting regally on his special cushion in pride of place in their stall, with a benign, yet superior look on his face. His favourite game was to lie across the entrance, waiting for someone to pass by – at which point he'd languidly reach out a paw and scratch the unsuspecting shopper. Poor Balthazar was petrified of him, and Ambrose and Eugene were forever apologising for Rochester's antics, but he was part of the Chipwell Barn family.

'Do you think there'll be cake?' asked Reuben as we pulled out of the school car park.

'I'm sure there'll be cake. Ginny baked muffins this morning – there's bound to be some leftover,' I said.

'What type of muffins?' Reuben asked.

My brow furrowed. 'Banana muffins, I think.'

'I think banana muffins are my absolute favourite muffins,' said Misty, her serious, almost-grown-up expression on her cherubic face reflected in the rear-view mirror.

'You said that chocolate ones were your favourite,' said Reuben.

'Well, they were last week, but this week it's banana.'

The two of them carried on in this vein for most of the drive back to Chipwell, bickering about nothing and thankfully keeping their hands to themselves. I tuned out to their chatter, my thoughts again on the painting. Even though it hadn't been attributed to any specific artist, there could be a signature below the frame – it wouldn't be the first time that had happened. I'd take it out of the frame and see if there was anything on the canvas that gave me a clue as to its provenance. Then again, I might be wasting my time – after all, the Yorkshire coast, in particular Whitby, Staithes and Robin Hood's Bay, had been popular with artists for hundreds of years, and plenty of examples came through the auction houses and dealerships. Even this painting had obviously come from a house clearance somewhere, so who knew how many similar views were languishing in attics around the county, their only value being historic – or the price of the frame.

The sun dipped below the horizon, casting an almost lilac light across the scene as we drove into the gravel car park at Chipwell Barn. I unbuckled Misty – Reuben declaring he was quite capable of removing his own seatbelt, thank you very much – made sure both children had their coats on and let them free to run inside the barn while I followed loaded up with my purchases.

Pausing at the open double wooden doors, I took a second to appreciate what we'd created. A traditional Yorkshire stone-built barn, we'd replaced the dirt and stone floors with wooden floorboards, exposed and stripped back the structural beams and whitewashed the walls, leaving us space for five dealers and a café.

Off a central walkway were our stalls. Heading down from the left, my space was first. While I filled my cabinets mostly with vintage china, glass and jewellery, I had a soft spot for art and kitchenalia – the sorts of products that would've been at home (no pun intended) in the Victorian and Edwardian kitchen.

Beside me were Ambrose and Eugene and their collection of (mostly) coins and military items. If it had any connection to military history – no matter how tenuous –

they were interested in it. Some of the most obscure objects we've had come through the doors of Chipwell Barn have found their way into Ambrose and Eugene's cabinets. Only last week they showed me a tatty leather satchel that held a rusty pile of what looked to be a lethal-looking barbed wire that, with the addition of two pieces of wood, became a trench saw. The short story is that most non-commissioned soldiers carried one for when they had to dig a hole or get out of trouble in a hurry. The long story was much more involved, with both brothers becoming extremely animated in the telling.

Simon Bridges filled the rear of the barn with furniture. If you were after a card table, a tea table or any sort of chair, he was your man. Simon loved the textures and natural ageing of wood and, while he was a gentle man, had been known to raise his voice when a piece came through his door where someone had thoughtlessly scraped away the patina of a hundred years of wear. Perpetually untidy, with once mousy hair that was now liberally peppered with grey and flopped haphazardly over his eyes, he wore his reading glasses on a chain around his neck (yet was constantly searching for them) and reminded me of a dog who, from time to time, forgot how tall he was. Simon lived in well-worn jeans and a succession of band T-shirts – few of whom I'd ever heard of – and ate more food than anyone I'd ever come across, at least some of which inevitably ended up on his clothes.

Henry and Tamsin Proctor occupied the opposite

corner. Their garden ornaments and, for want of a better term, agricultural bric-a-brac, sprawled out of their space and into the garden behind the barn. In their early forties, they'd met in high school and married while still teenagers. I didn't think I'd ever meet a couple more obviously in love as these two were; if I wasn't so happily divorced (and contentedly single), I might've envied them that. They finished each other's sentences, punctuating their conversations with a touch of the other's hand or arm. Tamsin was tiny and blonde, with bright blue eyes. Her hair was usually tied back in a long plait that ran down the back of her dungarees – which she had in a myriad of colours – and paired with black work boots and T-shirts (short-sleeved in summer, long and with a woollen jumper in the cooler months) all year round. She reminded me of the actor Felicity Kendal in the old TV show *The Good Life* – about the couple who decided to live off the grid. As for Henry, well, he was just Henry. Of medium height and stockily built with dark, thick, wavy hair and big brown spaniel-like eyes, Henry was, aside from Simon, one of the gentlest men I had ever met – which made him an absolute pushover for customers after a bargain. Luckily for their bank balance, Tamsin had a strong will and could haggle with the best of them.

Next up was Isobel Mayfield. Bell's specialty was antique and vintage clothes, fabrics and accessories and, like me, the magic for her is in the story. She gives each of her pieces a name and can look at a 1930s tea dress and imagine the life of the woman who wore it. If asked, she'd give you the backstory she's created for each garment – for some dresses, she'll write that story on a little card and include it in the tissue paper she carefully wraps each purchase in. She put most of her items online and sells her garments all around the world – some buyers coming back again and again for those special cards.

Finally, across the hall from me at the front of the barn, Ginny Wilding ran the barn's tearoom selling soups, pies and baked goods. She baked whatever she felt like baking, so every day's menu was a surprise. All anyone knew was that there'd be cake, scones, maybe a muffin, a pot of soup and always a pie or savoury tart. Ginny's Yorkshire cream teas, served in my vintage china and eaten from furniture supplied by Simon, were something special indeed, and people came from far and wide for them.

Everything in the café was for sale – from the vintage china and bric-a-brac (usually supplied by me) to the furniture (Simon, Henry and Tamsin) and table runners and cloths (Bell). As a result, the café looked different from week to week and that, plus the constantly changing menu, had resulted in the café becoming a destination in its own right – and we all benefited from that. Customers would come for coffee and a cake or one of Ginny's amazing pies and find their way into our stalls afterwards. In the warmer weather, we set out tables and chairs (from Henry and Tamsin's store) for patrons to enjoy the views over the hedgerows and across the fields to the Howardian Hills, and at this time of the year, the couches by the wood stove were in high demand.

A few years younger than my fifty-eight, Ginny liked to describe herself as vertically challenged but horizontally gifted – and by that, she meant nothing sexual. She was instead referring to the circumference of her waist. I preferred to think of her as comfortable. With hair that was still mostly brown and cut into a shoulder-length slightly wavy bob, when she smiled – which was often – her brown eyes twinkled; and when Ginny laughed, her mouth wide open, her hands clasped beneath her generous chest, you couldn't help but laugh with her.

Some people are like the Dementors in the Harry Potter novels – they suck the joy out of every situation and leave you feeling that the world is grey. Ginny was the opposite – she left everyone she met feeling happier just by being in her brightly clothed presence.

Right now, she was charming Stewart's children.

'You two sit yourselves down,' she said, 'and I'll get you both a hot chocolate.'

'With a marshmallow?' asked Misty.

'Absolutely,' she beamed. 'And it just so happens that I have two banana muffins left.' She tilted her head to the side and raised her eyebrows. 'I don't suppose you know anyone who might like to take them off my hands?'

'Me,' cried Misty, her hand shooting up in the air.

'I will!' chorused Reuben.

'Thanks,' I mouthed to Ginny. To the kids, I said, 'I'm just going to take these across the hall and find Balthazar, so you two stay here with Ginny, okay? I'll be back in a couple of minutes.'

'I take it Alison lets them eat cakes and hot chocolate,' Ginny whispered for my ears only once she'd given the children their muffins.

'I assume so,' I said dismissively. 'I've never asked.' I shared a complicit grin with her and walked across to my stall with a box balanced on each hip.

Placing them on the counter, I crossed the hallway to Bell's place and whistled softly to Balthazar who had been curled up on the cushion Bell keeps especially for him. After stretching luxuriously, he bounded across to me, his ears flopping and tail wagging. I bent down and gave him a hug that he tolerated for a couple of seconds and a tummy rub he insisted on prolonging.

'Thanks for keeping an eye on him,' I said to Bell who was sitting in a wing-backed chair busy sewing an oversized gold button onto a crimson velvet jacket. As she usually was, Willowy Bell was dressed entirely in black with black ballet flats. Bell always finished her outfit with a shawl – the colour of which reflected her mood for the day. If she was feeling on top of the world, her shawl would be in shades of orange and yellow; serene would mean the colours of the ocean; dramatic would result in sequins, velvet and chiffon. Very often she'd complete her look with a hat from her collection of vintage accessories – a fedora one day, a cloche the next and a bucket hat or a beret the day after that. I always wished I could wear a hat the way she did, but being not many inches over five feet, with short, tousled curls, hats made me feel even shorter and left my hair in a weird helmet shape.

With the poise and grace of an ex-dancer, Bell glided rather than walked. When I first met her (so long ago that I was still married to Stewart), I used to feel dowdy and clumpy next to her. These days it didn't worry me – I am what I am, and she's who she is. She wouldn't feel right in the jeans and Chelsea boots or wellingtons that are my working uniform, and I wouldn't feel comfortable in hers.

'No problems – it's been a quiet afternoon. Did you get the letterbox you were after?'

'I sure did.'

She looked up from the jacket, her eyes assessing my face. 'And something more?'

'Yes, a few bits and pieces and a mixed lot box. There's a nineteenth-century oil of Whitby harbour in there and goodness knows what else.'

'But it's the painting that has you interested,' she guessed.

'The hair stood up on the back of my neck,' I said, knowing she'd understand exactly what I meant.

'I see. Let me finish this, and I'll come take a look.'

'Don't hurry, it will still be there tomorrow. I had to

pick up Misty and Reuben from school. Ginny's doing what Ginny does best, but I'd better get back to them.'

'Feeding them and keeping them entertained, I assume. How come you had to collect them? That was last minute, wasn't it?'

I grimaced and balanced my bum against her counter. 'Don't go there. Nice chair – one of Simon's?'

'Yes, it came in this morning. Arts and Crafts, he said, and I think this fabric is a Liberty print.' Bell stood, laying her sewing on the counter, so I could see the upholstery, a riotous cottage garden with sunflowers, Queen Anne's lace, bluebells and a host of other flowers I didn't recognise against an ink-blue background.

'I think you could be right,' I said, 'but I don't think it's original.'

'Maybe not, but it is beautiful. Depending on how much he wants for it, I might buy it off him,' she mused, the forefinger and thumb of one hand pinching her chin, her hand on her other hip, her shawl (black with embroidered roses) slipping off her shoulder.

I chuckled softly. 'I'd better go and see what these kids are up to,' I said, patting my leg for Bally to follow – which he did, crossing to the other side of the hallway to avoid Rochester.

I need not have worried about the children. Both now had their hands around massive mugs of chocolate, their mouths stained brown. I chuckled to myself when Reuben wiped his mouth with his jumper sleeve. Alison wouldn't like that – not that she'd say anything to me about it. Where possible, she tried not to say anything at all to me. After the twin's birthday party one year, I'd commented on it to Ryan. He and Jordan had invited Stewart, Alison and the children – as they did to every family event. There was, after all, no getting around the fact that Stewart was Ryan's father and the twin's grandfather.

In any case, after they'd left this particular day, I'd made a (admittedly, snide) comment about how Alison had barely said a word to me, and Ryan snapped.

'Are you surprised, Mum? She's intimidated by you.'

I'd taken a step back, both in surprise at his tone of voice and at what he'd said. 'How can you say that? I'm the one he left,' I said.

'Maybe, but you were there for all the important things in his life. You had two children with him, and you shared a career with him in the police force until he was transferred to York. You run your own business, you're independent and capable, and you stand up to Dad in a way she never would. Instead of snarking about her, you should feel sorry for her.'

That was me put in my place. Ever since, I've tried to put her at ease and not give her any reason to feel inferior. Even so, I couldn't help smiling at the children's messy faces – both would need a bath when they got home.

Ginny was cleaning up around us, wiping down the

counter-top, collecting any stray pieces of crockery, when Alison breathlessly burst through the doors. 'I'm so sorry,' she said, moving to hug the children. 'My appointment in Harrogate went over time, and then there was an accident on the A59 near the ring road and –'

'Alison' – I smiled to put her at her ease – 'it's okay, the kids are fine, and they've been fed.' Albeit chocolate and muffins.

She smiled tentatively and took a few breaths, her shoulders dropping and forehead smoothed of the frown she'd worn when she arrived. 'Thank you for collecting them, Philly; I know it's an imposition, and Stewart wouldn't have asked, but –'

I waved away her thanks.

'It sounds like you've had quite the afternoon,' said Ginny. 'Why don't you sit down and have a brew before you go?'

'Thank you, but I can see you're all packing up, so I'll be on my way.'

As she spoke, Simon and Bell waved their goodbyes and let themselves out, closing the door behind them.

'It's no problem,' I said. 'You need to calm down before you get back in the car.'

'I'll be fine –' she said, interrupted by a knocking at the door.

'That will be Simon forgetting his car keys again,' said Ginny with a knowing grin. 'I'll go.'

'Okay, kids,' Alison said. 'Let's get packed up.'

'I want to play with Bally some more,' said Misty.

'I think Balthazar wants to go home and have his own tea,' said Alison.

Ginny soon returned with a large stranger in an ill-fitting suit and crooked tie. 'I'm sorry,' I said, 'we're closed.'

The man held up his warrant card. 'Mrs Barker?'

When Alison and I answered simultaneously, he looked from one to the other. Alison's cheeks glowed with embarrassment, and I just chuckled. 'I'm sorry, Inspector' – I took a closer look at the warrant card – 'Dawkins. We're both Mrs Barker, but this Mrs Barker is married to your boss.' I waved my hand towards Alison, and the inspector swallowed hard.

'My apologies, Mrs Barker,' he said uncomfortably to Alison. 'I didn't recognise you.'

'That's perfectly fine, Inspector Dawkins. I'm sure you weren't expecting to be confronted by two Mrs Barkers.' Alison smiled gently at him, putting the man at ease. 'The other Mrs Barker is teasing you.' That was me scolded.

'No,' he conceded, 'I certainly wasn't expecting two Mrs Barkers. I'm here to see Mrs Philomena Barker.'

'Which would be me.' I stepped forward, more curious than anxious.

'We'll leave you to it,' said Alison. 'Thanks again for collecting the children, Philly, and thanks for feeding them, Ginny.'

'You're very welcome. Inspector, would you like to come this way?' I waved my hand towards my stall, ignoring the curiosity in Ginny's stare.

'I'll be off too then,' said Ginny. 'See you tomorrow.'

I held up a hand in farewell.

Chapter Three

'Please take a seat,' I said, indicating the pair of oak captain chairs with dark brown leather seats that were the only seats in my space this week. 'How can I help you?' He sat, but before I did, I said, 'I haven't offered you a tea or coffee yet – would you like one?' After being married to a police officer for over twenty years – and being one for part of that time – I had no discomfort talking to one.

'No, thank you, Mrs Barker –'

'Please call me Philly,' I said, studying him closely. With close-cropped hair, thinning at the temple and liberally sprinkled with grey, I placed his age somewhere close to mine, late fifties, possibly early sixties. His hazel eyes looked kind, but the puffiness below them spoke of long days and broken nights, and the furrows on his brow ran deep. I knew first-hand how hard the job was that he did every day and the scars that sort of stress left. Stewart had always been ambitious and could rise above it; I had a feeling this man had not been able to do that.

He wore no wedding ring – not that that meant anything

these days – but there was something in his attitude that suggested he was single now, but perhaps hadn't always been. Divorced maybe? While large, in both height and breadth, he was solid rather than overweight, something which his navy suit obviously struggled with. There was also something familiar about him.

He nodded politely. 'Alright, Philly,' he said slowly as if he had to think twice about addressing the boss's wife, no matter how ex, by her christian name.

'Now we've got that settled; what can I do for you?'

He took out his notebook from the inside pocket of his jacket, and again, I had the feeling we'd met before. I wrinkled my nose as I tried to place him. 'We've met before, haven't we?'

'Well, yes, but –'

'No' – I held my hand up to silence him – 'let me think. I'm normally good with faces – especially if they've bought things from me in the past – and you have bought something from me, haven't you? Not here, though …' I held a finger in the air as it came to me. 'It was at the fair last summer, wasn't it? I had a stall, and you bought a … an art nouveau toast rack!' I caught his eyes for confirmation, and he nodded, his smile bringing his otherwise ordinary face to life. 'It was a beautiful piece in fabulous condition – hallmarked silver, wavy lines. Lovely. You have good taste,' I said, unsuccessfully hiding my smile as his cheeks coloured.

'And you have a good memory,' he said, shifting slightly

in his chair. 'Which leads me to the reason I'm here. There's been a spate of fake antiques doing the rounds and –'

'Again? What is it this time? You're seeing me rather than Simon or the brothers, so it must be art or pottery. Silver is usually top of the list when it comes to stolen goods.' Antiques and fine arts were subject to more than their fair share of scams, and whenever any surfaced – or there were rumours of stolen goods floating around – most of the dealers in the county received visits from the local constabulary.

'The brothers?'

'Ambrose and Eugene Ashton – they're into militaria and coins, and whenever there's furniture involved, Simon Bridges gets a visit.' I shrugged and sat back in my chair, placing my hands on the arms and swivelling it around.

'Right.' He nodded as if my logic made perfect sense – which, of course, it did. 'Well, the issue now is with fake Clarice Cliff pieces.' He consulted his notebook. 'We've had them turn up in salerooms across the county.'

I groaned inwardly. Clarice Cliff was a recognisable name and style, with pieces coming onto the market regularly. Plus, the apparent simplicity of the designs was a magnet to potential scammers – anyone who regularly watched programs such as *Bargain Hunt* or *Antiques Roadshow* probably thought they could spot one from a mile off.

'Links to money laundering?' That was usually the main reason. Fake a highly collectible piece – such as anything by the Staffordshire ceramic artist – and sell it at auction for substantially more than it's worth. The buyer was left thinking they had a bargain, and most never found out that what they'd purchased was an over-priced fake.

'Perhaps,' he said, leaning back in his chair and crossing one ankle over the other. 'Or it could be a scam to make money – let's face it, most people wouldn't know what they'd bought.' He narrowed his gaze at me. 'Would you know a fake if you saw one?'

'I'd hope so,' I said. 'It's particularly hard with Clarice Cliff, though. The first sign is, of course, the price. If it's too low, there's a reason for that. The figurines – which are rare – and some of the vases can fetch into the thousands. Then you'd check the weight – if you've handled enough pieces, you get to know whether it's too light. Hang on.' I stood and walked around to one of my cabinets. 'I have some in here.' I reached in and brought out a teapot and a sugar sifter.

I placed both pieces on the counter, and Inspector Dawkins stood to examine them. 'May I?' he asked and waited for my nod before picking up the teapot. 'How old is this?'

'This one dates back to the nineteen thirties,' I told him. 'What do you notice about it?' I asked.

'There are a lot of triangles,' he said with a hopeful smile. The teapot was from Cliff's modernist period in the Bizarre range. Mostly cream but edged in green, both the spout and the handle were solid triangles. Handpainted, the bottom third was terracotta with crocuses springing up from it in shades of blue, lilac and orange. 'And it looks as though a child could paint it – it's pretty simple.'

'You'd think so, wouldn't you? But look more closely at the detail. The design flows, and you can see the confidence in the brushstrokes. Then there's the colour – which is often a real giveaway. While it appears delicate, as though it's almost been watercoloured on, it still has oodles of body. See this?' My finger traced the petal work on the orange crocus. 'The colour is bold with almost an oily sheen – and that's because, at Clarice Cliff, they mixed their powder pigments with oil to produce such strong colours. If your orange is pale and flat, it's a good bet that it's fake.'

'I see,' he said. 'I think I understand what you mean by the painting too.' He turned the pot over to look at the backstamp. 'What about this mark? Can that be faked?'

'Yes, and that makes it even harder to detect. There was at one point a spate of backstamped blanks – that's what we call the unpainted ceramics – which found their way onto the market with new paintwork. The clever scammers can fake the backstamp too. It's made harder because legitimate reproductions also come onto the market.'

'Sorry? Legitimate reproductions?'

'Yes. Back in the early nineties, the Metropolitan Museum of Art in New York reproduced some pieces under licence – they're all marked with the letters MMA, though.'

He raised his eyebrows and pressed his forefinger into his temple. 'It's a wonder anyone can tell fake from real,' he finally said, picking up the oval-shaped sugar sifter in the same pattern. 'How much would these be worth?'

'These aren't particularly rare,' I said. 'I've got two hundred and sixty on the pot and eighty on the sifter.'

He picked the teapot up again. 'This solid handle isn't very practical,' he commented, the pot appearing dainty in his large hand. 'I'd have problems picking this up and pouring it.'

I chuckled at his assessment. 'It wasn't very practical, and now I come to think of it, it's another way of identifying a fake – many of the fakes have open handles. The same goes with the teacups from the range.'

I carefully placed both pieces back in the cabinet. When I turned back, Inspector Dawkins was examining the letterbox I'd purchased that afternoon. He ran his hand across the smooth surface of the oak, his fingers following the direction of the grain and lingering on the brass. 'This is nice,' he said. 'And what's in this?' He turned his attention to the box of odds and sods.

'No idea,' I said. 'I bought it for the painting, but I'm looking forward to seeing what else is in there. Although' – I turned to smile up at him – 'mixed lots like these are always a lucky dip.'

He glanced at his watch and widened his eyes. 'I'm sorry, Mrs … Philly, I've taken up more of your time than I should've done, but thank you.'

'You're welcome, Inspector.'

'Please, call me Robbie,' he said, the tips of his ears colouring slightly.

'Okay, Robbie. I'll keep an eye out and let you know if anyone calls by attempting to sell me any Clarice Cliff.'

'I'd appreciate that.'

'If I do, how do I contact you?' I prompted, a wry smile on my face.

'Sorry,' he said, reaching for his wallet. 'Here's my card. My mobile number is on here too.'

'Thanks,' I said, taking it off him. 'Drop by for a browse anytime,' I added, leading the way to the front door.

'Are you going home now too?' he asked. My lights were the only ones still on; the rest of the barn was in darkness.

'Yes,' I said, picking up the box with the painting in it.

'I'll wait while you lock up,' he said. 'Better to be safe – and I'll walk you to your car.' He took the box from my arms.

'It's perfectly fine,' I protested. 'I only live a couple of streets away.'

'No trouble at all.'

He waited as I whistled for Balthazar, switched my lights off and locked the door behind us.

'No alarm?' he asked. 'Or CCTV?'

'No,' I said. 'We've never thought we needed it – not in Chipwell.'

'Hmmm. You can never be too safe.'

I bit my tongue to hide my smile as I placed the box in the back of Libby. Robbie opened the back door for Bally, who jumped straight in, getting a ruffle on the head for being such a good dog. He then opened the door for me and waited as I slid behind the wheel.

'It's been nice meeting you, Philly. Have a pleasant evening.'

'You too,' I said, starting the engine.

As I pulled out into the darkness, Robbie's shadow watched me in the rear-view mirror, and I was surprised to be smiling.

Chapter Four

The house phone was ringing as I unlocked the front door a few minutes later, Bally clattering past me to wait at the back door to be let out. I ignored the ringing phone and placed my keys in the basket on the hall stand, the box from the auction on the kitchen counter, let the dog out and went to the fridge, removed a bottle of New Zealand sauvignon blanc and poured a large glass of wine.

I'd taken the first sip when my mobile rang. I reached into the back pocket of my jeans for it. Stewart.

'Hi,' I answered. 'Was that you who just rang on the landline?'

'Yes, I thought you'd be home by now,' he said.

'I'm just in. Did Alison and the kids get home okay?' I tucked the phone between my shoulder and ear and opened the fridge again. Unsurprisingly, the contents hadn't changed since this morning.

'Yes, she's not long in. Thanks for picking them up, by the way.'

'It's okay, they're nice kids, but don't make a habit of it, eh?' I sat on a bar stool and toed my boots off.

'Noted,' he said. 'She mentioned Dawkins came to see you. What was that about?'

I took another sip of wine and looked at my watch – nearly six, and I'd skipped lunch; it was no wonder my tummy was rumbling. 'Oh, just some business with some fake Clarice Cliffs floating around. Nothing for you to worry about.'

'Right, well, if that's all it was, I'll let you go.' He hung up without another word. Whatever.

My shoulders relaxed as I sipped at my crisp and fruity wine, my reflection in the kitchen window showing a tired-looking version of myself. How long had there been bags under the blue eyes that Stewart used to say he couldn't look away from? Had the lines that ran down from my nose become deeper, the slight puffiness at my jaw puffier? My cheeks, which used to be rosy and pinchable, were now hollow, and it was a long time since I'd been bothered to dye the grey out of my short blonde hair. I ran my fingers through it to give it some lift and volume and tucked the bits that poked out like wings behind my ears. At least my body was still in good shape, I supposed. While I didn't believe in taking exercise as such, I was constantly moving – country walks with Balthazar and all the lifting, carrying, and climbing of ladders that went along with my job. All the incidental exercise and occasional skipped meal kept everything where it needed to be.

Wardrobe-wise, today was a good day. Because it was an auction day, I'd teamed my usual well-worn jeans with a forest-green jacket with a matching belt that wrapped around my waist and had even applied mascara and a dab of blush in addition to my usual tinted moisturiser. I did a little shimmy-shake. What did any of it matter? I drained my wine and opened the back door to let Balthazar back in.

'Okay, fella,' I said, the dog wagging his tail as if he could understand every word I'd said to him. 'What say we leave this box for later and treat ourselves to dinner at the pub tonight?'

Our pub, The Chipwell Arms, had been serving the village for over three hundred years. For the last twenty years or so, it had been under the stewardship of Roger and Lynn Marsh. They arrived in town soon after Stewart and I did – although being from 'down south', they were treated as strangers for longer than we were – Stewart having been born in the north. I'd come from Australia originally so I was still excused from any mistakes. 'Aye, lass,' long-term residents would say, 'you weren't to know.'

About ten years ago, Roger and Lynn had attempted to turn The Arms into a so-called gastropub – to replace the ham and chips with something infinitely posher and more expensive. The locals grumbled loudly about incomers changing the way of things, and the gammon was soon back on the menu – as were other pub classics such as steak and ale pie in a suet crust, toad in the hole, haddock, chips, and mushy peas (a chippy tea), and the ubiquitous roast. These days, though, you found these sitting happily beside dishes like ham hock and black pudding terrine, slow-cooked belly pork, apple and potato rosti, cauliflower, kale, blackberry with red wine jus, and game sausage rolls.

It had happened so slowly that the regulars either didn't notice or had become used to the change – to the extent that they now grumbled if gravy replaced the jus on the pork belly.

Being a Wednesday night in mid-November, the pub wasn't busy, so after getting Balthazar settled in his usual place just far enough away from the wood heater, I made my way to the bar, stopping to chat with the friendly locals.

'Hiya, Philly,' said Lynn as she pulled a beer. 'What can I get you, pet?'

'A glass of red, thanks, Lynn. What's been happening?'

'Oh, you know, the usual,' she said. 'It's proper parky out tonight.'

'It's raw for sure. I'm only here for the fire.' I grinned cheekily.

'Away with you,' she laughed. 'Will you be wanting some tea?'

'Please. What's on the specials tonight?'

'How hungry are you?'

'As my mother used to say, my stomach's beginning to feel like my throat's been cut.' I rolled my eyes to illustrate the desperation of the situation.

'Like that, is it?' Lynn grinned at me and passed my wine across the counter. 'How about a War of the Roses?'

'A what?'

'The battles between the white rose of York and the red rose of Lancaster,' she said, referring to the legendary tussles for the English crown through the Middle Ages.

'I know what it is,' I said. The white rose of Yorkshire could be seen everywhere through the village – there was even one in wrought iron on the gate into my house. 'What I don't know is how you've turned it into a menu item.'

'Aye, well, you being Australian and all, I couldn't be sure you'd catch my meaning, like,' she said. 'It's a Yorkshire pudding filled with Lancashire hotpot,' she replied, her face deadpan, but her brown eyes were twinkling behind her pink-rimmed glasses.

'Oh, very funny,' I chuckled. 'It sounds lovely, but I'm not sure …'

'How about wild mushroom risotto with leek and parmesan?'

'Sounds good to me,' I said.

'Take a seat, and it won't be long,' she said before switching her attention to another patron.

Taking my wine, I cast a look around the vast dining room.

Roger and Lynn had begun decorating The Arms for Christmas. A tree (as yet unadorned) stood in the corner near the bay windows, and battery-operated candles with silvery pinecones sat on each round wooden table.

At one of these tables sat Detective Inspector Dawkins. The gentle light from the candles had softened his face, blurring the craggy edges. His suit jacket was neatly placed over the back of his chair, his cuffs were undone and sleeves rolled to his elbows, his blue-striped tie loosened with the end tucked into the pocket of his white shirt. In front of him was a half-eaten plate of ham, eggs and beans, and the remains of a pint of dark ale. He dipped a fat hand-cut chip into the yolk of his remaining egg and swirled it around to coat the end. As he lifted it to his mouth, a drop of deep orange yolk fell from the chip. Deftly he caught it with his forefinger before it could hit the plate and sucked the yolk off before eating the chip still held in his other hand.

Stepping forward before he could look up and see me watching him eat, I said, 'Inspector Dawkins, you didn't get far.'

He looked up from his meal with a start and made to stand up. I waved his efforts away. 'No, don't get up; I don't want to disturb you,' I said.

'Mrs Barker, sorry, Philly.' He reddened slightly. 'You didn't get far either. And it's Robbie, remember.'

'Aaah, but I live here in the village, and I suspect you don't.'

'No, I don't, but I was hungry and decided to grab my tea here rather than driving home to something microwaved.'

'No one waiting at home with dinner?' I grimaced inwardly as I asked the question.

His mouth curved slightly. 'No,' he said simply. 'What's your excuse?'

I shrugged lightly. 'I looked at the time and decided I couldn't be faffed either preparing or defrosting something. Besides,' I added, 'I live literally a few houses away so eat here at least once or twice a week. But don't let me keep you from your meal.'

'Have you ordered?'

'I have.'

'Then why don't you join me?'

I cast my eyes around the room. Bally poked his head up to see where I was, stretched, and loped across to where Robbie sat, resting his head hopefully on Robbie's knee.

'Balthazar Barker!' I scolded. 'You know better than that! I'm so sorry; he knows he's not supposed to bother people when they're eating.'

'He's alright, aren't you, fella?' Robbie idly scratched the dog's head. 'I bet you'd like one of these chippies, wouldn't you?'

'Yes, he would,' I answered for the dog, 'but he's not going to get one.' I shook my head and gave Bally a stern look.

Rather than taking my hint, he turned his limpid spaniel eyes on Robbie who simply laughed.

'You'd better join me now.' He waved his hand towards

the seat opposite him.

Placing my wine on the table, I caught Bally's eye and pointed in the direction of the wood heater. Reluctantly, he turned and made his way back to the rug that was always left for visiting dogs, looking back at us balefully.

'He's a lovely dog. How old?' Robbie asked.

'Five, and yes, I wouldn't be without him. Please, eat your meal; mine will be out soon, and you don't want yours to be getting cold.'

He smiled and picked his knife and fork back up. After taking a mouthful and chewing thoughtfully, he said, 'How long have you lived here for?'

'It would have to be getting on for twenty years. We moved here when Stewart was transferred to York. We didn't want to live in town, but it was close enough for Stewart to commute. Ryan would've been ten, I suppose, which would make Chloe eight.' It really didn't feel that long ago.

'And you stayed after … well …?'

'You mean after the divorce?' I laughed shortly, ruefully. 'Yes. I got the house; he got to keep his pension fund. Although naturally, it wasn't all as simple as that.'

'But you're obviously all friends now – Mrs Barker … Alison … was there this afternoon, and you'd picked their children up.'

'True. I don't make a habit of that, though. We all get on now but when it first happened, I couldn't look at either of them. Let alone speak to them. I blamed her, of course, although knowing Stewart as I did, I don't imagine she stood a chance. I had no idea, you see. They say the wife always knows, but for me, it was an absolute blindside after twenty-something years of marriage.' My gaze flicked across to check quickly on Bally. 'We're civil these days, though. We have to be – Ryan, our son, lives in York, and if I want to see my grandkids for their birthdays or Christmas, I have to tolerate Stewart and Alison and, to be honest, the more I get to know her, the more I respect her. I always thought she was a doormat and assumed that's what Stewart saw in her, but I'm not so sure now.' Robbie's head was tilted to the side, listening. Reminded of who I was speaking to I added, 'I probably shouldn't be saying any of this – after all, he's your boss.'

'It's okay, I'm a vault,' he said. 'Your secrets are safe with me. In fact, I've forgotten already.'

I chuckled at that. 'Unless it affects a case, that is.'

'Naturally. Where does Chloe fit into it all?' Robbie picked up a slice of his buttered bread, folded the triangle over and used it to mop up the remaining yolk and sauces on his plate.

'From a distance. She's in Australia, on the Sunshine Coast with her husband. She went over there on her gap year, fell in love and never came home.' I paused as Lynn's daughter Josie brought out my risotto. As she placed the steaming bowl in front of me, she took in my companion, raised her eyebrows and gave me a cheeky smile.

'Thanks, Josie,' I said pointedly. Unabashed, she shrugged, grinned and left us to it.

Once she'd retreated to the kitchen, I leant forward and inhaled the earthy richness of the mushrooms and parmesan.

'That smells good,' said Robbie.

I dug my fork in, gently blew on it and took a bite. 'It tastes good too. Do you want to try some?' The question came out automatically, and he seemed taken aback.

He shook his head quickly and then, as if to change the subject, said, 'How long ago did you leave Australia?'

'The accent isn't that strong, is it?' I asked.

His lips curved, but he didn't answer me.

'Let's say I did the same as Chloe, but from the opposite direction. I came over on a gap year, met Stewart and stayed. He'd just finished his basic training, so there was no question of him moving to Australia. I didn't know what else I wanted to do, so I joined the force too and because I had British citizenship – my father was born here – it was easy for me to stay.'

His eyes widened in surprise. 'How did you go from being on the force to being an expert on Art Deco pottery?' Plate cleaned, he pushed it away and settled back in his chair.

'You must be very good at your job,' I said, aware that I'd been dominating the conversation.

'I'm sorry; am I asking too many questions? A bad habit, I suppose.'

'I'm happy to answer them, but I've been talking about myself since I sat down. You know almost all there is to know about me –'

'Except how you came to be in the antique game,' he quipped.

'Okay, except for that, but I know absolutely nothing about you.' I took a sip of wine and rested my cheek against the back of my hand, my elbow on the table.

'Ah, I'm not very interesting,' he said, picking up an errant bread crumb from the table and placing it on his plate. 'Just a middle-aged copper. There's not much more to know.'

'I don't believe that for one second.' I retorted and sighed. 'Alright then, if I answer that, I get to ask you some questions.'

'It's a deal, but as I said, you'll be disappointed.'

'I'm not so sure about that.' I had another mouthful of risotto and chewed thoughtfully. It was delicious. 'I left the force because we came here. Stewart was moving through the ranks and, well, I don't need to tell you what a detective's work/life balance is like, and the kids were getting to the stage in their schooling when they needed more structure than I'd been able to give them.'

He shook his head and chuckled, the sound deep yet knowing. 'You certainly don't need to tell me about balance.'

I returned his laugh. 'I know, right? Anyway, I also wanted to do the university course I hadn't gone back to

Australia to do, so that's what I did – left the police and enrolled in a fine arts degree. I took a part-time job at the auctioneers in York – Young and Johnson's – and fell in love with the trade. I met Bell – she has the vintage clothes stall – through my work with Young and Johnson's, and we became good friends. We'd been talking about setting up a cooperative of dealers one day, and when the barn came on the market, it seemed like a now or never proposition, and Bell approached the Proctors and Ashtons. Ginny came in later when we decided we needed a café. While it's been hard work, it's all gone far better than we could've hoped it would.'

'And Stewart has been supportive of it?'

'Well, it's not really any of his business, but yes, although at first, he thought it was a hare-brained idea. Once he knew we were serious, his tune changed. I don't think he ever thought we'd make a success of it, but as I said, it's none of his business anymore. Now,' I said, 'I've answered your questions; it's time for you to answer mine.' He sat back in his chair and rested his clasped hands on his belly. The action was designed to show how open he was to talk about himself, but the sudden tension in his jaw told a different story.

'You said you would've had a microwave meal tonight. Does that mean you're not married?'

'That's right; we'll make a detective of you yet.'

I rolled my eyes good-naturedly. 'Sooooo,' I said slowly, 'have you been married?'

'I have.'

It was as if a shutter had come over his eyes and took the twinkle away and brought the hard edges and the furrows back.

'She died,' he said. There was something in the simplicity of those two words that sounded as bleak as the bleakest of February days. Something in his tone also told me he didn't say the words very often.

'I'm so sorry,' I said. 'How long?'

'Five years. You didn't ask how she passed.'

'I don't think it matters how she passed – well, obviously, it does, but the fact that she's gone is sad enough.'

He searched my face for a few beats. Had I said the wrong thing? Finally, he said softly, 'Thank you for saying that. It matters, but at the same time, it doesn't.'

I nodded, both in understanding and relief. 'Do you have children?'

'Just the one, a son.'

'Does he live nearby?'

He shook his head sadly. 'No, like your daughter, he's in Australia. In Sydney, though. He's married, and she doesn't like the cold, so he doesn't come home very often.'

He turned away from my gaze, shifting in his seat, but the loneliness was in his voice. Somehow I knew he wouldn't welcome my sympathy, that he was more used to being a support for others than asking for it himself. 'I see. Chloe's the same – it's why she doesn't get home much.'

Robbie broke the ensuing silence and said, 'Maybe you

should've stayed in the force – you'd be good at my job too – you're a great listener.'

'Aaah, but you see, that helps in my trade too,' I said with a smirk.

He laughed at that and got to his feet. 'Can I get you another wine? You're not driving, are you?'

'No, I'm not, and thank you.'

While he was at the bar, I finished the rest of my meal. I wasn't in the market for a relationship – and I didn't think he was either – but I could always do with another friend, and I got the feeling that was something he needed more than anything.

When he returned with my wine and an orange juice for himself, I steered the conversation onto safer grounds, and we spent the next hour entertaining each other with war stories from our chosen professions.

When I yawned for the second time at around nine, Robbie said, 'I'd best be getting off home. I've enjoyed tonight though, Philly, thank you.'

'Yeah, I did too.' I stood and whistled for Bally. Robbie held my coat, waiting as I slid my arms in before dealing with his own.

When he said, 'I'll walk you home,' it didn't occur to me to argue about it.

'You weren't joking about being so close, were you?' he said when we got to my gate.

'No, I wasn't. And before you start thinking I must be

lazy to drive to work, I only had the car there today because I had an auction to attend in York.'

'Oh aye.' He chuckled, and the warm, rumbly sound of it made me smile.

He waited until I'd unlocked my front door and switched on the light before stepping forward and shaking my hand awkwardly. 'I'll be seeing you, Philly Barker.'

'See that you do, Robbie Dawkins.'

He lightly touched the side of his head in a 'right you are' gesture and turned to walk the short distance back to his car.

When the front door clicked shut behind me, I was still smiling, already looking forward to our next encounter. The box on the kitchen counter taunted me, but it could wait until tomorrow.

Chapter Five

The following morning, I lugged the same box back into work that I'd taken home the previous night. I'd taken the first few items out – a couple of brass trivets and some books that appeared to be tourist guides – when Bell sailed in wearing a benign smile on her face, an ink-blue fringed shawl smattered with stars over her shoulders and a navy cloche on her long black hair. 'So, sweetie,' she said. 'What did the constabulary want last night?'

'Good morning to you too.' I smiled at Bell's suggestive tone. 'Detective Inspector Dawkins was just warning me about some fake Clarice Cliff pieces doing the rounds of the salesrooms.'

'Oh, is that all?' She flung herself into the captain's chair, crossed her long legs and swivelled a full three hundred and sixty degrees. 'Ginny said he had kind eyes.'

'Did she? Well, I guess she's right; he does have kind eyes.' I pulled out another item and unwrapped the newspaper that was around it. 'This is rather nice,' I said, picking up my magnifying glass. 'A lovely teaspoon hallmarked …

Sheffield, 1890. What do you think this animal is on the handle?' I passed the spoon across to Bell.

'Could it be a stoat? It's really quite sweet.' She handed it back and resumed her swivels.

'Yes, it is, isn't it? I'm not sure there's much else of value in here. Some books, some horse brass and a couple of brass trivets, nothing special, maybe a hundred quid worth, I'd say.' I picked up one of the trivets and inspected the markings. 'These should clean up well, though.'

'Some nice things, but hardly enough to get your spider senses going yesterday,' Bell commented, rising from the chair to flick through one of the tour guides, it's cloth cover discoloured with age. 'Perhaps there's something special about these,' she said, wrinkling her nose as she flicked through the pages. 'I know people are supposed to love the smell of old books, but they make me want to sneeze,' she said, placing it back on the table.

'No, I don't think it's got anything to do with the books,' I said, picking up the one she'd discarded. 'This has some age, and you can see how some pages haven't been cut properly, but … no.' I shook my head. 'I still think it's to do with this painting, and I'm going to need to have a good look at it.'

Simon loped in; I recognised today's band T-shirt – the Australian rock band AC/DC – and this morning's breakfast – a bacon and brown sauce butty. 'I heard we had a visit from the forces of justice last night.'

'Nothing exciting,' said Bell. 'Some fake pottery.'

'Again?' Simon clapped before I could answer. 'Before I forget, did I tell you what the Proctors bought yesterday?'

'No,' I prompted, giving him my full attention.

Before he could enlighten us, Ginny arrived carrying a tray of teacups and a pot of tea. 'Simon, be a dear,' she said, 'and bring through the plate of parkin I've laid out.'

'Sure, as long as there's a cup there for me,' he said. He was halfway down the hall before he doubled back and said, 'Actually, Bell, do you want to get the parkin, and I'll grab another couple of chairs.'

'You might as well get enough for everyone,' I called.

'Tamsin and Henry aren't in yet,' he said, 'but I'll tell the brothers.'

By the time he was back with chairs for all, Bell had collected the parkin, and tea was poured; the gang was all there.

'What did the police want?' asked Ambrose.

'Have you been up to no good again, lass?' teased Eugene.

'Okay,' I said. 'Now everyone's here, I'll tell you.' Ginny sat forward in her seat, her eyes eager. 'Inspector Dawkins was only here to warn me about some fakes. That's all, nothing more to see here, but keep your eye out in case anyone comes in wanting to sell cheap Clarice Cliff.'

Ginny sighed, her shoulders falling back into position. 'That's a pity; he had such kind eyes, and you were naughty teasing him like that.'

'Like what?' This time it was Bell leaning forward with an anticipatory look.

'Nothing,' I retorted. 'He said he was here to see Mrs Barker and because Alison was there picking up the kids, it was too good an opportunity to waste. Now, Simon, what were you going to tell us before Ginny so rudely interrupted us with tea?' I grinned cheekily at Ginny, who shrugged.

'I was going to tell you what Tamsin bought yesterday – but now they're here, they can tell you themselves.' He pushed his hair out of his face and reached for another piece of parkin.

Tamsin pulled at her plait and twisted it around. 'Would you believe we bought some bricks?'

'Bricks?' asked Bell. 'Why?'

'They're not just any bricks; these are commemorative Charles and Diana royal wedding bricks,' said Henry. 'Does anyone want this last piece of parkin?'

'No. Way!' I said. 'Please tell me it's not true … about the bricks, that is.'

'What on earth will anyone do with commemorative bricks?' asked Bell.

'Maybe they're building a commemorative brick wall,' suggested Ginny, trying – and failing – to keep a straight face.

'I don't know,' mused Ambrose. 'I can see a market for them. What did you pay?'

'Twenty quid for ten bricks – two of them were for the royal wedding in 1981, one was for the jubilee, and the others were football teams,' Henry said, looking pleased with himself.

'Maybe you need to ring Inspector Dawkins with his kind eyes and tell him some fake bricks are doing the rounds,' Ginny suggested to me.

'Oh, ha ha,' I said.

'It's a good point, though,' said Bell. 'How do you know whether they're genuine commemorative bricks or just bricks someone's stamped some writing into?'

Tamsin shrugged. 'No idea. We bought them for a laugh but should make some money on them as well.'

'What's their estimate?' asked Eugene.

'There's always plenty of interest in anything Diana related,' Tamsin said. 'I'm thinking we'll get seventy-five to a hundred.'

'That's a great result,' I said, trying to cover the surprise in my voice.

'Well, it looks like we've sold that leather kitbag and suitcase we bought yesterday,' said Eugene. 'Sir Antony will be here on Saturday to collect it.' He named a price that even Bell sat up and took notice of. 'He wants first refusal of what was in the mixed lot we bought as well.'

Ambrose looked at his watch. 'Speaking of which, we need to go through that before we open this morning. Come on, Eugene.'

The rest of Thursday passed as it usually did until a call came through late in the afternoon from Becky at Young and Johnson's.

After greeting me, she talked just long enough about the weather for me to say, 'Becky, what's up?'

She gave a nervous-sounding giggle and said, 'Look, this is awkward, but we were wondering whether you'd be interested in selling the letterbox and mixed lot you bought yesterday – the one with the Whitby oil in it. Catherine will pay what you bought it for, plus a ten percent premium.'

Words failed me. This wasn't just an unusual request; it was downright weird. No wonder Becky sounded uncomfortable asking me.

'It's too late for that,' I finally said. 'I've already sold the brass from the box.' They'd sold this morning before I could clean them up and put them on display – a couple had declared they were exactly what they'd been looking for to decorate the fireplace in the home they were renovating in Pickering.

'Oh,' she said. 'Hang on a minute.'

There was a muffled conversation, presumably with Catherine. Becky was soon back. 'I'm sure that's okay – if the rest of the lot is intact.'

I allowed the silence to hang for a couple of seconds. 'What's this about, Becky?'

'To be honest, Philly, I have no idea. Catherine has asked me to see if you'll sell the items back, that's all.'

'Does that mean the letterbox came from the same place as the mixed lot?'

'Aye.'

For all the plausible reasons Catherine would be desperate to get the goods back, none sounded like the Catherine I knew. 'Did she have authority to sell?' I asked tentatively.

'Absolutely.' Becky sounded almost personally affronted.

'I'm sorry,' I said, 'but I had to ask.'

There was another long moment of silence before Becky continued, 'I probably shouldn't be saying anything, and I don't know if I'm on the right track, but I think those items belonged to a deceased estate, and now another family member has come forward and said they would've liked them for sentimental reasons.'

'I see. Well, if that's the case, they can buy them back off me. I'm still not sure what's in the mixed lot – other than the brass and the painting, that is.' I crossed my fingers as I told the lie.

'If that's the case, you might be left with a whole lot of nothing,' Becky said quickly, a tone of desperation creeping into her voice. 'Those trivets were probably the best of the lot.'

'Hmmm,' I said slowly. 'I think I might have a look at what else is in the box before I make a call on that. It sounds as though there's something in particular they want back.' And that might be worth more than the ten percent premium on what I'd paid.

'You don't get to pick and choose, Philly. It's an all-or-nothing deal. Besides, knowing you, you've probably already made your money back and more on the brass – the rest might be rubbish.' Was that an edge of panic in her voice?

'If it is, then why do they want it back so badly?'

'I don't know,' she admitted. 'I suspect it's a family estrangement, and now they want anything that belonged to the dearly departed.'

No, there was more to it than that. 'The answer is no, Becky. I won't sell it back. If the family wants it, they can buy it back directly from me.'

'But –'

'No buts, my answer stands.'

After hanging up, I pondered the call for another few minutes, idly swinging from left to right in my swivelling chair. What was it that was of so much interest? The brass had gone, and Becky and Catherine (if it had been Catherine with her) hadn't seemed overly concerned about that. Was it the silver spoon? Surely not. It was a nice thing, but not rare. The other spoons in the box were later – Edwardian – and nice, but not special. As for the horse brass, it came in all the time. It looked great in old pubs, but enamelled signs did better at sales these days.

I swivelled back to rest my elbows on the table, my fingers pressing into my temple. Becky had specifically said she wanted the letterbox and the mixed lot with the Whitby oil. What if it wasn't the goods they wanted back, but something that had been in the goods? Boxes, books and the backs of picture frames used to be common hiding places for documents. But if they wanted it all, it meant they didn't know what piece held whatever it was they were looking for.

'I'd clear that frown if I were you,' said Bell who had glided in without me noticing. 'What's up?'

I told her about the conversation I'd had with Becky.

'That doesn't sound like Catherine,' she finally said. She'd lost the cloche during the day and now reached behind to twist her hair into a thick makeshift ponytail. 'No wonder she got Becky to make the call.' A speculative smile came to her mouth. 'What do you think it could be?'

'I don't know. A letter or a will? What if it's a lost will that leaves everything to someone else? That would be why they don't know what item it's in.'

Bell lifted one shoulder. 'Perhaps, but you're assuming what they want back – whoever they are – is a document. What if it's the piece itself that's special?'

'True. If it's a family estrangement, perhaps they'd always heard talk of something that was never sold – rainy day money. Plenty of families did it – held onto a special piece of jewellery, art or furniture until they were desperate for money.'

'Perhaps,' Bell said, picking up the little silver stoat spoon. 'But it's not this spoon. What about the brass?'

'Already sold, and Becky didn't seem too perturbed about that.'

'Already? Good price?'

'Let's just say I've already got my money back on both lots.'

'Okay, so you have nothing to lose by hanging on until you know more.' Bell stood facing a cabinet containing some silver and jewellery, perfectly still, a tall, elegant sculpture in black. She turned to face me. 'What if it really is just about getting some family pieces back? Let's face it, plenty of people have been unable to travel over the last couple of years and might not have been able to make it back in time for a funeral. Would you want to profit from that?'

'Probably not,' I conceded.

One eyebrow cocked, she said, 'So, rather than jumping to conclusions, why don't you talk to Catherine tomorrow and find out what's going on? Then you can make your decision.'

I nodded slowly, tapping my finger on my bottom lip. 'You're right, of course. I'll call her tomorrow.'

Once she'd left, I picked up one of the books from the box and weighed it in my hand. A small cloth-covered book – about the size of a paperback but much thinner – it was a recipe book published by the Women's Institute in Cornwall in the 1930s and somehow had found its way here, to north-east Yorkshire. I turned it over. For a book that was almost a hundred years old, it was in good condition; there was some yellowing on the pages, some wear and tear on the cloth cover, but otherwise good condition.

Inside the front cover was an inscription:

Dearest Peggy,
To remind you of home …
Your loving sister
Beatrice 1938

These sorts of books were published by WI branches across the country, so the only value (to anyone other than family) was as a piece of social history. I made a mental note to email the WI in Cornwall to see if they had a copy; if they didn't, I'd send it down. From experience, the north-south divide was such that I'd have trouble selling this book up here.

My instincts were telling me there was nothing special about this book – or the others, what appeared to be travel guides to Yorkshire, the Yorkshire Dales and the Derbyshire Peak District from about the same time. Yet my skin prickled each time I glanced at the painting – it had to be that. I'd take it home again tonight and have a proper look. Something was sending my senses into overdrive, and I wouldn't rest until I knew what it was.

Chapter Six

'I'm really sorry about yesterday,' Catherine said after greeting me. She'd phoned me before I had a chance to call her. 'It wasn't something I was comfortable about asking.'

'Which is why you got Becky to call?' I guessed.

'Yes,' she replied in an embarrassed voice. 'You know me well enough to know that's not how I do business,' she said.

'I must say, it surprised me. What was the story?'

She sighed heavily. 'To be honest, I'm not sure.' There was a moment of quiet. It was as if she needed to get her thoughts straight in her head. 'A woman came into the office yesterday morning wanting to look at the items we'd had from a deceased estate from Malton. I explained everything had been auctioned the previous day, and the proceeds were sent to the executor for disbursement. I'd no sooner said it when she began crying – and not a few tears either; she was out and out sobbing. I tried to calm her down, but she was having none of it.' I imagined Catherine grimacing as she recalled the scene – Catherine wasn't a big one for scenes.

'Finally, she stopped crying for long enough to tell me the estate had belonged to her grandmother, and she and her husband hadn't been able to get to England before now – apparently, they've been living in Australia, and you've had your borders closed so they hadn't been able to leave the country.'

The way she added the last sentence was the way everyone did – as if I personally, being an Aussie, had something to do with the borders being closed for as long as they had been. Each time it was mentioned, I wanted to wail that I hadn't been able to get back to see my family either. Now, though, I let the comment go.

'She said there were things that had been special to her grandmother that she wanted to keep,' Catherine continued.

'Did she specify what things?' I asked.

'No. I asked the same question, and she said she just wanted to look at them, although she said she wasn't interested in the few pieces of furniture – it would be too difficult to get it home. When pressed, she said there were some books and paintings she remembered and boxes that she said were like treasure chests to a child. I showed her the catalogue, and she could identify the letterbox, a couple of paintings – yours and another one – and a travelling vanity case. Then she got upset again and said she'd pay whatever it took to get some of it back.'

'I see,' I said, although the situation was no more apparent than before. 'How much over the hammer price was she offering you?'

Catherine paused again before saying in a small voice, 'Twenty-five percent.'

'Not bad,' I said. 'You've already got your sale commission, and now you get another bite at it.'

'Come on, Philly,' she said defensively. 'Business isn't that good that I can turn it away.'

'Did anyone agree to sell it back?'

'No. I got Becky to ring you, but I know for a fact the other box – a lovely Victorian ladies travelling vanity case, one of those that would contain all the necessities for a week in the country – was bought as a wedding anniversary present so I didn't bother calling the purchaser and couldn't get hold of the buyer of the other painting.'

'What did she say when you told her?'

'Mrs Wainwright?' Catherine exhaled. 'Forget I mentioned that name,' she added quickly. 'That was the strange thing. She didn't leave me with any means of contacting her. Something about how she hadn't bought a UK phone card and it would cost a fortune, but that she'd call in today with her husband to see how I'd gone.'

'And did they come back?'

'Yes, although minus the husband, and very contrite she was too. She said she was sorry for my trouble, that she'd been overwrought, but now understood that it was for the best and how were they going to get it all home again anyway? And that was that.'

'Okay,' I said, perplexed by the whole situation. 'I hadn't been able to see what they would've wanted with my lots anyway – the letterbox is unusual enough, but there's nothing special about the rest. A couple of old books, some spoons, and I sold the brass.'

'That oil looked alright,' Catherine said.

'Yes, it's sound, and I think there's something in that, but …' I wasn't sure what else to say. I'd had a good look at it last night and was convinced it was special. There was something familiar about the brushstrokes, but I'd need to do a lot more research. It was sitting on an easel at home, ready for me to look at it over the weekend in daylight.

Catherine apologised again and rang off. That, I decided, was that. Nothing more to see here.

At least that's what I told Bell when she asked.

'That makes sense,' she said. 'She was probably feeling guilty because she'd ignored her grandmother for the past twenty years, and now she's been left nothing.'

'We don't know that,' I pointed out.

'No, we don't know it, but I'd like to bet it's true. So she's dragged her husband out from Australia to try and buy a picture or a box that she says she remembers from rose-coloured holidays with old gran – that in truth she probably complained about every year – and then when it's all sold, she's overreacted. I'd say she's gone back to their hotel, calmed down and realised it's all probably junk anyway.'

'What if it isn't junk?'

Bell shrugged, her black velvet shawl sliding off her arms. 'She's never going to know, is she?' she said wryly before gliding back to her stall.

A York-based tour company had recently added us to their shopping day trips – in the prized lunch stop on account of our tearoom and toilets – so we were kept busy for much of the morning. Aside from increased business, the other positive of the bus tour deal was that Ginny always had something special on the menu – which meant we all ate well. Today there was Thai red curry lentil soup, a chicken chorizo and cider pot pie, and clementine and poppy seed muffins.

The sales were good, mostly from the cabinets – silver and jewellery did particularly well on these tours – and the others also had good trade. The Proctors triumphantly declaring that one shopper bought every single one of their commemorative bricks. We discussed how they managed to get them on and off the bus at length.

It wasn't until later in the afternoon that I could sit down and pull out the letterbox. 'Not that I expect to find anything,' I told Balthazar as he sat with his head on my knee and watched me pour over every square inch of oak. To be completely honest, I don't know what I expected to find. A secret drawer, perhaps. They often had them in writing desks and ladies' travelling cases, so it wasn't beyond the realm of possibility, but I couldn't see where one would fit in this box. It didn't appear to have a fake bottom to the box section, and I couldn't find a hidden catch for a second drawer. As to what I'd find in there if it even existed? A secret will? A photo? A love letter?

When I was doing my antique training, I used to drive Catherine mad with my incessant searches for hidden compartments in writing desks and the like – I found a few too, but none had anything interesting in them. I did, however, still live in hope.

I pushed the box to one side and stood to help a customer who was peering behind a mahogany dressing table mirror I'd had balanced on an early twentieth century shipping chest. 'Can I help you with anything?' I asked.

Smartly dressed in a silky emerald blouse with a floppy bow at her neck, well-cut black pants and heels, and a coat that looked so expensive it must be cashmere, the woman turned to me and smiled slightly. 'I'm not sure what I'm looking for, but ...' Her voice was as well-cut as her clothes – not exactly from the best of schools, but certainly from a good one.

'You'll know it when you see it?' I finished.

'Exactly. My husband and I have recently purchased a home not far from here, and for the first time, we have a proper library room – so I'm after some proper library furniture.' She smiled widely. 'And I've been told Chipwell Barn is the place to come, so here I am.' She opened her arms, her palms facing upwards.

'If it's furniture you're after, you're probably best

visiting Simon – at the back of the barn.'

'I'll work my way down there. I'm also looking for accessories and art – and maybe some old boxes. I have a large mahogany desk and would love a box to sit on top of it.' She cast her eyes around the room. 'And old books – the kind that are cloth covered. Do you have anything like that?'

A bell began ringing in my brain – pealing so softly that I had to strain to hear it. 'I do – you'll find books in that corner.' I pointed to the bookshelf in the rear of the stall. 'Unless there's a specific title or genre you have in mind?'

She frowned and pursed her lips as though contemplating the question. 'Well, now you mention it, I'd love something regional – an old-style recipe book or traveller's guide. They'd look quite fun on the shelves, don't you think?'

The ringing in my head grew louder. She'd described the books I'd bought in the mixed lot. Could this be the relative who'd called on Catherine? Mrs Wainwright?

'I'm afraid that all I have is what's on the shelves,' I said, my fingers crossed behind my back.

'I see.' She ran her finger lightly along the backs of the books, scanning the titles. She turned back to face me. 'I don't suppose you've seen any paintings come through of the Yorkshire coast? I'd love something from Whitby – maybe turn of the last century, a little older? It would suit the room and also' – she lowered her voice as if she were telling me a secret – 'my husband is from Whitby, and he has a milestone birthday coming up, so it would be a lovely surprise to give him something that reminds him of home.'

I wasn't sure what made me say it, but I said, 'No, nothing's come in recently – although we get some from time to time. Would you like me to take your number?'

She waved the offer away. 'No, it's fine; I'll keep looking.' Her gaze swung to my desk. 'Now, *that* I'm interested in. What is it?'

'It's an oak letterbox,' I said. 'It would've sat on the hall table in a large country manor house.'

She ran her hand across the wood, her fingers tracing the brass hardware. 'This is rather lovely. Is the key original?'

'Yes.'

She nodded in approval. 'What price do you have on it?'

I wasn't sure what made me say this either, but the words, 'It's not for sale,' came out of my mouth.

'Oh, really?' She sounded surprised in the way that people who didn't want to sound surprised sounded. 'I'm sure there's a price at which it might be for sale.'

'I'm afraid not; I've already sold it,' I said, the lie coming from my lips easily.

She lifted the box and tapped at the bottom. 'It's a lovely piece. You said it would've come from a country house. Do you know which one?'

'No, I bought it at auction.'

'Hmmm,' she said again. 'Did you buy anything else that might've come from the same source?'

By now the hairs were standing up on the back of my

neck – and not for a good reason. 'There's some silver here; I believe it came from the same place,' I said evenly, opening the cabinet and taking out the stoat spoon. 'This is quite lovely. I had some brass fire tools and trivets, but they've been sold. Why do you ask?'

'No reason. It's just that sometimes when you get a quality piece like this from a deceased estate, often there'll be other interesting things too – other boxes, books, paintings and the like.' She might've been attempting to sound nonchalant, but there was something in her tone I didn't like at all. That bell was positively clanging.

'Who said anything about a deceased estate?' I asked.

She laughed a fake laugh. 'Oh, didn't you say it was a deceased estate?'

'No,' I said, straightening to my full five feet and a few inches. 'I didn't.'

'Silly me, I must've misunderstood.' She picked up the spoon and flipped it over to see the price tag. 'I do like this, though, and think I'll take it.' She tilted her head to the side and focused her gaze on me. 'Are you sure you can't be persuaded to part with the box?'

My return smile was thin. 'I'm sorry, but as I said, it's been sold.'

'Perhaps you could ask your buyer if they'll reconsider. I'm happy to make your – and their – trouble worthwhile.'

'You must really like the box,' I said with a quizzical stare. 'To go to that effort to get it.'

'I really do. Will you ask them – or, if you like, give me their phone number, and I'll call them myself.'

It was as if she knew I was lying. 'I couldn't do that – that would be a breach of my client's confidentiality.' I returned her stare, trying to project more confidence than I felt. 'But leave me your name and number, and I'll let you know how I go.'

She cast her eye around the space one more time. 'I'll take one of your cards and call you,' she said, taking a card from the holder on my desk and sliding it into her oversized handbag. 'Now, you're sure you don't have any local oil paintings or books? Perhaps in your storeroom? Something new that you haven't looked at yet properly?'

By now, I was absolutely positive this woman was Catherine's Mrs Wainwright – even though this Mrs Wainwright had said she lived locally and Catherine's visitor had travelled from Australia. Surely she had to know that Catherine would've spoken to me? Maybe she was arrogant enough to assume that none of us spoke to each other.

'I do have a couple of paintings in my storeroom,' I admitted. 'A couple of still lifes and an abstract nude. Would you like to look at them?' Her look was one of impatience. 'I also have some enamel signs which work well in period renovations depending, of course, on what look you're going for.'

Hopefully, my expression was as guileless as hers. She searched my face as if she was trying to decide if I was as open as I was pretending to be. After a moment's silence, she said, 'No, that's okay. I'll take this spoon with me and call you tomorrow to see how you've gone with the letterbox.'

'No problem.' I rang up the sale and wrapped the spoon in some tissue before attaching a sticker with my logo to it.

'Thank you … Philly,' she read my name from the sticker. 'What's that short for?'

'Philomena,' I said.

'Unusual. And is that an Australian accent I hear?'

'It is. But I've been here so long I forget I have the accent. If I go home, they think I speak with an English accent.' I hesitated before adding, 'Have you ever been? To Australia?' Cheeky, yes, but I couldn't help but ask.

'Me? No, it's such a long flight, and we do like Spain for our holidays.'

I pulled together a smile and pretended to believe her. She smiled the same smile – as if she was pretending to believe that I believed her, and then she was gone, leaving behind a weird energy that made me feel chilled to the bone even though it was comfortably warm in the room. A shiver trickled down my back, and I collapsed back into my chair, exhausted after the battle of wills that had taken place. Bally, who had not moved from his mat the whole time she was here – but also had not taken his eyes off her (dogs always know) – rose and padded to where I sat. I patted his head and said, 'I know, fella, that was strange. I think we both need some fresh air after that.'

Chapter Seven

While Bally was doing his doggy business, I wrapped my arms around my waist in feeble defence against the chilly breeze. In my rush to get outside, I'd left my jacket hanging on the hook behind the door. And now ... What to do about Mrs Wainwright – if that was her name? I could call Catherine and get a description of the woman who'd called on her; I could even find a way to ask if Catherine, Becky, or someone else at the salesroom had given my details out. If the description didn't match, I'd sound awfully foolish, though.

No, I'd say nothing. I doubted whether she'd call me tomorrow. It had been uncomfortable, though. I leant back against the wall of the barn and exhaled puffs of steam as Bally sniffed around the garden, making sure nothing new had happened in his world since he'd last been there. A documentary once said that smells were like text messages to dogs – it was how they kept up with everything, and spaniels, according to the same program, had some of the best noses of all the breeds. It's why they were used as mountain rescue dogs in the peak country. I concentrated on trivia like this until the cold air blew away the sound of that ringing bell in my subconscious. When it was silenced, I listened to a more rational voice telling me I was blowing the whole thing out of proportion. It was just a coincidence that this afternoon's customer had been browsing for items like those I'd bought at the sale the other day. After all, they were the sorts of items that anyone doing up a country home would search for – ask any interior designer in the county, and they'd tell you the same thing.

Taking a deep breath and letting it out with a huff, I whistled for Bally and went back inside to close up.

As I walked through the front door, changing the open sign to read 'Closed', Ginny called out. 'Fancy a brew?'

'You don't need to make me tea,' I said, blowing warm air into my hands to warm them. 'Have the others gone?'

'They have. I've just boiled the kettle for myself, and I thought you might like one.' Her smile was as sunny as the yellow knit she wore and warmed me immediately. 'I'll bring it through,' she said.

'I'm not sure I could possibly love you more,' I said a few minutes later, taking the saucer and cup from her – two-thirds of an Edwardian Shelley trio. It didn't matter whether it was vintage or not, but there was something special about sipping your tea from a fine china cup – especially when it was as pretty as this one was.

'You look like something's on your mind,' Ginny said,

cradling her mug which would be filled with her favourite hot chocolate.

'You know me too well,' I said, my eye wandering again to the letterbox.

'It fascinates you, doesn't it?' she said. When I nodded, she asked, 'Why?'

I exhaled loudly. 'I don't know. Maybe it's because you don't come across many of these, or perhaps it's because of the stories it could tell.'

'There's more, though, isn't there?' she guessed.

'Yes. Someone wants this quite badly, and I don't know why.' I told her about my call from Catherine and this afternoon's visitor.

'Is it worth a lot of money?' She asked, placing her mug down on a coaster and picking up the box.

'Not particularly,' I said. 'I've seen some command big prices – over two thousand pounds – but they were larger and had a better provenance.' At her raised eyebrows, I added, 'The ones I've seen do well at auction had come from one of the major houses – somewhere like Castle Howard or Blenheim Palace. I'm not sure of the history of this one, but I'd be surprised if it weren't from a local manor. This one is in excellent condition, and I'll probably be able to get five hundred for it on a good day – but it would need to be a very good day. I'll be putting that price on, but knowing I'll probably take a bit less.'

'I get the slot for posting letters, but what about these

gaps? What would've been here?' Ginny asked, pointing towards the vertical pigeonholes.

'The house labelled stationary. It would've been quite the thing to write – and receive – a letter from one of these houses. Being invited to the house parties was an honour, especially if it was during the hunting season. The men would go out with the guns and the women –'

'Would stay back and wait for them and write letters,' she finished with an intrigued look on her face.

'Pretty much.'

'Didn't some of these boxes have secret drawers and the like?' Ginny held the box to her ear and knocked at the panels.

'Yes, some did. I wondered whether there may have been a hidden drawer where the telegram drawer is or a false bottom in the letter section, but I've checked there.'

Ginny used the key to open the letter box itself and tapped hopefully at the base panel. 'No, nothing here either. So' – she pulled out the telegram drawer and ran her hand around inside the resulting space – 'if it's not worth a lot of money and it doesn't have anywhere to hide secrets, why do they want it?'

I shrugged. 'Who knows.' I sipped at my tea. 'I could be jumping to conclusions that aren't there, and it could all be a coincidence, but –'

'Your instincts are telling you it isn't.'

I pressed my lips together and nodded.

'Then go with them.' She went to put the box back on the table, but it wavered on the edge, and then it clattered onto the ground. Ginny's hand flew to her mouth, and her eyes widened in horror. 'Oh my god, I'm so sorry.'

My heart was in my mouth as she bent to lift it, exhaling in relief when it appeared to be in one piece and with no visible dents. 'It's okay,' she announced with a shaky breath. 'No thanks to me. I should be banned from coming in here and touching things.'

'Don't be silly,' I said, taking the box from her to examine it for damage. 'It seems fine. Hang on, what's this?' One of the carved decorative spindles that sat on either side of the letterbox itself, separating the stationary pigeonholes from where the letters were stored for posting, was loose. Damn.

'Is it broken?' asked Ginny, sounding as devastated as I was beginning to feel.

'I'm not sure.' I jiggled the wood. Could it be? My heart was beating double time as I pulled my magnifying loupe out from its case and examined the carving more closely. 'Ginny, can you pass me a paperclip, please?'

'Have you found something?' she asked, grimacing sightly.

'I think I have.' I straightened the bends and folds in the paperclip and inserted it into the tiny hole I'd found in the carving, my ear as close to the wood as I could get it. Yes, there was a click. The panel popped forward to reveal a narrow space an inch wide and the depth of the letterbox. I looked up at Ginny and smiled widely.

'Oh. My. God. Really?' She moved her chair closer to mine so she could see what I was doing.

My pulse racing, I picked up a silver letter opener that was only on my desk for decorative reasons and, holding my breath to control my shaking hand, inserted it smoothly into the space, gently dragging out the contents.

'What is it?' asked Ginny.

'I'm not sure yet. Photos, I think. There's definitely more than one.' Taking my time, I removed the photos from their hiding spot.

There were three photos. The first was of three people – two fresh-faced young men and a girl. One of the men, more of a teenager than a man, was looking at the camera; the other had eyes only for the girl – who was, in turn, looking into his eyes with as much intensity. I turned the photo over. *Billy, Johnny and Peggy Spring 1944.* The second was of the same girl, but this time she was cradling a baby. The inscription on this one was simply *Jonny December 1944.* The third was (presumably) the same baby smiling in that way that babies do when all is good in their world. Again, the inscription on the back was *Jonny December 1944.*

'Do you think these are what they were looking for?' asked Ginny, taking the photos from my hand and studying the images.

'I suspect so.' I already had the loupe and paperclip at the ready for the other carved plinth. This one was harder to open; the years had jammed it shut. With the help of the letter opener, I could release the catch, though. Inside the drawer was a document – a birth certificate.

I unfolded it, taking care not to rip the fading paper. 'Look at this,' I said. 'Jonathon Edward Sykes born December 1944. The mother's name is listed as Margaret Sykes, and the father is unknown.'

Ginny leant in closer to read. 'It says that she was a servant, and there's an address, but it's difficult to read.'

I peered through my magnifying glass. 'I think it's a Malton address,' I said, 'but I'll need to look it up.' I turned to Ginny. 'This has to be what she's after – if the woman I had here this afternoon is the same as the Mrs Wainwright who Catherine dealt with.' I refolded the birth certificate and put it, plus the photos, into an envelope. 'I'll take these home, I think, and if Mrs Wainwright, or whoever she is, calls tomorrow and wants this letterbox, I'll give her a price and see what happens.' I pushed the carved panels back firmly into the box. No one looking at it now would know it had been tampered with.

'And tomorrow I'll call Catherine too and get a description of her Mrs Wainwright. I might also see if she'll give me any information on where the items came from.' I tapped the envelope with my finger. 'Let's see if we can't somehow find out who these originally belonged to.'

Chapter Eight

When Bally and I arrived at the barn the next morning, the Ashton brothers and the Proctors were standing outside, and Rochester was complaining loudly from inside the plastic carry box he arrived in each day.

'What's going on?' I asked, Bally straining the lead to be further away from the cat.

While they all smiled weakly at my arrival, it was Tamsin who answered. 'We've had a break-in,' she said. 'The police are on their way.'

'But how?' Even as I asked, I could see how the perpetrators had gained access – they had cut the padlock on the timber barn doors off, and the sliding glass door that sat behind it had been jemmied open. 'Is there any other damage?'

'We don't know,' said Ambrose. 'When we arrived about twenty minutes ago, we saw the door and rang for the police. None of us have been inside yet.'

Over the next ten minutes, the rest of the crew arrived, so by the time the police car turned up, we were all milling around outside – and it had begun to drizzle.

Beside the squad car, another car pulled up, and Robbie got out. After chatting with his colleagues, he walked across to where we were watching.

'Good morning, Mrs Barker,' he said, flipping a large umbrella open, attempting to cover us both.

'Inspector Dawkins.' I greeted him with a smile, echoing his formality. 'Other than Ginny, you haven't met the rest of the crew, have you?' I introduced him to the others, giving him a quick rundown of who collected and sold what.

'Who was the first here this morning?' he asked.

'That would be us, Inspector,' said Eugene.

'And you haven't been inside?'

'No, we haven't. Once we saw the door had been tampered with, we stayed out here until the others arrived – just in case anyone was still in there.'

Robbie gave a quick nod. 'A wise decision. We've ascertained there's no one inside, and at this point, it appears the only stall that has been broken into is yours, Philly. The glass doors to each of the other tenancies appear secure, so the rest of you are free to open up.'

My head jerked up at his words, my tummy teetering. 'What did you say?'

'Yours appears to have been the only stall that's been targeted,' he said again, his eyes burning into mine.

'That would make sense, I suppose,' said Simon. 'Philly and the brothers are the only ones with portable stock that has any value.' He shot Bell a look of apology. 'No offence Bell, but unless you have something worn by Princess Diana, there's not massive money in vintage clothes, but some of the jewellery and silver that Philly gets in and the coins and military memorabilia the Ashtons hold can easily be carried out and resold.'

Ambrose was nodding, a serious look on his face. 'That's true. Perhaps they were disturbed and only had time to turn over Philly's place. That's what they call it, don't they? "Turning over"?'

Robbie appeared to be trying to keep a straight face. 'Yes, that is a term sometimes used.' To everyone else, he said, 'I'm happy for you all to open up. Can I ask you, though, to check and make sure nothing has been tampered with? I still have some questions I need to ask Philly.'

The Proctors and Simon drifted off, full of chatter about what had happened. Ambrose and Eugene, with a complaining Rochester, followed.

Bell and Ginny hung back. 'Are you okay, Philly?' asked Bell, resplendent today in peacock blue – in fact, today's shawl looked as though there was a peacock printed on it.

'I'm fine, thanks,' I said, including them both in my smile, a smile that was becoming more tremulous the longer I stayed out here thinking about what had happened.

'Do you think this has anything to do with –?' Ginny started, her voice trailing off when she saw my face. 'I'll put the kettle on, shall I?'

'And I'll take Bally with me,' said Bell.

I nodded absently, and they left us to it, Bally trotting contentedly beside them.

'Philly?' Robbie said slowly. 'Is there something you need to tell me about?'

I sighed. 'I think that depends on what's missing,' I said, toeing at a stone on the path with my boot and feeling the stare he was directing at me.

'I see. Well, let's get inside and have a look then, shall we?' His tone was so different from how it was on Wednesday night at the pub. Then it was open and friendly; now there was a tinge of suspicion to it.

I wasn't sure what I'd expected to see – overturned cabinets perhaps, broken china, shattered glass – but while the cabinet doors were opened and they had obviously picked through the jewellery, nothing was missing. When I told Robbie this, I wasn't sure he believed me.

'You're saying nothing is missing from these cabinets?'

'Not that I can tell. I'd need to check my records, but no.' I shook my head and bit my lower lip. 'Everything is here.'

The same couldn't be said for my bookshelves, where the contents had been pulled out and thrown on the floor. As I'd expected it would be, they had forced the door to my storeroom open, and the room had very obviously been searched – and not at all neatly.

The letterbox was gone, as were the books that had

come from the mixed lot. I stood in the middle of the room – which was no larger than a dressing room – and put my hands over my face.

'Philly, what's missing?' Robbie asked firmly.

Expelling a long breath, I held my hands almost prayer-like at my mouth. Removing them, I said, 'An oak Victorian letterbox, a 1930s copy of a recipe book published by the Cornwall WI and a few travel guides to Yorkshire and Derbyshire published around the same time.'

He rubbed at the back of his neck, his brows drawing closer together. 'Are you sure that's all?'

'Yes, I'm almost positive.' Before he could say anything else, I said, 'Let's go and sit down, and I'll tell you what little I know.'

Ginny chose that time to bring in a tray with a teapot and two cups. 'I wasn't sure if you were a tea or coffee man,' she said, 'but decided that as Philly likes her tea, that's what you'll get too.' Before Robbie could thank her, she continued. 'There's milk and sugar and some parkin. It's parkin weather, don't you think?'

'Thanks, Ginny,' I said with a tight smile.

She touched my arm lightly, set the tray down and backed out of the stall.

'Shall I pour?' I didn't wait for his answer and poured tea into the cups. I waved vaguely at the milk and sugar – which he refused – and the parkin – which he took. 'Good decision,' I said. 'Ginny makes a lovely parkin. I think it's the combination of oats and flours ...'

'Philly ...'

'I know, I'm rambling.' I sat down and swivelled in my chair, my finger to my lips as I pondered where exactly to start.

'How did you know what would be missing?' Robbie prompted. 'You *did* know, didn't you?'

I picked up my cup and sipped at the tea allowing the strong, earthy scent of the brew to soothe my mind, slow my heartbeat and warm me from the inside. 'I'll need to go back to the beginning for that,' I said. He nodded for me to continue. While he still sat back, notebook poised, his face more closed than open, I still got the impression that while he was wary, he wanted to believe whatever I had to say.

'When you called in the other day,' I started, 'I wasn't long back from a sale at Young and Johnson's in York – I'll give you the details when we're done. I bought several items at that sale, two of which I now believe came from the same deceased estate – an oak Victorian letterbox and a mixed lot box that I'd bought as a lucky dip. That's the thing with boxes like that, you don't know what's in them. They're a mix of odds and sods, and sometimes there are nuggets of gold in them, while at other times, well ...' I shrugged. 'I wanted this one because there was a framed painting in there that no one had attributed to any particular artist, but looking at it had made my neck prickle.' He raised an eyebrow in question. 'You know when you just know something is special or off or about to happen? Those little spider senses.' I took another sip of my tea. 'Of course you know – you're a detective; you would've had to learn to listen to them.'

'Yes,' he said simply, 'I know what you're talking about.'

'Anyway, I thought there might be something special about the painting, so I went for the whole box.'

'You didn't mention that the painting had been stolen,' he said, almost accusatory.

'No, because I'd taken it home so I could have a good look at it.' I set my cup back in its saucer. 'She wanted it too, though,' I said.

'Who wanted it?'

'We'll get to that. I hadn't long been back from the auction when you arrived to warn me about the fake pottery, and then, as you know, I went to the pub that evening, so I didn't get a chance to look at what else was in the box until Thursday morning.'

'And what was in the box?' he asked, leaning forward, curious.

'A few silver spoons, some horse brass – actually, a lot of horse brass – and some brass fireside trivets and tools. There were also some books.'

'The cookbook and the travel guides,' he guessed.

'Yes. That's right. The brass sold quickly – almost before I could put a price tag on it. That's the thing about brass – it only suits pubs and certain kinds of houses, so you need the right buyer or it takes up room for months. I tend not to buy it if I can help it.'

'So it's not particularly valuable?'

'No. It generally wipes its face, but that's about it,' I said dismissively.

'Wipes its face?'

I grinned at his look of confusion. 'Makes its money back, perhaps a little more. And that's all this brass did – paid for the box and a little more. Anyway, that afternoon Becky – she's the saleroom assistant – called and wanted to buy both lots back with a ten percent premium on what I'd paid.'

'Can they do that?'

'Sure, for the right price. It's unusual, though, really unusual. I told her I'd already sold the brass, and I wasn't interested in selling the rest. It had been busy, and I hadn't looked at the letterbox or the painting properly, and I wasn't letting either go without checking them over.'

'Did she say why she wanted to buy it back?'

'Not really. She thought some disgruntled relative wanted what Gran had always told them they could have, but she didn't really know. I thought little more about it until Catherine Young – the auctioneer – rang and told me to forget about it, that the potential buyer had changed her mind. She also accidentally dropped a surname – Wainwright – and said she'd been a granddaughter of the person who had passed away, but because she and her husband lived in Australia, they hadn't been able to come across for the funeral.

'Now Mrs Wainwright wanted some of the things she used to love when she was a child visiting her grandmother. Catherine said she got quite distressed when she was told everything had sold and offered Catherine a twenty-five percent premium to get some of it back. There was furniture too, but she didn't want that – just the paintings, the letterbox, a ladies travelling vanity case and the books.'

'There were more paintings than the one you have?'

'Yes, apparently another one which was sold separately. I remember it from the catalogue – a beautiful oil of Goathland Station, which there was quite a bit of interest in because of the Harry Potter connection. It's Hogsmeade station in the movies,' I explained. 'I almost bid for it myself.'

'It was also in some other TV show too, wasn't it? The one set in the 1960s?'

I nodded. 'Yes, *Heartbeat*. Of course you'd remember that – it was a police drama.'

He returned my grin. 'And the travelling vanity case? What's that?'

'I remember that one too – mainly because I was outbid on it as well. Come to think on it, I'm surprised it had come from the same place as my box, though,' I mused, tapping my finger against my teeth. 'It seemed a better quality piece than the rest.' I set my teacup back on the tray. 'Do you want another cup?' I asked. When he shook his head and placed his cup and saucer on the tray, I moved it away and dragged over my laptop. 'The results might be online now, and if they aren't, the catalogue should still be ...' I navigated to the auction website.

'Here we are.' I turned the screen so he could see it. 'Boxes like these would hold all the toilet necessities a lady needed when travelling – her brushes and combs, any lotions, that sort of thing. The French called them *necessaires*. This one is mahogany so that immediately spells class. The lady who owned it would've had money. Plus, the lining is fully intact; there doesn't appear to be any rips or tears – and you'd certainly expect to see some in a working box that's one hundred and fifty years old.

'You can't see it from this picture, but see the velvet under the lid? That's a little velvet-backed mirror that would detach and could sit on top of the closed lid in case wherever you've ended up doesn't have a proper dressing table. They usually came with silver-lidded cut-glass bottles and other beauty tools, but it's rare to find one complete.' Wondering if I was rambling, I looked up from the laptop and caught Robbie's face. He nodded once, indicating for me to continue. 'And if you do, it would be worth a couple of thousand rather than a couple of hundred.'

I returned my attention to the laptop and scrolled through the other lots to show him the paintings I'd been talking about.

'Nice,' he said. 'But not, as you say, worth more than a few hundred quid.'

'Exactly. I'm not sure what furniture came from this

deceased estate, but I'd be very surprised, having seen the other lots, if it was the quality of this vanity case.'

'The auctioneer said they'd changed their mind about buying it all back?' he asked.

'That's where this gets interesting – well, I think it does, anyway. I'm pretty sure Mrs Wainwright paid me a visit yesterday afternoon, but this woman said she was doing up a house she and her husband had bought and when I asked, said she'd never been to Australia. She knew, though, exactly what she was looking for.'

He sat back in his chair, his hands clasped, the fingers in a steeple resting against his mouth. 'Go on.'

'She pretended to look around but was only interested in the letterbox – I'd had it on my desk. She was also after vintage books – she specified old cookbooks and travel guides – and wanted to surprise her husband with a painting for his milestone birthday. Something older, in oil, of Whitby or the Yorkshire coast. If I hadn't already spoken to Catherine, I wouldn't have thought anything of it. But everything she mentioned was in that box I'd bought, Robbie.

'When I told her the letterbox was sold, she offered to pay me extra to sell it to her instead. I asked for her number, but she said she'd call me today to see how I went with the other buyer.'

'But there was no other buyer,' guessed Robbie.

'No. I'd only said that because I wanted to have a

chance to look over the letterbox properly.' I closed the lid of the laptop and met his gaze. 'And she won't call me today because she thinks she has what they want.'

He narrowed his eyes. 'What do you mean, she thinks she has what they want?'

I took another breath, debating whether to tell him the whole truth. 'It occurred to me that if they weren't interested in the silver or brass, and that the other items weren't worth a whole lot of money, it mightn't be the item itself they're after, but what's inside it.'

'Go on,' he encouraged.

'People used to use the spines or pages of books as hiding places for letters and the like. The backs of paintings or under the frames was another safe place. Mostly though, secretaires and writing boxes, and vanity cases like the one I showed you often had built-in secret drawers where valuables could be hidden. You wouldn't know it from the outside, but there'd be a catch somewhere – often under the escutcheon, that's the metal around the keyhole, or within one of the visible drawers. I've seen examples with inbuilt sovereign cases where your money can be held so securely that the coins don't jangle against each other when moved.'

'And you think they were looking for something they thought might be hidden in one of those compartments or in the books or in one of the paintings?'

'I know they were.'

'And how do you know?' He smiled a slow, wry smile as

if he already knew the answer to the question he was about to ask.

'Because I've found what I think they were looking for.'

'What have you done, Philly?' Robbie asked sternly.

'Firstly, can I say that I don't think I've done anything I shouldn't have done – I did, after all, buy the box fair and square. And secondly, how was I to know these people – if it was Mrs Wainwright and her husband, of course – would do what they've done to get it?'

'Okay, I'll give you that. What was it you found?'

'It was in the letterbox – I still haven't checked the painting, but I found two compartments behind the carved spindles on the letterbox. Here, I took photos ...' I located the photos on my phone and showed him. 'They were well hidden, and if Ginny hadn't accidentally dropped the box, we would never have found them. The hole for the catch was so tiny I only found it with a magnifying glass.'

'Are you going to tell me what was in there?' he asked in a way that told me he wanted me to get to the point.

'These.' I dug into my handbag for the envelope I'd put in there last night.

'You kept it?'

'Of course, it's mine to keep – at least I think it is. I owned the letterbox after all, and whoever hid these would be long dead.'

He exhaled – in exasperation? 'I'm not disputing that the property is yours; I'm simply wondering why you didn't put it back where you found it – not that you've told me yet what you found.'

'That's an easy question to answer – I wasn't sure I'd be able to find the catch again easily. Plus, I was going to do some research to find out who the people in the photographs were, and I couldn't do that if I had to continually lug the box back home. And finally, I'd bought the box to sell.' I handed the envelope to him. He opened it and pulled out the contents, carefully unfolding the birth certificate.

'Is this it?' he asked in surprise.

I nodded. 'It was all I could find, but it must be important if they're prepared to steal for it.' I pursed my lips. 'Unless there's more to be found. I think you're going to need to get in touch with whoever bought the vanity case and the other painting – if they find nothing in the letterbox, they'll probably head for those. Catherine could give you the details.'

He grinned and shook his head. 'You know, that hadn't occurred to me,' he drawled.

Embarrassed heat bloomed across my cheeks. Of course he would've thought of that – he had, after all, been doing this detective work for a long time.

'What has also occurred to me,' he said, the cheeky grin making way for something more serious, 'is that if they weren't able to find the painting here, they might go looking for it elsewhere.'

My heart stopped for a beat as what he said sunk in.

'You mean like at my house?'

Expression concerned, he nodded and opened his mouth to say more, but the ringing of his phone stopped him. He answered it, sneaking another look at me. 'Good morning, Sir. Yes, Sir, I'm here now. She's fine.' It must be Stewart. 'No, Sir, no damage to any other stall; it looks as though Phi ... Mrs Barker's stall was the only one broken into. No, not a lot of damage – the thieves seemed to know what they were after. Yes' – he shot me a wry smile – 'she's cooperating.' He gave Stewart the short version of what had happened. Then he said, 'Yes, Sir, I'll do that. I'll put her on now.'

He handed the phone to me. 'Good morning, Stewart,' I said. 'What are you up to on this fine Saturday morning?'

'Don't worry about what I'm doing,' he said. 'What's going on? You haven't been buying anything you shouldn't be, have you?'

'Absolutely not!' I exclaimed. 'How stupid do you think I am?' My voice rose at his accusation, and I took a breath to calm my rising anger. 'It was just a couple of lots from the sale on Wednesday. Nothing special.'

'Well, someone thinks they're special. Either that or they think you have something else worth stealing. Once Inspector Dawkins finishes there, I'm going to ask him to accompany you back home.'

'But –' I began.

'No buts, Philly. You and I both know you have a habit

of taking items home with you – too many of which don't end up back in the stall – and it wouldn't be that difficult for someone to find out where you live. Dawkins will take you home and check your locks – it's not as if you'll be trading today anyway.'

'I suppose not,' I admitted grudgingly.

'Right, so no more arguing. Put Dawkins back on, please.'

'Yes, Sir!' I made a face at the phone and handed it over.

Picking up the tray of tea things, I motioned across the hall, indicating I was taking them back to Ginny. He nodded, turned his back on me and continued his conversation.

Saturday morning trade was brisk in the tearoom with plenty of people in for Ginny's sausage rolls, savoury muffins and this morning's scone special – blueberry and Stilton.

In the small kitchen, I unloaded the tray and put our cups into the dishwasher, stashing the tray on the shelf where it belonged. Ginny came in as I was heading out. 'Are you okay?' she asked.

I nodded, a lump suddenly rising to my throat. She rubbed at my arm, and her warm sympathy almost brought me undone in a way that Robbie's calm practicality hadn't. 'I'm fine, and there's not a lot of damage. The door repair people will be out this afternoon to secure everything and Robbie, Inspector Dawkins, will leave an officer here to supervise that.'

'What was taken?'

I didn't need to tell her; the look on my face must have said it all.

'Oh Philly, no. The letterbox?'

I nodded mutely. 'And the books?'

Then she said what I'd been thinking and what I knew Robbie had been thinking. 'And they've been so obvious about it they mustn't care that you'll know who did it.'

I attempted a tremulous smile that didn't quite work, which was when she said the other thing that I'd been concerned about and that I knew had Robbie concerned too, but that neither of us had said. 'What are they going to do when they find out the letterbox is empty?'

'Come after the painting,' I said flatly.

'As long as they don't come after you.' Ginny grabbed for one of my hands. 'Do you and Bally want to come and stay with me for a few days?'

I shook my head. 'Thank you, lovely, but I'll be fine. Stewart has given strict instructions that Robbie's to come home with me now and check my locks. I'm perfectly safe. Besides, when they find nothing in the letterbox, they might decide that the document and the photos have been lost sometime over the years.'

I'd said it as if I believed it, and Ginny nodded in agreement as if she did too.

'You haven't told anyone about what we've found, have you?' I asked her.

She shook her head. 'There hasn't been time to.'

'Can you do me a favour and keep it to yourself for now? Just until this is all over?'

'Sure.' She looked bemused. 'What if Bell asks?'

'If she asks straight out, tell her, I'd never ask you to lie to anyone for me, and Bell is as safe as can be. The fewer people who know about this, the better. At least for now.'

Ginny tapped the side of her nose. 'Your secret is safe.' She kissed my cheek. 'You get out of here, and I'd better get back and help Jemima with these orders!' She inclined her head towards the tearoom where there was now a queue for coffee.

Chapter Nine

Bell was helping a customer when I ducked in to collect Balthazar. She excused herself briefly and said to me, 'Okay?'

I nodded and told her it was all under control and that there'd be someone through later in the day to fix the door and secure the premises.

'It's time we got CCTV, isn't it?' she said. 'Can your policeman help with that?'

I ignored the part about Robbie being my policeman and said, 'Yes, he's arranging for someone to come out and give us some quotes.' As well as being a deterrent, it might've helped us identify the perpetrators.

Ambrose came out of his stall as I walked past. Rochester was lying in the doorway, so Bally took a wide berth and sat on the other side of the corridor where he could keep an eye on both the cat and me.

'Anything we need to be worried about, lass?' he asked.

'No. It seems to be about that letterbox I bought on Wednesday – that and some books that were apparently from the same deceased estate were all that was taken.

They've got what they came for,' I said.

'Hmmm, I hope Catherine didn't give your name and details out,' he said. 'After all, we don't want to be in a position where if people aren't successful at auction, they think they can acquire what they want by more nefarious reasons.'

'I think we're fine,' I said. Keen to change the subject, I asked, 'Has Sir Antony been through to pick up the purchases you made for him yet?'

'This afternoon,' said Ambrose with a broad smile. 'He was over the moon when I told him what we'd found.'

'I bet. Anyway, I'd best be off. Inspector Dawkins is going to make sure my home is fully secure too – not that I'm worried about it, of course.'

'Naturally,' he said. 'You can never be too safe.' Then in an unusual (for him) moment of warmth, he said, 'Take care, lass.'

Robbie was off the phone and had completed his notes when I made it back with Bally.

'Are you done?' he asked.

'Yes. I'm ready whenever you are.'

'I'll follow you home,' he said. 'But don't go into the house until I'm there.'

It was overkill, and I told him so.

'You might think that,' he said, 'and that's your right, but I'm under orders to see you home safely, and that's what I intend doing.' He smiled as he said it, and it was a smile intended to make me feel better about everything that was going on. It was a smile that confirmed my initial impression of this man – that he'd be the best person to have on your side in the middle of a crisis.

Even though I shouldn't be, there was a part of me that was disappointed knowing he was only following orders issued by my ex-husband. I shrugged it away and headed out the door.

Each time I checked the rear-view mirror on the short drive home, Robbie's car was there. When I pulled up and got out of the car, he said, 'I'll go in first and make sure everything is fine.'

I nodded and wordlessly handed him my keys, keeping Bally in the car.

Of all the strangeness this morning had brought with it, knowing that Robbie was walking through my house, seeing it for the first time without me was the most uncomfortable. What sort of state had I left my bedroom in that morning? Yes, I'd made the bed and hung my towel after my shower, but had I put my dirty clothes in the basket? Had I washed up after my dinner for one last night, or did the empty bottle of wine and single wine glass on the sink tell the story of my (inactive) social life?

I pictured him opening the front door, having to jiggle the key that always got stuck no matter how many times I tried to fix it. He'd wipe his feet on the mat inside the door, but rather than hang his jacket on the hook, I guessed that he'd keep it on until invited to do otherwise. He'd turn right and head into my kitchen with its warm terracotta tiled floor, free-standing double oven and hob, and the wood-topped island that ran up the middle of the room. He'd check that the back door was locked and make a mental note to warn me about the glass in that door that would render any lock useless.

He'd walk down the short hall into the dining room with its fireplace and large timber table with bench style seats with plaid cushions – the same oatmeal plaid that was in the curtains – that had been the scene of so many family dinners in the past yet had only been sat on a couple of times this year. He might linger over the art in the alcoves beside the fireplace and probably not notice how well the deep sage we'd used on the walls worked with the plaid and the timber on the table, the fire surrounds, and the floorboards. He'd pass through to the lounge room with its chocolate leather two-piece suite, another fireplace and the burgundy feature wall – a colour that was echoed in the thin stripes on the plaid curtains. Being a man, he probably wouldn't notice how I'd softened the wood and the leather in there with stripes and florals. He might, however, notice the easel in the corner upon which I'd placed the Whitby painting. Perhaps he'd pause to look at it, but probably he'd wait for me.

After checking that the double doors out to the garden were locked (and with another mental note made to discuss the efficacy of this lock as well), he'd retrace his steps back up the hall to the stairs.

On the landing, he'd turn left and find himself in my bedroom. He'd walk through quickly, purposefully, probably taking care not to linger too long in my personal space. He'd check that the room and ensuite was clear and then do the same for the other two bedrooms and the main bathroom.

As I was leaning against the car murmuring to Bally, who couldn't understand why he wasn't allowed out yet, Robbie reappeared. 'It's clear in there,' he said. 'You're right to come in.' He stood aside, not making eye contact with me as he spoke, waiting as I liberated Bally, shuffling awkwardly as I walked past him into the house and Bally bounded through.

I turned at the door and said, 'Are you coming in?'

He smiled tightly, wryly, as I held the door open, closing it behind us. 'Is everything as it should be?' I asked.

'You do know these back doors would be easy to gain access through,' he said as we walked into the kitchen. 'And given you don't have CCTV at the barn, I doubt you have it or an alarm here either.'

'I've never needed to worry about security before,' I said. 'This is a small village, and nothing normally happens here, but yes, I take your point.' I switched on the kettle. 'Tea?'

'Please.'

'Did you see the painting?' At his blank look, I clarified. 'The one I bought at the auction – the one I think they were after.'

'I didn't like to go looking around without your permission,' he said.

'What do you think will happen?' I asked as I poured hot water over tea bags. 'With the painting and the documents I found in the letterbox?'

'Nothing,' he said, and I appreciated his honesty. 'We can investigate the break-in, but that's all. No other crime has been committed.'

'But we know they're after these things?' I protested.

'Maybe, but we can't take any action. All we can do is investigate the break-in. The team has dusted for prints – although I doubt they'll find any. I'll need a description of this Mrs Wainwright, so we'll start with your auctioneer friend for that. Hopefully, her description will match yours – but it still doesn't prove she and her husband are the perpetrators; we need evidence for that.'

'What about warning the other buyers?' I asked. 'Surely we should let them know in case the Wainwrights come knocking.'

'At this point, they're just offering to buy the goods,' he explained patiently. 'We've no evidence they've committed any crime – or intend to commit a crime.' When I sighed heavily, he added, 'I understand you're frustrated, Philly, but there's not much more we can do.'

'Yet you're here, and you're checking my locks. Would you normally do that in this sort of circumstance?' He shifted his eyes from mine. 'And don't tell me it's because my ex-husband asked you to.' As he would've opened his mouth to say something, I stopped him. 'No, you're here because even though you might not be able to investigate this officially, you believe what I'm saying, don't you?'

He hesitated slightly and then nodded. 'Yes, I do.'

'And you think that when they don't find anything in the letterbox, they'll come looking for the painting?'

He nodded again. 'It has crossed my mind.'

'I see.'

'I might not know you very well – yet' – he grinned as he added the clarification – 'but it's also crossed my mind that you might go looking for the owner of this photo and birth certificate on your own – even if I asked you not to.'

'Maybe not on my own …' I said, hoping I projected an innocent look. 'I'm sure Ginny and Bell would want to help.'

'Why doesn't that make me feel better?' he asked, his grin a tolerant one.

As I was searching for an appropriate response, my phone rang. 'Philly Barker.'

'Philly, how are you?'

I'd recognise that voice anywhere.

'It's her,' I mouthed to Robbie and switched the phone to speaker.

'I'm not sure if you remember me, but I called in yesterday and was interested in your letterbox.' Robbie twirled his finger in a circle, indicating to keep her talking.

'Yes, I remember you. You were also interested

in paintings of coastal Yorkshire – for your husband's milestone birthday.'

'That's right, I was. You mentioned you'd ask the buyer if they'd sell the letterbox to me – how did you go with that? Any success?'

I made a face at the phone. 'Unfortunately not. I had a break-in last night.'

'Oh really? I hope there wasn't too much damage. Was very much taken?'

Robbie and I exchanged a 'you've got to be kidding' look, incredulous at the woman's gumption. 'Luckily no, but the letterbox was one of the things taken.'

'I'm sorry to hear that,' she said and, to my ears at least, she sounded genuine.

'I had some luck in locating a Whitby seascape for you, though – if you're still interested, that is.'

There was the briefest of silences on the other end of the phone as if she'd put her hand over the mouthpiece to talk to someone else.

'In fact,' I said, 'I owe you an apology. I'd bought a mixed lot at auction the other day and hadn't had the chance to go through the box but did so last night. I think it might've come from the same place as the letterbox.' I shrugged when Robbie rolled his eyes at my lack of subtlety. 'There's a lovely oil painting in there – late nineteenth century. I took it into work this morning so I could examine it properly, but as I'm unable to open the stall for now, there's little chance it will be sold before you get a chance to look at it.'

'I'd be very interested in having a look at it. What sort of money were you after?'

'That will depend on my assessment of it,' I said, mouthing 'what?' to Robbie when he shook his head. 'And given that I haven't yet had a chance to look at it, there are no guarantees I'll sell it through the stall. I have a feeling it could be extremely special – in which case I'll send it back to auction.'

'Hmmm, I doubt that very much. I would, however, be prepared to pay whatever you're asking. Can I look at it tomorrow?'

'I'm afraid we're not open tomorrow or Monday – but I'm hopeful of being able to open on Tuesday. The police are still there collecting fingerprints, and we've employed a security guard to keep an eye on the place until Tuesday, just to be on the safe side. We're getting some CCTV installed then too. It's never crossed our mind that we'd need CCTV, but there you have it. Anyway, if you want to leave me your name and number, I can message you and confirm that I'll be in on Tuesday. I'd hate for you to come all this way and for me not to be open. Or,' I added as if it had only just occurred to me, 'I'm happy to duck into work and take a photo of the painting and message it to you.'

I waved my free hand to encourage Robbie to applaud how clever I was. It earned me another good-natured eye roll.

'That's alright,' she said. 'I want this to be a surprise, so I can't risk him seeing any messages. I'll take my chances on you being there and will drop by on Tuesday afternoon.'

'Okay,' I said, 'I'll see you then.'

She hung up, and I put my phone down with a triumphant smile.

'Brilliant!' said Robbie. 'Not only have you told her that the painting is no longer in your house, but you've made her think twice about calling in out of hours to try and get it.'

'How cheeky was it of her to call?' I asked.

'That was all designed for you to rethink any suspicions you might have had,' he said. 'And when you offered her the painting, she would've been put completely at ease. Nice work – you obviously haven't forgotten your training.'

He looked at his watch. 'Okay, will you be right here now? I'm heading into York to chat with Catherine Young. I might even strike it lucky and they'll have CCTV and can show me a picture of this mysterious Mrs Wainwright. What will you do with yourself now?'

'I'm going to take advantage of the daylight hours to have a good look at this painting,' I said.

'Okay, but don't do anything else until you speak to me. I'll call you later to check in.'

'Deal. Hey, if you're not doing anything, why don't you come for dinner tonight? It's my way of saying thank you.'

When he began looking anywhere but in my direction, I said, 'Don't worry, Robbie, I have no designs on your virtue. I'd like to thank you in the way that friends thank friends for helping them out. I know I've only known you a few days, but I think that's what we could be – friends. Besides,' I added, 'it'll just be a beef and ale stew with some dumplings – nothing special.'

'In that case, I'd love to,' he said, his smile chasing away all the craggy bits on his face.

Chapter Ten

I wasn't sure what to do once Robbie left. It wasn't so much that it felt weird not to be at work on a Saturday, but that the house now felt empty and, despite what I'd said to convince the mysterious Mrs W I had nothing in the house worth breaking in for, I felt exposed and rattled. It was that last feeling that annoyed me most of all. I'd lived alone for several years – both the kids were away at university when Stewart left, and although they used to come home for holidays, they hadn't lived at home for any length of time since. While there was no denying the loneliness from time to time – hence why Balthazar came into my life – being alone hadn't worried me from a security viewpoint. Until now.

When I jumped up from my chair in response to a noise in the garden, I gave myself a good talking to. For a start, there was no way anyone would attempt to break in here during the day, and secondly, Mrs W now believed the painting was at the barn. The only reason I would be in danger is if she somehow found out that I'd already found the photo and the birth certificate and, given that this business was a small one, it was probably best if I kept that to myself. I was confident Ginny wouldn't tell anyone, and if she did, she'd only tell Bell. As for Robbie, he wouldn't say anything unless it became pertinent to a case which, currently, it wasn't.

Gazing out my kitchen window, I smiled at Balthazar barking at a squirrel who had surprised his slumber in the weak winter sun and smiled to myself. No one would get past him without me knowing about it – although in all honesty, once they did, he'd probably lick them to death, not that any prospective burglar would know that. He had a bark that belied his size.

What I could do now, though, was put together the stew I'd promised Robbie, and once that was done, I'd take a good look at that painting in the daylight.

Taking the beef from the fridge, I cut it into cubes and tipped it into seasoned flour and tossed it around to coat. I pulled out the expensive canary yellow cast-iron casserole dish Ryan and Jordan had bought me for Christmas last year and began browning the beef in small batches in a mix of oil and foamy butter. I loved this part of the process – it was almost meditative ensuring each cube was evenly browned. That was a mistake too many people made – hurrying the process along. On the surface, stews and casseroles might sound simple, but the time you take at the beginning is repaid in the depth of flavour of the final dish. Besides, once the meat was browned, the rest was quick – toss in some chopped onions, carrots and celery, pour in the

Worcestershire sauce, beer and beef stock, pop the lid on, bring it all to a boil, and then let the oven do the rest of the heavy lifting. I'd make the herby dumplings when he was here and finish it all off. Too easy.

Stew in the oven, I cleaned down the kitchen bench, laid a clean towel over the surface and retrieved the painting from the easel. Before I did, though, I took some photos of it and scrutinised it in the light from every angle. The description in the catalogue had been:

Whitby Harbour and Abbey

British 19th century Victorian landscape oil painting

The artist was unknown and was from what was collectively termed the British school – mainly to distinguish it from the French-influenced impressionist movement of the late nineteenth and early twentieth centuries. The painting might have been a good example of this but was too dark for my taste. I certainly wouldn't hang it on my walls. Even so, there was something about it that made my nerves tingle. I'd seen this style before, studied it; I knew I had.

The primary subject was Whitby harbour, with the cliffs rising behind and the ruins of Whitby Abbey sitting atop East Cliff facing out to the North Sea. The image was a winter one with grey skies and a smattering of snow on the sides of the cliffs drifting down to the harbour itself. The artist, who had probably painted the picture from about where The Magpie Café stood now, had depicted the harbour as it had been – a working harbour. Timber-hulled ships with tall masts waited to be loaded or unloaded. Wooden tenders ferried workers and goods from the harbourside out to the waiting ships.

If I closed my eyes, I could imagine Whitby as it was then – at the tail end of its importance as a ship-building port. Regardless of the historical facts and figures, it was certainly a different Whitby than the one you'd see today. While the ruins of the abbey still stand as a sentinel of sorts over the town, these days, both sides of the harbour were filled with pubs, restaurants, guesthouses, amusement arcades and gift shops selling the usual tourist tat plus the jet – a polished black, coal-like rock – that Whitby was known for.

The frame itself was gilded, and while some in this style could be hollow, this one was too narrow to hide anything.

I lifted the painting carefully from the easel and carried it into the kitchen, lying it face down on the kitchen bench. The back was as I'd expect it to be – hardboard attached to the frame itself with tape. There was a packing label on the back dated 1901. Although I couldn't decipher the name and direction, I took a photo of it anyway. The rest of the backing had the usual wear and tear you'd expect to see over a century or so.

The tape, though, didn't. While not clean and new, it appeared to be younger than the board it was securing. I reached for the loupe that was rarely far from my side and leant in. There were faint marks on the board where previous tape might've been and which this tape didn't quite cover.

Someone had removed the original tape at some point. But for what reason?

I took a step back and thought it through. The backing board hadn't been replaced – I could tell that from the packing label. The frame was, I believed, original too. The only reason someone would've removed the tape would be to lift the board – and thereby place something between the board and the canvas.

If I was to do the same – lift the existing tape and replace it – it would be obvious to anyone looking at the back of the painting that I'd done so. I could, of course, claim ignorance if I was asked by Mrs Wainwright and tell her it had been like this when I purchased it – that might also send her in a different direction if she thought a previous owner had removed the materials, assuming, that is, there was something to remove.

I flipped open my laptop and navigated to the catalogue for Wednesday's auction. Just as I thought – there were no photos of the back of the painting and nothing stopping me from cutting the tape and having a look inside.

I was contemplating slicing the tape when my phone rang – Catherine Young. I let it ring for a couple of seconds. Robbie would've been there by now, so she'd know I'd been broken into – and who we suspected.

'Hiya,' I finally picked up.

'Hi yourself,' she said. 'I understand you've had some trouble today – I had a visit from the police earlier. A

Detective Inspector Dawkins.'

'Yes, we were broken into last night.'

'I got the impression from the inspector it was only your dealership that was targeted.'

'Yes, that's right – and the only things that were taken were the letterbox and a couple of books that came from that mixed lot I bought.'

'That's why he came to see me, I suppose.'

I sat down on a stool at the kitchen bench. 'He also came to see you because I think the woman who asked you to buy back the letterbox and the painting also came to visit me.'

There was silence at the other end of the phone. 'He did ask if there'd been anyone interested in those lots, and I told him about her.' There was a tapping sound on the phone, and I pictured Catherine sitting at her desk tapping the surface with her acrylic nails. 'But it couldn't be her because she'd specifically asked about art works as well, and the Whitby oil wasn't stolen.'

'No, because I had it here at home.'

'Is it still there?' she asked.

'It's somewhere safe now.' I told myself it wasn't really a lie at the same time as I questioned why I hadn't told Catherine, someone I'd known and trusted for years, the truth.

'I see.' More tapping. 'It doesn't make sense to me though Philly, none of it was particularly special – a few hundred pounds worth, five hundred on a good day. I told the inspector she was trying to get back some family pieces. I couldn't see anyone stealing for that.'

'Me neither,' I said.

'Perhaps it was a different person who came to your stall, and this is all a coincidence, and the only reason they didn't take more was that they were interrupted. No offence, Philly, but if I was going to break into the barn, I'd probably be concentrating my efforts on the brothers Ashton and then move onto your silver and jewellery – not the other way around. In fact, I don't think you've been targeted; it's just that yours is the first stall they would've come to when they got through the front door.'

'Suppose it was the same person,' I said, annoyed she didn't seem to believe my theory. 'What did your Mrs Wainwright look like? How did she sound?'

'She didn't say a lot – she was way too upset to speak once she found out she was a day late for the auction. But she spoke nicely – not plummy, but definitely not from around here. Classic shoulder-length bob – bronde.'

'Bronde?'

'Was once brown and is now highlighted blonde – it helps with the grey, darling.'

'Of course it does.'

'I do recall she was wearing a pricey-looking coat I'm positive was cashmere and well-cut black pants with a stack heel boot.' Catherine, always immaculately dressed, could spot a designer label from ten feet. If ever you needed to know what someone was wearing, Catherine was your woman. 'What surprised me, though, was the animal print pussy bow. They're huge this winter, of course, but they're so new that I wouldn't have thought they'd be a thing in the Australian winter – maybe next year, but not yet. You know I said something like that to her – to try and distract her – and she perked up and thanked me for noticing. She said they'd had a night in London before driving up and she'd bought the blouse there. Then she teared up again and said she wished they'd come straight to York instead.' She paused and said, 'You think it's the same woman, don't you?'

'I'm almost positive,' I said, 'although I won't pretend to understand about the pussy bow.'

She laughed a high tingling sound. 'Oh, darling, you and I need to go shopping someday. How on earth are you going to find a replacement for that philandering husband of yours if you don't dress in something other than denim and boots? And a pussy bow is a floppy tie – like what Maggie Thatcher used to wear – you've seen *The Crown*, haven't you, darling?'

'Well, yes. Hasn't everyone?'

'Then you've seen a pussy bow. They were big in the eighties and are back again now, but with more of an edge.'

'Right, well, thanks for that education,' I said, 'but for the record, I'm not interested in replacing Stewart anytime soon, and I'm too short for a pussy bow.'

'How long has it been? Ten years? It's time, darling.'

I ignored her comment and said instead, 'She was wearing one when she came to the barn yesterday – an emerald green one – with that coat and black slacks. The thing is, she said that she and her husband were doing up a house they'd bought, and when I asked her if she'd been to Australia, she told me she hadn't.'

'Curious and curiouser,' pondered Catherine. 'We didn't give her your name, though, so unless she's been going from dealer to dealer. Oh, hang on … god I'm sorry, darling, but she might've got it from us. Why have I only remembered this now?'

'Remembered what?' I asked impatiently.

'I'd been working through the catalogue sheet before Mrs Wainwright arrived, and while I was talking to her, a man who had been looking in one of the bookshelves toppled a stack of books onto the floor. I rushed down there to check that he was okay – people sue for absolutely nothing these days, darling, and they shouldn't have been lying in the middle of the floor. She didn't follow me down straight away, and when she did, he recovered quite quickly.'

'Let me guess, they left soon after.'

'Yes, they did. Separately though. She would've had plenty of time to take a quick photo of the sales sheet. I'm so sorry.'

She sounded genuinely apologetic. 'You weren't to know,' I said. 'Besides, I'd told Becky that if they wanted those items, they'd need to buy them from me.'

'So,' she mused, 'if the lots weren't worth very much, why would they be so desperate to get them back?'

'Perhaps they think there's something hidden in there,' I said.

'You and your secret compartments. Remember when you worked for me, you'd check every desk and box that came into the place.'

'And I found a few too,' I pointed out.

'With nothing in them,' she countered. 'It made for a good narrative at sale time, though.' She sighed. 'I suppose you're going to tell me I can make it up to you by giving you the details of the deceased estate they came from?'

'Now Catherine, why didn't I think of that?' I said cheekily.

'Oh, away with you. I'll text it through.'

'Did you give it to Inspector Dawkins too?' I asked.

'Yes, as a matter of fact, I did. By the way, since when does the constabulary send an inspector around on a Saturday for a piddly little break-in like yours?'

As I racked my brain for an appropriate answer, she said, 'I suppose it helps when your ex-husband is the Chief Superintendent.'

I laughed at her accurate assumption and said, 'There has to be some upside to having been married to Stewart.'

'Other than two beautiful children, of course,' she reminded me.

'Of course.'

Before she hung up, we arranged to catch up for lunch in the next week or so. 'Only if we can go to Betty's,' I said, naming a café that was an institution in York. 'I'm hanging for a Fat Rascal.' Betty's Fat Rascals – a cross between a rock cake and a scone – were legendary.

'Eat too many of those, darling, and you'll be a fat rascal.'

The rest of the afternoon was taken up with phone calls and visitors. Stewart phoned to check on me and reiterated what Robbie had said about Mrs Wainwright. 'Whoever it was must have worn gloves as we have no fingerprints, and you have no CCTV. You've always had good instincts, Philly, and I think you're right on this occasion too, but there's only so much we can do.'

'Because it's a little break-in that wouldn't normally warrant the attention of a detective inspector,' I said.

'Unfortunately, yes.' There was a momentary pause before he added, 'Dawkins says you've invited him for dinner tonight. I know it's none of my business, but –'

I bristled at Stewart's insinuation. 'You're damn right it's none of your business!'

He sighed loudly. I pictured him casting his eyes to the ceiling as he debated his choice of words. Maybe Allison was in the background and he was rolling his eyes at her. 'As I was saying, I know it's none of my business, but if you …

how do you say it? … fancy him, go carefully – he hasn't had an easy time of it.'

'He mentioned his wife had died,' I said, the fight going out of me.

'Did he?' Stewart sounded surprised. 'When did he tell you that?'

'The other night – I ran into him at The Arms, and we talked.'

'Interesting. Did he mention how she died?'

'No. Are you going to tell me?' I asked.

'It's not my story to tell. All I'm saying is I'm not sure that he's looking for a relationship, so go carefully. He's a good man, and I don't want to see him hurt.' The anger rose in me again. 'Not that I'm saying you'd hurt him,' he added in a conciliatory tone that somehow managed not to sound patronising.

'I'm not looking for a relationship either,' I said. 'We're friends, I think. I got the impression he could do with some friends, and while I'm not great at relationships, I am good at friendships.'

'Oh, I don't know, Philly,' he chuckled. 'You did okay in ours for over twenty years.'

I bit my tongue to stop the retort, 'It's a pity you didn't,' from spilling out.

Five minutes after Stewart's call, Ryan's name flashed on the phone screen. 'Dad told me what happened,' he said. 'Are you sure you're alright?'

'Positive. I wasn't there at the time, and locks can be replaced. Besides, it's given me a day off I otherwise wouldn't have had.' I forced a laugh into my voice to ease his concerns.

'If you say so. Jordan was only saying the other day how we haven't seen you properly since the twin's birthday, so we'll come over tomorrow if that's okay.'

Ryan and Jordan shared custody of Ryan's four-year-old twins with his ex-wife. It might've sounded complicated, but theirs really had been an amicable parting of the ways. Jenny had since remarried, as had Ryan, but they were completely devoted in their commitment to ensuring Ada and Alfie weren't impacted at all. Now they were no longer married, Ryan and Jenny were the best of friends.

'I'll do a roast,' I said.

'No, don't go to any trouble Mum, we can pop next door to the pub.' Ryan's protests were half-hearted at best.

'It's no trouble. I was only thinking earlier about how long it's been since this table was full. Besides, the kids can play with Bally in the garden when they get bored sitting at the table. It's supposed to be another fine day.' My mind was already busy planning what I'd cook for them. If I left now, I'd make it to the butchers in Malton before closing time. A proper Sunday lunch – complete with extra Yorkshire puddings for Jordan who loved them even more than Ryan did – what a treat.

I'd just pulled into a car park in Malton when Bell

phoned, so I went through the same thing with her. Yes, I'm okay and, no, they didn't take very much; yes, I was lucky they didn't take much; yes, I'd be back at work on Tuesday, and no, she didn't need to bother coming over. I hung up with the excuse that I was out shopping and promised to call her on Monday.

Chapter Eleven

As I pulled Libby to a stop in the driveway, Ginny was walking back to her car. 'I took the chance you'd be home,' she said, 'but when you weren't, I left you something.' She waved at the tea-towel-wrapped parcel on the doorstep. 'It's an apple and rhubarb crumble, and I thought it might cheer you up tonight.'

I gave her a grateful hug. 'Come in for a cuppa?'

She looked at her watch and nodded. 'Just a quick one,' she said, looking away before she could meet my eye.

'Virginia Wilding, could it be that you have a date tonight?'

Her blush was answer enough.

'Tell me more,' I said, picking up the crumble and almost pushing her through the front door.

In the kitchen, she sniffed the air. The oven was doing its job; the rich aroma of slow-cooked beef filled the space. 'You've been doing some cooking, too.'

'A beer and beef stew. Robbie's coming for tea, so this crumble will save me making something for pudding.' I'd turned my back on her to put the crumble in the fridge so I couldn't see her face – not that I needed to to know what she was thinking. 'And don't you go thinking those things either,' I said. 'We're just two friends getting together for a bite to eat on a Saturday night.'

'And an exchange of information?' she guessed, spying the painting I'd left on the kitchen bench.

I moved it onto the dining table before passing a mug of tea to her. 'Possibly. Now, tell me about this date of yours.' I couldn't remember Ginny dating in the whole time we'd worked together. While Bell dated often and casually, neither Ginny nor I made a habit of it. Stewart had burnt me, but as for Ginny? I had no idea. As much as she could brighten the day of anyone who came across her, she was also one of the most private people I knew. To the best of my knowledge, none of us knew much about her past before she came to us.

'His name is Richard, and he's an old school friend,' she said, pouring some milk into her tea. 'It's not a date so much as a catch-up.'

'An old school friend you used to date?' I guessed.

'Maybe.' She gave a one-shoulder shrug, and then her smile slid off her face. I watched as she tried to catch it.

'What's wrong, Ginny? Are you worried about meeting this man?'

'Aye,' she said simply. 'I mean, look at me, Philly. When I knew him, I was twenty and gorgeous. Now I'm fat and fifty-three. He's probably still as hot as he was back then, and I'm short, frumpy and invisible.' She waved her hands down her body. 'I know I've aged badly, but –'

'You stop right there, Virginia Wilding.' I rested my hand on hers and gave it a gentle squeeze. 'You are beautiful inside and out. When you smile, it lights up the entire room. Besides, you've still got your own hair which is something few fifty-year-old men can boast. If he's looked you up after all this time, he's probably feeling as nervous as you are about tonight. Where are you going?'

She named a restaurant in Malton.

'That's good – they specialise in traditional Yorkshire portions which tells me he's a man with an appetite. You'll be absolutely fine.'

Ginny laughed one of her belly laughs. 'I hadn't thought about it that way. I was wondering how I'd order a salad there.'

I shook my head, an exaggerated look of horror on my face. 'Don't even go there! Ryan and Jordan took me there for my birthday earlier this year, and their Whitby fish pie was the stuff legends are made of. Go, enjoy, and tell me all about it.'

'And will you tell me all about that?' She inclined her head towards the painting.

'Maybe not,' I said honestly. 'If there is something to all of this, the fewer people who know what's going on, the better. I don't want to tempt trouble for anyone else.'

She nodded her understanding. 'But you'll be careful?'

'Absolutely. I have Yorkshire's finest on my side; I'll be fine.'

'What if they decide to come here to look for that once they realise there's nothing in the letterbox?' she asked, concern etched on her face.

'Don't worry,' I said, reaching across the counter again to pat her hand. 'She called me this morning – Mrs Wainwright, or whatever her name really is – and I told her I had a painting, and I'd taken it into the stall this morning, but I could show it to her on Tuesday. She won't be coming here – she has no idea I suspect her of anything.' I spoke with more confidence than I felt.

'If you're sure,' Ginny said. 'I better be off to let you get ready for the good inspector.'

'This is me done,' I said, waving my hands down my body to show I was dressed and ready. 'Take me or leave me.'

Ginny exhaled heavily and shook her head. 'Philomena Barker, this might not be a date – as you're so quick to remind me – but you're still having a guest for dinner, so the least you can do is change out of the clothes you've been wearing all day and put some make-up on.'

'But I don't want him to think it's a date,' I said, noticing a dust of flour on my jeans.

'You're hopeless, Philly. I bet he's having exactly the same thoughts as you, but he'll turn up here looking like he's made an effort because that's what you do when someone has gone to the trouble of cooking you dinner. If I invited you to mine for dinner, would you bother changing first?'

'Of course I would.' Not that I'd ever been to Ginny's house – for dinner or anything else.

'My point exactly.' She gave me her best stern look which wasn't very stern at all. 'Are we clear?'

'Crystal.'

When she left, I went upstairs and had a shower, swapping my jeans for loose black pants and a floaty top. I put on some light make-up – mascara, blusher, and a swipe of lip gloss, and then – so he wouldn't get the wrong impression – slid my feet into sheepskin boots.

When Robbie arrived, I was still rolling out parsley dumplings for the stew. In a fancy silver gift bag was a bottle of red wine which I accepted with gratitude.

'I'm sorry to put you to work, Robbie, but you'll need to get your own drink.' I waggled my sticky, floury fingers at him. 'There's beer in the fridge if you prefer.'

'No problems. And point me in the right direction of your glasses,' he said.

I was glad I'd taken Ginny's advice and changed for dinner – even if I'd caught Robbie's grin when he spied my sheepskin slippers. He'd changed out of the suit and tie he'd been wearing earlier and was now dressed in a pair of black jeans, navy canvas shoes and a dark blue shirt with the top few buttons open. Dressed more casually, he looked different, younger, less serious.

'Something smells good,' he said after he'd poured us both a drink – beer for him, red wine for me.

'I hope it tastes as good as it smells,' I said. 'It's been simmering away most of the afternoon. I just need to pop these on top, and once they're cooked through, we can eat.' I pulled the casserole out of the oven and placed it on a trivet. Lifting the lid carefully, I stood back to let the steam dissipate and closed my eyes briefly as my nose filled with the heady aroma of slow-cooked beef and beer.

'Can you pass me that plate of dumplings, please?' I asked.

'Of course.'

A look of fascination came over his face as I placed the dumplings evenly over the surface of the stew before replacing the lid and putting it back in the oven.

'Are you going to sit down now?' he asked, the curve of his mouth telling me of his efforts to put me at ease.

'Absolutely,' I said, pulling a stool out from under the kitchen bench and planting my bum on it. 'Happy now?'

'Much better,' he said.

And then we were both lost for words.

'Why don't we –' I started.

'This calls for –' he said at the same time.

A nervous giggle slipped from my lips, and I shook my head. 'This is hopeless,' I said.

'It is,' he agreed wryly. 'It's just that I'm not –'

'And neither am I.'

He chuckled self-consciously; the tips of his ears tinged pink.

'Robbie, I might only have known you for a few days, but I've decided that you're a nice man. I like you, and as someone I like who I think is nice, I'd also like to share the occasional meal or a drink with you. I meant what I said this afternoon – I'm not looking for a relationship, and I don't think you are either, but I am looking for a friend, someone to cook for occasionally, and someone who can tell me what they found out at Young and Johnson's.'

Somehow I kept a straight face throughout my little speech – until he laughed. It was a lovely sound – warm and rumbling as though it had begun down in his belly and bubbled out.

This time his grin was open and sincere, all diffidence gone. 'I knew there had to be a catch,' he said.

I shrugged lightly. 'I don't cook beef and beer stew with fiddly little dumplings for just anyone you know.'

'I'm pleased to hear it. Now' – he took a thoughtful sip of his beer – 'if I was a betting man – which I'm not, mind you – I'd put good money on the fact that Catherine Young would've been on the phone to you almost as soon as I left her place this afternoon. Am I right?'

'You could be.'

'And I'm also guessing that because the two of you are

friends – she told me you used to work for her –'

'She taught me everything I know about the business.'

'Then she'd also tell you what she told me about Mrs Wainwright who – and this might come as a shock to you,' he added with a lift of his eyebrow and a wry smile, 'probably isn't even Mrs Wainwright.'

'She did and if I was a betting woman – which obviously I am a little being in this business – I'd say that I'm almost ninety-five percent certain that the woman who Catherine knew as Mrs Wainwright, the bereaved relative just back from Australia and the woman who called on me who had never been to Australia are the same person.' I took a sip of the bold red and added, 'She also gave me the name and address of the buyers of the vanity case and the other painting.'

Robbie tilted his head to the side, his eyes narrowed. 'Go on …'

'I also happen to know that the person who bought the vanity case was broken into on Thursday night.'

He sat taller in his chair, his mouth a firm, straight line. 'How does she know this and, more importantly, why didn't she tell me this?'

I shrugged. 'Because *she* doesn't know,' I said simply, thoroughly enjoying myself. I stood and walked around to the other side of the bench to open drawers for cutlery and placemats. 'Do you want to eat here or in the dining room?' Smiling benignly, I glanced across at him. His brown eyes were twinkling, and I got the impression that few people teased him as I was doing now. 'Actually, I think we'll eat at the table – it will be much more comfortable. I lit the fire in there earlier in case we decided to.' I'd also moved the painting off the table and back onto the easel.

'Wherever is fine with me.' From the curve of his lips, he was determined not to rush me to expand on what I'd begun to tell him. That was probably a technique he used in interrogation – leave spaces for people to jump into. He'd be very good at it too. Sitting at my kitchen bench drinking beer, Robbie radiated a stillness that was quite comforting to be around. It was a stillness that said you could rely upon him, that his were a safe pair of hands. How many people had trusted him with what they knew, only for it to be used to ensnare them?

'Do you mind setting the table?' I asked.

'Of course not.' He picked up the cutlery I handed him. 'Anywhere in particular you like to sit?'

When I shook my head, he left the room, coming back briefly for our glasses and, at my nod, the bottle of wine.

With my oven gloves on, I placed a trivet on the bench and pulled the stew from the oven. The dumplings were cooked perfectly golden and were still light and fluffy, the scent of the herbs mingling with the rich earthiness of the beef and beer. Into a cane basket, I popped some cheddar and rosemary scones I'd made earlier.

'I hope you're hungry,' I said when he returned to the kitchen.

'I certainly am,' he replied as I ladled generous servings into bowls.

'If you take these through, I'll put Ginny's crumble into the oven and be with you in a second.'

Once seated at the table, steaming bowls in front of us, I picked up my glass and held it in a toast. 'Here's to new friends and good food.'

'I'll drink to that.'

As he clinked his glass against mine, our eyes met in the dim light, the flames from the fire crackling, the light flickering across the table. In that second, I knew instinctively that I could trust him, and he wouldn't let me down or betray that trust. I could also trust Bell and Ginny and the others at the barn, but somehow it felt different – and safer – to share what I knew with Robbie.

'This is wonderful, Philly.' He said as he took a mouthful of stew, nodding slowly in appreciation.

'I'm glad you like it,' I said, my fork sliding easily through the beef and swirling it around in the rich sauce.

We ate for a couple of minutes in companionable silence – that quiet that's necessary when you first begin a good meal. It was, however, time to explain, so I took a sip of wine and spoke. 'The man who bought the vanity case is named Tom Ainsworth. He's a lovely man, and he and his wife, Beth, are regulars at the barn.' Robbie was chewing thoughtfully and motioned to me to continue. 'Beth was in yesterday morning – she collects Shelley trios, you know those cup, saucer and plate sets, and I had a new one I thought she'd like that I'd put aside for her. She was flustered when she came in and told me they'd disturbed a burglar the previous night. They were both upstairs asleep in bed, and she heard a crash downstairs. She woke Tom, and apparently when he switched the lights on as he came down the stairs, whoever it was ran off. All he saw was someone dressed in black. Nothing was taken, but it had clearly shaken her – as it would've done. They're both in their seventies, you see.' I paused for another forkful of food.

'I asked Beth if they'd reported the break-in to the police, and she said they had, but nothing had been taken, so they were putting it down to opportunistic kids.'

'Did she happen to say how they got in?' Robbie asked.

'Yes, apparently they broke a pane of glass in the back door.'

He looked pointedly at the doors leading out to my garden – like those of the Ainsworths.

'I know … Anyway, the police came and did the usual checks and said they had little to go on. Beth said she got the impression it would all go in a report that would go nowhere. While she was at the barn, Tom was back at the house waiting to get the door fixed.'

'And she said nothing was taken?'

'That's right. At that point, I didn't know about the vanity case, so …' I shrugged and reached to pour more wine. Robbie put his hand over his glass and reminded me he was driving.

'I didn't think anything more about it,' I said, 'until Catherine told me who the buyer of the vanity was.'

'And the painting? Do you know the buyer of that one?' he asked.

'No, the name's not familiar to me, but I wondered whether they'd also had an uninvited visitor.'

Robbie nodded slowly. 'Yes, that thought had occurred to me too. I'll make a call in the morning and see if there have been any reports from that address. I'll dig out the report from the Ainsworths too.' He pinched at the bridge of his nose, something he must do when he's thinking.

'Maybe,' I said slowly, 'I can call in on Tom and Beth – just to check on them, of course.'

'And, presumably, ask about the vanity case?' he guessed, his wry look one of resignation.

'Only if it comes up in conversation,' I said lightly.

'Naturally.'

He wiped the last of the sauce from his plate with the scone and sat back in his chair with a satisfied smile. 'That was the best stew I've had in years,' he said.

'I'm pleased to hear it; do you have room for seconds?'

'Not if I'm to leave room for pudding – I caught sight of that crumble you put in the oven earlier.'

'Ginny brought it over this afternoon for me – her crumbles are worth leaving room for.' I stood to clean the plates away, but he stopped me.

'Let me,' he said. 'You did the cooking.'

Rather than argue, I allowed him to gather the plates and take them through to the kitchen, listening as he opened the dishwasher and stacked the plates within it. I'd wager his house was tidy, with everything in its place. It would be too easy (and completely sexist) to say his wife must've trained him well, but I couldn't help but wonder whether that was the case. Somehow, though, I knew it was how he was – methodical, practical.

He was soon back and sitting down opposite me. 'According to the timer, the crumble has another five minutes to go.'

'Thanks for that.' I sipped at my wine and grinned. 'How's my form? I invite you for dinner, and you have to set the table, clean up after us and report on the progress of the oven.'

He chuckled. 'If that's what it takes for you to cook for me again,' he said with a teasing grin. If I didn't know better, I could've thought he was flirting with me.

'Are you going to warn Florence Miller?' I asked. When he looked blankly back at me, I added, 'The purchaser of the other painting – although I don't suppose you can.'

'I can't; I have no grounds to. All we have is supposition rather than evidence.'

'I suppose you're right,' I said, my brain ticking. 'There has to be a way …'

'Don't get too far ahead of yourself,' he chided gently.

'Let's wait until I check if there have been any reports at her address first, eh?'

The oven chimed in the background. 'Okay. I'll go dish out the pudding, and then I thought we might see if we can't get the back off this painting.'

'Sounds about right to me,' he said.

Chapter Twelve

With the pudding plates cleaned away and the kitchen wiped down, I removed the painting from its easel and placed it on the kitchen bench.

'So this is what all the fuss is about,' Robbie said, looking at it as if trying to understand what was so special about this painting. 'Who's it by?'

'I don't know. There's no signature that I can see on the canvas – although that might be hidden by the frame. There might be one on the back of the canvas – which is where some artists left their signature.' I stood back to view it properly, feeling that same ripple of excitement. 'There's nothing special about the subject – Whitby was probably the most important port on the east coast at that time – although its importance was waning by then. At the same time, though, tourism was hotting up, so plenty of people would've been painting this very scene – or one like it up the coast in Staithes or Robin Hood's Bay. As for the artistic merit, well, it's good, but unless we can attribute it to anyone …' There it was again, that prickling at the back of my neck.

I pulled out my trusty loupe. 'There's something about these brushstrokes, though. They remind me of JT Wilson's work – he's hugely collectible now, and I know he worked on the docks in Whitby in his youth. See these boys in the tenders?' I pointed to the foreground of the painting. 'That's what he was employed to do – row out to the ships waiting in the harbour and ferry in goods and people. I don't recall seeing any of his work from that time, though; most of his later works – and the paintings he's most known for – are based further up the coast. If I can find a signature somewhere on the canvas – and he was renowned for signing under the frame – then this painting could be worth quite a bit more than what you'd think.'

'Do you think Mrs Wainwright knows? It could be why she wants the painting,' Robbie suggested.

'No, she'd have no idea; I'm almost positive of that. She wouldn't be as keen to get her hands on the boxes and books if she knew what this is worth – if it is a Wilson, that is.'

'Are we talking thousands?' Robbie asked, leaning closer and squinting as if searching for the elusive signature.

'More like tens of thousands. There are Wilson collectors out there who'd snap up an earlier work like this. On a good day, it could make close to six figures. That does, of course, assume that I'm right, but I think I am. The hairs on the back of my neck stand up when I look at it closely, and it's not just because I think the frame could be hiding something more than a signature.'

'Do you think there's something behind the backboard?' Robbie asked.

'Back when this Peggy slash Margaret person had baby Johnny, there weren't many options for her to keep the information safe. If she wanted to hide documents, letters or photographs, she would've needed to be creative. The very fact that the birth certificate for this baby has father unknown and that she'd hidden both the birth certificate and the photo tells me this was a love affair that was supposed to stay secret. She loved him enough to keep his photo, and she obviously loved the baby enough that she wanted to be able to remember him – assuming, that is, that she'd had him adopted. If there aren't love letters to be found, I'll be very surprised indeed.'

'If that's the case, we're going to need a sharp blade,' said Robbie. 'Plus, we'll need some tape to replace the tape we're removing – are you able to get any of that?'

'Too easy. I can deal with that. I've got the perfect tool for the job. Back in a sec.' The toolbox lived in the alcove under the stairs. 'Here we go.' I handed the blade to Robbie. 'I think your hand might be steadier than mine,' I said.

'Okay, if you're sure.' He waited for me to nod before making the first slice into the tape. Once he'd traced the tape the whole way around the board, he carefully peeled it back to expose the metal catches that held the board in place.

Our eyes met. Robbie's brows knit together. 'These

have been moved – not recently because they're still quite stiff, but you can see the marks on the backing board where they've been slid across at some point.' There were distinct scrape marks on the board.

'You're right. You can also see where the board has been forced in or out of the frame by where it's buckled along the side,' I said. 'Let's have a look at the canvas. The board is in so tightly though … we'll need something to prise it out.' I scanned the kitchen, my eyes falling on a butter knife. 'This will do for leverage.'

I passed it to Robbie who slid it into the narrow gap left by the tape and eased the backing board out far enough for me to slide my fingers under and pull it off completely, exposing the back of the canvas to our gaze.

'Nothing there,' said Robbie, sounding as disappointed as I felt.

'No, but let's pop the canvas out and see what's been hiding under the frame.' Carefully, I turned the canvas the right way up again. Before touching it, I pulled on the blue silicone gloves I'd left out for this very purpose. 'My CSI gloves,' I joked to Robbie who chuckled in response.

Gently I pressed at the front of the canvas and, after some initial resistance, felt it give way from the frame, allowing me to lift the frame off it and move it to one side. My pulse quickened as the canvas was laid bare for my inspection. Could it be? I picked up the loupe and leant in closer. There, on the bottom right-hand corner of the canvas, behind where the frame sat, was what I was looking for.

'Is it what you think?' asked Robbie, peering over my shoulder.

My breath caught in my throat.

There were some in the antiques business who were referred to as being a 'divvy' – mythical beasts who have an innate ability to divine antiques from junk, the fakes from the real thing. Sort of like a water diviner but with art and antiques. A true divvy operates on instinct, with experience to back that up. Most of us use a combination of knowledge we've acquired – either through being in the trade or having studied a related subject at university – and what our instincts were telling us. I might not be a divvy, but my instincts had been screaming at me ever since I saw this painting peeking out of the box it was sold in.

Like everyone who has ever traded in antiques, I'd dreamt of the day I'd have *that* find. Not exactly the long-lost Rembrandt found in the stables or Van Gogh's forgotten sketches in an attic, but the day when I'd buy a piece that was more than it purported to be. A treasure in the trash, so to speak. This, it appeared, was my moment.

'It is,' I said simply. 'It's also worth stealing.'

We stood back, shoulder to shoulder, and contemplated the canvas, looking remarkably unremarkable out of its frame.

'Are you sure?' asked Robbie.

'I am. Absolutely. I'll get it verified by someone, of course, but this is a Wilson, and it's rare because of its subject matter. For now, though, I need to get it back in its frame and somewhere safe. Can you pass me the board, please?'

'Sure,' he said, reaching for the board. 'Um, Philly?'

There was something in the tone of his voice that made my tummy flip – and not in a good way. I turned towards him with trepidation. 'What's wrong?'

Instead of answering, he pointed at the board where taped securely in place was an envelope. We'd missed it when we first took the board from the back. Now, though, we both stared at it, neither willing to rip off the yellowed sticky tape that held it in place.

'I think we've found what Mrs Wainwright was looking for,' he said.

With my gloves still on, I gently removed the tape that had held the envelope in place for years. Decades, probably. Pushing the envelope to one side, I carefully placed the canvas back into the frame and slowly manoeuvred the board back into place.

'Robbie, can you please have a scrounge around in the fourth drawer down? There should be some tape in there that will do the job until I can get this repaired properly.'

Together, we taped the board back onto the frame, matching as best we could the line that the previous tape had held. I carried the painting through to the lounge and placed it back on the easel. Confirming that the painting was more valuable than I'd dared to hope, would change everything. It did, of course, mean that I'd need to come up with a story for Mrs Wainwright when she called on Tuesday, but I could think about that later. Shaking that worry away, I joined Robbie back in the kitchen.

'You can't leave that here, Philly,' he said, concern deepening the furrows in his brow.

'I know. I'll take it to Catherine on Monday and get her to store it securely for me. It will be safe there until I can get it appraised and into the right sort of sale.'

'Can you trust Catherine?' he asked, placing the tape back in the drawer.

'I've known her for years, and while she can be completely ruthless in business, yes, I trust her. The painting will be safe with her. She'll be kicking herself though that they missed it in their appraisal.' The gloves made a loud 'thwack' sound as I removed them. 'Right, the letter. But first I think I need another glass of wine. Robbie?'

'I'm fine, thank you, Philly,' he said. 'I still need to drive home. But I could go a brew if you put the kettle on.'

Drinks in hand, we sat back down on the stools near the bench. I reached for my reading glasses, surprised to find I didn't feel at all self-conscious about doing so. Robbie pulled his from the pocket in his jacket.

'Okay,' I said. 'Let's see what this is all about.'

Picking up the envelope, I slowly lifted one side and

slid my fingernail along the yellowed seal and pulled the first of the letters out. The pages, some of which looked as though they'd been torn from a notebook, had been folded for so long that as I straightened them, they were in danger of tearing along the creases.

Written in ink, some words were hard to decipher, but the meaning was clear. What we had were love letters.

My hand flew to my chest as I understood. 'Oh Robbie, this is so sad. He's written to her and sent back her last letter to him.'

'How about we start from the beginning?' he said with a soft smile.

I nodded slowly and began to read.

May 1944

Darling Johnny,

These last few months have felt like a wish has come true even though it's a wish I didn't know I had, but one that had been growing inside of me. I love you, Johnny, and I can't believe I have the right to say that now. I love you. I'll never forget our day in Whitby – I haven't been to the sea since leaving Cornwall, and it felt as though I'd come home. To breathe in the sea air with the sound of gulls swirling above us; the whole day was like a holiday from our real world. I'll treasure forever that special day and the moment we became one for the first time.

I know I promised not to write, to trust you to arrange everything, that we'll be together soon, but there's something I need to tell you – something important. Can we please meet?

Don't try and see me in the house – that would be too dangerous – but I'll be in the folly on Friday at 3 pm.

Yours forever,

Peggy

'I wonder who these people are,' I said with a heaviness in my heart. 'The one thing Catherine didn't tell me was the name of the deceased estate, but I'm guessing it was this Peggy lady.'

'This letter was obviously to the father. What does the other one say?'

I flattened out the pages and read aloud.

Dearest Peggy,

I'm so sorry about how I reacted to your news yesterday – our news. It has brought me a pleasure I have no right to feel. Our child. It's something I would never have believed to be true.

I only wish I could be here to support you, but I can't. I report for duty on Monday, and I don't know when I'll next see your face, darling Peggy.

If only things were different, if only I was free, if only this war was over. I'll sort it out, I promise. Until then, I've included a little money – all I can spare – with this letter in our hiding place. I've also arranged for you somewhere to stay in town – you won't be able to stay working here once you're showing. I've sent ahead the painting of Whitby you love so much, Grandmother's vanity case and a little silver I've managed to take from the house. It won't be missed, but you will be my darling. They're for you to sell if you need funds before I'm home to look after you. And I will make it home, my love. I'll come home for you, not for her.

If the worst happens and I don't come home, know that I thought of you always. Billy knows to look after you and will see you right.

Please let me know you've got this message in the usual way. I'll check one more time before I leave. I love you, darling girl. I always will.

Yours forever,

Johnny

'This must've been how they communicated,' Robbie said. 'Notes in the letterbox and meetings in the folly.'

'That means she would've worked in the house where the letterbox was.' I pursed my lips in thought. 'Not many houses still had servants by that stage of the war – or follies, for that matter.' The possibilities swirled. 'Johnny, whoever he is, was married by the sounds of this. In the picture, he's young, so I'd say he's the son of the house rather than the master.'

'It explains how she got the vanity box and the picture, but not the letterbox itself,' Robbie said. 'Or the other painting.'

'It might not have even come from Johnny. Like the brass, it might've been something Peggy had acquired over the years. Maybe the boxes and the Whitby painting were the only things left of Johnny's. There certainly wasn't much silver – unless she sold some of that.' I sighed deeply, suddenly caught up in the plight of these two lovers from so many years ago. 'I wonder what happened to baby Jonny?'

'I don't think we'll ever know,' said Robbie. He looked at his watch. 'I need to be going, Philly, but I've really enjoyed myself tonight.'

'Playing detective with me?' I asked cheekily.

He laughed his deep, rumbly laugh. 'Well, I have to say it's different from what I usually work on. I'll check all your doors before I go, but I think you'll be safe tonight. Call me if you're worried, though.'

'Thank you, I will. My son and his husband and family are over tomorrow for lunch, and I'll make sure I take the painting to Catherine's first thing on Monday.'

He nodded once. 'Okay.'

'And after that, I'll call in on Tom and Beth.' As he would've opened his mouth to say something, I added, 'I'm only going to ask about the vanity if it comes up in conversation.'

'Good – just don't go seeing this Wainwright woman – if that's what her name is – without talking to me first. I'll check in on the reports of other burglaries too.'

'Will you let me know if there's a result?'

He smiled benignly. 'I shouldn't, of course.'

'But you will?' I raised my eyebrows.

He nodded again. Putting his jacket on, he kissed me lightly on the cheek. 'Thank you for dinner, and be safe, Philly Barker.'

'I will, Inspector Robbie Dawkins. Good night.'

Chapter Thirteen

The roast beef was perfectly medium-rare, the potatoes golden and crisp on the outside and soft and fluffy inside (thanks to the duck fat). As for the Yorkshire puddings, they rose a treat, and both men went back for extras – which they filled with gravy. 'Can't have these going to waste,' Jordan said with a wink.

'I honestly have no idea where you two put it,' I said. Both men were tall and lean, without an ounce of fat between them. Other than that, they were absolute opposites – architect Jordan with his caramel skin, short black curly hair, neat beard, and a mischievous twinkle in his brown eyes; and Ryan, blonde and blue-eyed like me, with black-rimmed glasses lending his face a serious edge that was perfect for his role as an accountant. His colouring might've come from me, but when I looked at him, I saw Stewart when he was Ryan's age. Although Stewart was much more the life and soul of the party than Ryan ever has been – Chloe took after her father in that regard. Ryan had always been quieter, more studious, more sensitive even. I'd been concerned when, at twenty-four, he married Jenny, but they'd been good together and, I supposed, still were but in another completely different way. Jordan, though, brought Ryan out of himself and gave him a confidence that had always (in hindsight) been missing.

'I don't suppose –' started Ryan.

'Yes, I'll package up the rest of the beef for you to take home for your tea.'

'Only if you're not going to eat it, Mum.'

After pudding – Ryan's favourite chocolate self-saucing pudding with lashings of homemade custard – we sent Ada and Alfie out into the garden to play with Balthazar, opening the doors wide so we could keep an eye on them.

'Although,' said Jordan with a grin. 'We only need to worry when we can't hear them.'

'Isn't that the truth.' Ryan rolled his eyes. 'Now, Mum, tell me what's really happening here.'

'I don't know what you're talking about,' I said, my halo positively shining.

'The innocent look doesn't fool me. I know there's more to this break-in than you've told Dad. For a start, why was it just your stall?'

'That's what I've been wondering too,' said Jordan. 'What was taken?'

'A couple of books and an oak Victorian letterbox,' I replied.

Both men were silent for a beat and then another.

'Sorry?' Ryan said as if he'd misheard me. 'You're telling me that someone broke into the barn and then into your stall, which is full of jewellery and silverware, and all they took was a box and a few old books?'

'Ah-ha.'

'And let's not forget they bypassed the brothers Ashton who would also have plenty in their dealership worth stealing,' added Jordan.

'I suppose when you put it like that,' I said airily.

'What was it they were *really* after?' asked Ryan, his eyes narrowed. 'And don't try and tell me they wanted a – what did you call it? An oak Victorian letterbox and some books.'

'Oh, but that's exactly what they were after,' I said matter-of-factly. 'And a painting. They were after a painting too.'

'Which painting?' Ryan almost growled the words in his frustration at me. Not that I blamed him, I was making out it was much less of a worry than it was.

'That painting.' I used my thumb to point to the easel in the corner.

'What's so special about that painting?' Jordan asked, standing to walk across and peer at it.

'As it turns out, a lot. It's a JT Wilson – something I didn't know when I bought it. What they were after, though, was what was hidden in it.'

Ryan took off his glasses and cleaned the lenses with the bottom of his T-shirt. 'Presumably, that was why they took the letterbox and books – in case there was something in there too.'

I nodded. 'And there was, but I'd already found it.'

'Mum! That means if they can't find what they're looking for, they'll come after you – and this painting that's sitting here in this house without any sort of protection.'

I waved away his concerns. 'I don't think they know exactly what it is they're looking for and where exactly it's hidden,' I reassured them.

'How do you know that?' Jordan asked, mirroring the concern on Ryan's face.

'Because there was nothing in the books – I checked. I'm hoping that when they find the letterbox empty, they'll assume that whatever was once there is long gone.' I shrugged my shoulders to make him think I wasn't worried, so he had no need to be. 'You know these family mysteries – they get handed down over the years. Granny says that there's a treasure hidden in an old box, and centuries later, someone goes looking for it and finds an old document that these days is worthless.'

'You've also told stories of family fortunes changing because of a will or a birth certificate found in a secret drawer in one of those boxes or hidden behind the frame of an otherwise worthless painting – or even pressed between the pages of an old book.' My eyes must have widened in surprise because Ryan then said. 'I have been listening over the years, Mum, and I remember how you used to go through every box and every writing desk that came into Catherine's saleroom. I bet she remembers too. Is that where you found the documents these people are looking for?'

I glanced across at Jordan whose grin was wide, his dimples deep enough that if I'd wanted to poke a finger into his cheeks, it would disappear. He gave me a look that said I was getting no support from him on this one. 'Yes,' I finally said. 'I found some photos and a birth certificate in a compartment in the letterbox and some old love letters taped behind the painting.'

'I knew it!' Ryan fist-pumped the air in triumph. 'Good old Mum. You might've left the force, but you've always loved a good mystery.' To Jordan, he said, 'Mum's always been addicted to mystery shows on TV – *Midsomer Murders*, *Rosemary and Thyme*, anything that needs solving. In fact, if she was ever on *Mastermind*, her special subject would be *Midsomer Murders – The Tom Barnaby Years*.'

'I think you're exaggerating, darling,' I scoffed, knowing he wasn't.

'I knew we were kindred spirits, Philly,' said Jordan. 'Who's your favourite sergeant?'

'Definitely Ben Jones,' I said. 'Who's yours?'

'Mum! Don't try and change the subject. There's more you aren't telling me, isn't there?'

'I might just check on the kids,' I said, rising from my chair. 'Do you think they're warm enough? You know they're saying we could get some snow over the next few days.'

'Mum …' Ryan warned. 'The kids are fine, and they're plenty warm enough. We can see them from here. Alfie is throwing the ball for Bally and Ada's chasing after them both. Now, let's go through this logically. Where did you buy this stuff from? Catherine?'

I nodded and slumped back into the chair. 'At the auction on Wednesday.'

'And you say it came from a deceased estate?' said Jordan.

'That's right.'

'What else came from there?' asked Ryan. 'And don't try and bluff me on this; I know you would've asked Catherine.' Ryan always had the gift of scolding me as if I were the unruly child rather than the other way around.

'A ladies travelling vanity case and another painting, plus some furniture,' I said.

'I take it you've discounted the furniture?' I nodded. 'And the other two lots? Do you know what happened to them?'

I nodded again.

'And?'

I hesitated before answering in a small voice. 'The buyers have both been broken into.'

'What?' My normally mild-mannered son's fist hit the table with so much force that the teacups rattled, and Jordan started in surprise. 'Does Dad know?'

I lifted a shoulder, biting my bottom lip. 'I have no idea

what your father knows or doesn't know.'

'Mum …'

'Okay, so maybe he doesn't know. I found out about one of them by accident and the other this morning.'

Robbie had phoned this morning to tell me that not only had Florence Miller been robbed, but that she'd been injured in the process – she'd fallen down the stairs when she'd ventured down to investigate the noise. The burglars took her painting, and she'd assumed (as had the police) that the thieves had been disturbed before they could take anything else. Ryan probably didn't need to know that Florence Miller was in hospital – he'd only jump to conclusions he didn't need to jump to.

'How did you find out?' He asked slowly, putting a gap between the words, almost as if he needed to ask the question, but dreaded the answer.

'My friend Robbie told me,' I said simply.

Ryan sighed heavily. The sigh of the long suffering. 'And who is your friend Robbie?' His question sounded patronising, as though I was someone who needed to be spoken slowly to.

'Don't you take that attitude with me, Ryan Barker. You're not so big that I can't put you over my knee.'

Jordan stifled a laugh. 'That's you told, babe,' he said. 'And for the record, Mrs B, I think he might be a bit large for *your* knee.' He waggled his eyebrows, and it was my turn to chuckle.

'Seriously though, Ryan, I'm nearly fifty-nine, not eighty-nine, and my friend Robbie is Inspector Robbie Dawkins. And don't look at me like that either; there's nothing else going on. Robbie called in the other day to warn me about some fake Clarice Cliffs doing the rounds –'

'Aaah, that old line,' said Jordan, his expression innocent, his eyes dancing.

'And your father asked him to come out yesterday when the break-in was called in.'

'And?' prompted Ryan.

'He came for dinner last night, and we took the back off the painting and found the love letters,' I said, beginning to feel as though I was being interrogated.

'Is that what the kids are calling it now?' said Jordan. I shook my head and lightly punched him on the arm. 'Ow,' he said and rubbed at the spot, grinning the whole time.

'Oh, for goodness sake, you two,' I said. 'There's nothing like that going on. We're friends, and neither of us are looking for a relationship.'

'Why not?' asked Ryan. When I responded with a blank look, he said again, 'Why not Mum? You and Dad have been divorced for years. You can't still be hoping he'll come back.'

'Of course not!' I snapped. 'We might never be the best of friends, but I'd hate to think that Stewart would put Alison through anything like what he put me through. No, I'm completely over your father; I'm just not in a hurry to rush into anything else.'

'It's been over ten years, so it's not exactly rushing into anything, though, is it?'

When I took an involuntary inward breath, Jordan laid his hand on Ryan's arm. 'Steady,' he said.

'Sorry, Mum, that wasn't meant to come out like that. I was just wondering whether … Has there been anyone? Since Dad?'

I poured myself a fresh glass of water before saying, 'No. Not really.' I met Ryan's sympathetic eyes. 'And before you go thinking that I'm still hung up on your father, well, I'm not. I won't deny he hurt me badly – I hadn't seen it coming, was completely blindsided – but that's not the complete story.' I bit at my top lip before adding, 'The truth is, I haven't felt ready to trust again, let alone to love. Besides, I'm happy on my own. I have a job I love, good friends, you two and Chloe – when she deigns to ring me, that is – and Bally. I don't need a man.'

'But what about …?' His cheeks flushed a delightful shade of rose.

'Sex? You can say the word you know, Ryan.' I debated how much to say but then decided he'd brought up this line of questioning; he could deal with the answer. 'Yes, I miss sex, but I've gotten used to that, and, well, there are other ways to… you know.' When his cheeks tinged even pinker I took pity on him and added softly. 'Thank you for caring, but I'm okay, really I am, and Inspector Dawkins, Robbie, and I are just friends. I hope that we'll be good friends, but neither of us are in the market for a relationship. Okay?'

'Okay.' He gave a quick nod and sculled his water.

'And in the meantime, while there's nothing really for him to investigate, it's a comfort for me to know he's at the other end of a phone if I need him.' I smiled. 'Now, do either of you want another coffee?'

'No, thanks, Mum, and I'm sorry if I sound like I'm ...' He lifted a shoulder and let me fill in the blanks.

'It's okay, Ryan darling. I'm glad you cared enough to ask and to be concerned.'

'Promise you won't go looking for trouble, Mum – and don't look at me like that; I know exactly what you're like. All I'm asking is that you're careful.'

'I promise,' I said. 'Besides, between your father and Robbie, I'm being taken care of. You don't need to worry,' I assured. 'Either of you.' My tone was firm, and their expressions lightened; the termination of the subject aligned neatly with Alfie's descent into tears in the garden.

Chapter Fourteen

The following morning I rugged up and took Balthazar for a long walk behind the village, letting him off the leash to duck through the gaps in the hawthorn hedgerow to run across the fields, his ears flapping, in pursuit of a pheasant. Once back home I wrapped the Whitby painting with some large bath towels and stowed it safely in the back of Libby. Leaving Bally in the garden with a bone large enough to keep him occupied for at least a half an hour, I set off for York and thirty minutes later pulled up on the gravel drive outside Young and Johnson's.

'Hiya, Philly,' greeted Becky as I pushed the large glass door open. Her gaze flickered to the towel-wrapped painting under my arm, but she was too well used to the goings-on of the saleroom not to bat an eyelid. 'How are you?'

'All good, and you?'

'I'm grand. What brings you here?'

I readjusted the bulky painting under my arm. 'Is Catherine around?'

'Aye. Go on through.'

I held up a couple of fingers in thanks and made my way through the salesroom to Catherine's office. The next auction wasn't due for a fortnight, so the showroom was almost empty. From experience, most of the work would be happening in the background – choosing which items to hold out for a specialist auction and which to include in the next general auction.

Catherine was seated amongst a flurry of paper and journals at her grand mahogany desk, her elbow on the table and cheek resting against the back of her hand. Her opposite shoulder making jerky circles while navigating the mouse. As if sensing my presence, she peered up and over her laptop screen. 'Philly! What brings you here? Have you come to save me from death by spreadsheet?'

'Do you need saving?' I asked, already knowing the answer. Catherine hated paperwork. Whenever she was doing her accounts, we all knew better than to go near her.

'God yes.' She puffed out a weary sigh. Then, upon spying my towel-wrapped parcel, 'What's that?'

'Can you take care of this for me? I'll put it in the next sale, but I'll need to have it authenticated first.'

'Sure, but what is it?'

Catherine pushed the papers into a messy pile on the edge of her desk, allowing me to lay the painting. When I unwrapped it, she glanced up at me, her brow furrowed. 'Isn't this the painting that was in the mixed lot you bought the other day – the one that all the fuss was about?'

'Yes,' I said. 'But have a closer look at it,' I urged.

'Okay.' She scooted back on her chair and stood to come to my side of the desk. 'What am I looking at? It's Whitby, obviously, late nineteenth century, British.' She sent me a quizzical look. 'Alright, what's got your heart beating faster about this that we missed?'

'It's in the brushstrokes,' I said. 'What would you say if I mentioned the name JT Wilson?'

Her eyes widened. 'I'd say I haven't seen one from Whitby before, but we get good prices for his seascapes – not that we get many of them in. Are you sure?'

'I've taped it back up for now, but here's a photo of what I found under the frame.'

Catherine gave a low whistle. 'This is some find, Philly. We'll need to get it authenticated, of course, but I think you might be right.' She straightened and rubbed at the back of her neck. 'Is this what Mrs Wainwright was after?'

'Possibly. But do you see why I need you to pop it into your safe for the time being?'

'Absolutely. I'm not happy that we missed it, but it took a good eye to catch it, and I'm glad it was you.'

'Besides,' I said with a grin, 'you'll pick up the commission the next time round.'

'There is that.' She pinched at her chin, a slight curve to her mouth. 'I can see this headlining the next fine arts auction. I don't think I've ever seen an early Wilson go to auction. There was always the suspicion that he might've painted some scenes from when he worked on the docks, but ...' She nodded slowly, meaningfully, and then a smile broke over her face. 'We might have missed this the first time round, but this could be good for us and, if you're right, I can see it going for a saleroom record price.'

'Don't feel bad about missing it,' I said. 'It's the fault of the framing. I wouldn't have known if I hadn't taken it out of the frame.'

'But you trusted your instincts enough to do that.'

She didn't need to know that I'd been looking for something else in the frame. 'You'll look after it until the auction?'

Still poring over the painting, she answered absentmindedly. 'Absolutely.' She looked up, her gaze narrowed. 'Am I assuming you don't need anyone else to know it's here?'

I gave a quick nod. 'If this could be between us, that would be great.' I hesitated and then said, 'I don't suppose you could give me any information about where it came from in the first place. It would help with establishing provenance, of course.' I rushed to add the last sentence, provenance in some cases being the difference between a good sale and an exceptional one – dollarwise. 'It would be one thing to have the painting authenticated, but to prove where it came from ...' I didn't need to spell it out to Catherine. 'Especially if it had come from a grand house originally.'

'Absolutely. I don't suppose it will do any harm to tell

you as the old lady apparently had no direct descendants.'
She let out a disbelieving laugh and shook her head slowly.
'I'm an idiot.' She held up a finger of warning. 'Say nothing!'
I giggled as I was supposed to. Catherine continued, 'I
don't know why it hadn't occurred to me before now. Mrs
Wainwright said she was a granddaughter, but now I think
on it, I recall the solicitor telling me there were no known
direct descendants. The alarm bells should've been ringing
from the outset.'

She sat back down behind her laptop and moved the
mouse, clicking and typing around until she found the
file she wanted. 'Here we are. The previous owner was a
Margaret Bishop. Hang on, I'll get you the address of the
house and the solicitors who were acting for the estate.' She
scribbled a Malton address and a solicitor's name on some
scrap paper and handed it to me.

When I thanked her, she said, 'I have no idea what
you're going to do with this, and I'm pretty sure I don't want
to know.' She glanced at her watch, a slim, gold Edwardian
timepiece. 'I tell you what, seeing as how you're Balthazar
free today, let's talk about this over a Fat Rascal and a pot
of tea.'

'Sounds good to me, although why they won't allow
dogs into Betty's is beyond me.'

It was a refrain she'd heard before, and this time she
patted me on the arm and said, 'Well, Philly, they don't;
however, feel free to continue your campaign to have that

state of affairs changed.'

The Ainsworths lived a few miles out of Chipwell on the Malton Road in a village that would've once been part of the great Castle Howard estate. Their home, a lovely two-storied bungalow constructed from local limestone almost three hundred years ago, stood proud at the end of a narrow lane directly opposite a quaint stone church surrounded by yews that probably dated back to the same time. I wouldn't have been surprised if the Ainsworth home was once upon a time the vicarage. I'd visited the Ainsworths several times before – to deliver items they'd purchased from me and to attend Christmas drinks parties – their Christmas drinks parties were fabulous.

Beth answered the door on the first ring, disappointment clouding her face when she saw who stood there. 'Oh, it's you, Philly; I thought it might've been the police.'

'The police? Is this about the break-in the other night?' I asked, worried by the tired and weary look on her face.

'No,' she said and briefly covered her face with her hands, her chest heaving with emotion.

I reached forward and put my arm around her, leading her into the house. 'Beth, what on earth is wrong? Is it Tom?'

She nodded, her shoulders shuddering under my arm. 'Oh Philly, Tom's in hospital. I've been there with him, but I needed to come home to get changed – the police are sending someone over to take a statement.' She wrung her hands. 'I don't know what I should be doing.'

'Alright, Beth. I've brought you some of Betty's shortbreads, so you take a seat, and I'll make us a brew. Then you can fill me in. Okay?' I smiled encouragingly at her, and she nodded mutely, seemingly happy to be given an instruction – any instruction.

I navigated my way around Beth's kitchen with ease and soon returned to the living room with a tray of tea things. I waited until she'd taken her first sip of tea and nibbled on her shortbread before I spoke.

'What happened?'

She took a deep, shaky breath before answering. 'You know I told you there'd been an attempted break-in the other night?' I nodded. 'Well, last night they came back – at least we think it was the same people. There were two of them – and they took the box that Tom bought me for our anniversary on Saturday. Such a beautiful box. It was in our bedroom on the dresser –'

My hand flew to my chest as my breath hitched. 'Are you saying they were in your bedroom while you were asleep?' It didn't bear thinking about.

'Yes, I woke up and saw a black shadow with a light – like the ones on a phone – over by the dresser. At first, it was like in a dream when you want to scream but you can't, your voice isn't working. Finally, I cried out, and Tom woke. The figure by the dresser grabbed the box and ran. There must've been another person waiting by the door, and when

Tom got out of bed and went after them, he punched Tom, and he fell and hit his head badly on the edge of the bed. Philly, I was afraid he was dead, but I felt for a pulse, and there was one, so then I called the ambulance.'

'Oh, Beth, that sounds terrifying. How is he?'

She shrugged, fresh tears pooling in her exhausted eyes. 'They're keeping him in for observation because they're not sure … and there was a lot of blood.' She attempted a tremulous half-smile. 'But he's a tough bugger is my Tom. It will take more than a burglar to bring him down.'

The doorbell rang. 'Oh Philly, will you see who that is, please? I suddenly don't have the strength to stand.'

'Of course,' I said gently and stood to go to the front door.

'Philly! I forgot you'd said you might call around.' It was Robbie.

'I came to see how Beth was doing after the break-in the other day. I don't need to ask what you're doing here,' I said sombrely.

'Indeed. Is Mrs Ainsworth around?'

'Philly,' Beth called. 'Who is it?'

I motioned with my head for Robbie to follow me. 'It's Inspector Dawkins, Beth,' I said. 'He's here to take your statement.'

'Good morning, Mrs Ainsworth,' said Robbie, holding his hand out for Beth to shake.

'Please call me Beth, Inspector Dawkins.'

'Right,' I said. 'I'll leave you to it.' I went to get my coat and bag from the hall stand.

'Please stay, Philly,' said Beth, grabbing for my hand. 'I'd like you to be here.'

I raised questioning brows in Robbie's direction. At his nod, I said, 'Okay, Beth. But how about I get a fresh cup for Inspector Dawkins first.'

Robbie smiled his thanks, and I left them to go into the kitchen. When I reappeared, I poured tea for Robbie and topped up Beth's and my cups.

'Are you ready, Beth?' I asked softly.

She pressed her lips together, nodded, and I removed the teacup from her shaking hands and placed it safely on the coffee table.

'I know this will be difficult,' Robbie began, 'but it's important you walk me through everything that happened last night. Any small detail could be important.'

Beth nodded again and swallowed hard before speaking – faltering at first and then gaining confidence when she saw Robbie was listening earnestly, taking the occasional note, and gently prompting her to clarify a point at other times. Watching him was a masterclass in how to actively listen. He'd put Beth at ease and drew from her information she didn't know she had.

'Would you say there was a difference between the build of the intruders?' he asked.

'What do you mean?'

'If you close your eyes and see them again – one by the dresser, the other waiting by the door. You've said they were both dressed in black and wore balaclavas over their faces, but how did they move? Were they light on their feet, one taller, shorter, stockier, thinner than the other?'

'Are you asking if one could have been a woman?' She raised her eyes from her lap and looked across the coffee table at Robbie. Before he could answer, she said, 'One of them could've been a woman. The one at the dresser. That person seemed leaner than the other and moved more lightly. The one who hit my Tom, that was a man. He was broad across the back, and there was something in the way he pulled his arm back to throw the punch that made me think he'd punched people before. When I heard it hit my Tom's cheek ...' I gripped her hand tightly until she could collect herself.

'Yes, Inspector,' Beth continued with renewed resolve. 'One of them could have been a woman.'

He closed his worn notebook and rewarded her bravery with a smile that was encouraging, empathetic and sympathetic all at the same time. 'You've done well, Mrs Ainsworth. I can only imagine how hard that must've been for you. Now, do you have anywhere to stay tonight? I'd prefer you don't stay here on your own until we ensure the doors are secure.'

'Thank you, Inspector. I'll go into the hospital now and check in on Tom. Our Julie is meeting me there, and I'll go to hers until Tom is well enough to come home. Joe, our boy, is on his way up from London too.'

I stood to gather the tea things and take them back to the kitchen. 'Don't you do that, Philly,' said Beth. 'You've done enough. I can manage from here.'

I reached for her arm and patted it. 'Are you sure? I don't mind staying and helping.'

She shook her head. 'No, but thank you for calling in, and thank you for staying while the inspector was here.'

'No problems at all, Beth.' I leant forward and kissed her smooth cheek lightly.

'Oh away with you, Philly,' she said with a smile that told me she appreciated the gesture. 'Thank you, Inspector,' she held her hand out for him to shake. 'I expect we'll hear from you in due course.'

I held back a smile at Beth's recovery from shaken and frail to resolute.

'That you will, Mrs Ainsworth.'

Robbie and I left the house together, me carrying my coat over my arm for the short walk to the car. Robbie's expression was inscrutable. 'It's the same people that broke into the barn, isn't it?' I asked.

'I think so; now we need to prove it.' When we reached Libby, he stopped and spoke. 'It worries me that this has turned violent. Mr Ainsworth is lucky to be alive. He's not a young man, and that blow was a hard one. He's still not out of the woods.'

'Beth would be lost without him,' I said, tears springing to my eyes at the thought of it. 'They've been together since they were teenagers and married at twenty. It was their fifty-seventh wedding anniversary on Saturday, and they're still very much in love. You don't get that much these days.'

'No, you don't.' He turned to face me. 'I'm concerned for your safety, though, Philly. Is there anywhere you can go?' He'd held my arm as he said it, staring earnestly into my face.

'Thank you, Robbie, but I'll be fine. At this point, they think the painting is safely locked away at work. Nothing will happen to me tonight.'

He removed his hand and rubbed at his temple, the lines on his face deep with concern. 'And what about when they find out you no longer have the painting? What then?'

'We'll cross that bridge when we come to it,' I said with more courage and confidence than I felt.

'What if they discover you've already found the documents?' he asked, his eyes not leaving mine.

I shivered involuntarily, hugging my coat for warmth. 'I don't know,' I finally admitted.

'Don't do anything without talking to me first,' he warned.

'I won't,' I said, faking a bright smile. 'I'll be fine.'

'Be safe, Philly Barker,' he said. 'I'll be seeing you.'

'You certainly will, Inspector Dawkins,' I replied before climbing into my car.

I might've believed I was perfectly safe – for tonight at least – but I kept Balthazar close that night and woke with a start at every little noise.

Chapter Fifteen

There was no sign there had ever been a break-in when I unlocked the barn's front door on Tuesday morning. Everything had been repaired, and a security company had installed the new CCTV cameras. No one was getting in again without us knowing about it.

The situation in my stall was a little different – cabinets needed dusting and straightening, and the storeroom needed tidying. Balthazar supervised it all from his cushion in the corner.

Bell floated in – today's shawl was a magenta velvet one that had me itching to run my fingers over its soft folds – and sat swivelling in the chair as I worked. Somehow, knowing I wouldn't want to talk about anything remotely connected to the events of last Friday, she told me of a find she had been put onto over the weekend.

'The wardrobe belonging to a society "It" girl of the twenties, darling. It's been in suitcases in an attic for decades – dresses, hats, coats, the works. I've negotiated a price for the lot, so I'll drive down there tomorrow. I've got Lily coming in to watch the stall for me.'

'Where is it?'

'Brookford, in The Cotswolds. I'd say you could come too for the ride, but I'm not sure about having Balthazar in the back seat if I have hats in there. Sorry Bally, no offence sweetie.' Balthazar thumped his tail twice on the ground to acknowledge her.

'Thanks for the offer, but I've got a bit going on here,' I said, closing the door on the final cabinet. 'There, that looks all back to normal, doesn't it?'

Bell swivelled and cast a critical eye over the space. 'Not a trace of fingerprint dust remaining. Nice job.'

I slumped onto the other chair with a sigh.

Bell directed her focus on me and tilted her head slightly. 'Everything *is* okay, isn't it? With you?'

'Yeah, fine,' I said. 'Why do you ask?'

'Don't shoot the messenger, sweetie, but the bags under your eyes have their own luggage. Not sleeping?'

I contemplated lying to her or shrugging it off but opted for the truth. 'I had a rough night. I was over at the Ainsworth's yesterday – they had a break-in on Sunday night while they were asleep, and Tom was injured.'

'Not Tom!' Her eyes were wide with horror as she brought the swivelling to a sudden halt. 'I can't imagine what it must've been like to wake up and see someone in your room! Did they take much?'

'No.' I hesitated for half a beat before adding, 'Just

a ladies travelling vanity box Tom bought at auction on Wednesday.'

Bell's shoulders slumped as she let out a great sigh. 'Let me guess, from the same place your box came from?' I nodded. 'And the painting? Where's that now? Please tell me it's not at home?'

'No. It's at Catherine's for safekeeping. It's turned out to be rather special.'

Before she could ask more about that, Ambrose and Eugene walked in. Today the brothers were dressed down and had opted for leather patch tweed jackets instead of suit jackets. Ambrose's tie was olive green, and Eugene pushed out all the stops in purple.

'Philly! It's good to see you back.' Eugene gripped my arms and looked earnestly into my face. 'Ow do's, lass?' he asked, slipping into the Yorkshire vernacular that lived beneath his tweed suits.

'I'm fine, thanks.'

'Good. Good.'

Eugene released me, and Ambrose patted my back and smiled reassuringly. 'It's a bad business, lass. And all for an oak box and a couple of books?'

'And a painting which wasn't here at the time,' added Bell.

'The one from the mixed lot?' asked Ambrose.

I nodded. 'I think it might be a Wilson.'

The brother's eyes were like saucers. 'You don't say?'

said Ambrose. 'Are you getting it checked over?'

'Yes, it's at Catherine's in the meantime.'

'Aye, best place for it,' said Eugene. 'Do you think that's what they were after?'

I shrugged. 'Possibly.'

Simon loped in, his usual well-worn jeans and trainers topped with the touring T-shirt of a band I'd never heard of but assumed was heavy metal judging by all the black and red. 'What have I missed?'

'Philly's mixed lot painting has turned out to be a treasure,' said Bell.

'Now that's the way to start a working week,' said Simon, watching Bell swivel around in the captain's chair. 'Umm, Philly …?'

'Yes.'

'Are you terribly attached to those chairs?' he asked.

'Why?'

'I've sold them. They're being picked up this morning, so I'll bring you up something else.'

'No worries at all.' And that was how it went here at the barn. Next to arrive were the Proctors. Tamsin had a hug for me while Henry patted my hand awkwardly, earning him a poke in the arm from his diminutive wife. 'You can hug her, you know,' she teased.

'It's okay, Henry,' I said.

'What's okay?' Ginny bowled in.

'Henry was too embarrassed to hug Philly,' said Tamsin.

'What's in the tin you've got there, Ginny?' asked Simon hopefully.

'Orange and cinnamon biscuits,' she said. 'But you'll have to make your own tea – I need to make sure this one is okay.' She gave me a one-armed hug.

'I'm fine,' I said, sneaking a biscuit from the tin.

'She's better than fine,' said Eugene. 'That painting the burglars didn't get looks like it's worth a lot of money.'

Henry perked up. 'Really? Who's it by?'

'Have you heard of JT Wilson?' Bell said.

'I have. Is it really?'

'Aye. An early piece,' said Ambrose.

'Nice.' Henry nodded slowly and respectfully. 'Good one, Philly.'

I sat back and swivelled in my captain's chair (while I could) and smiled contentedly. These people were my people. We looked out for each other and were happy about each other's successes. It would never occur to any of the dealers in the barn to be resentful of my find – we all knew it could happen to any of us at any time. We knew our product; we knew our market – the rest was trusting ourselves and our instincts and being in the right place at the right time with the courage to stick our finger in the air and have a bid.

As the others drifted off to make tea, I took Ginny to one side. 'How did it go the other night?'

Her wide smile was all the answers I needed. 'You were

right. It was lovely. We caught up on Sunday too – for a pub roast.'

'As you do,' I said with a chuckle.

'And he phoned me yesterday too. We're going out again on Friday night.'

I impulsively hugged her. 'I'm so glad.'

'What have I missed?' asked Bell, rejoining us.

'I'll let Ginny fill you in,' I said.

Balthazar knew she was there before I did. I was taking advantage of a lull in trade to catch up on some social media posts when Bally rose from his mat and came to sit beside me, his chin on my leg. 'What's wrong, buddy?' I asked, scratching him behind the ear, and looked up to see Mrs Wainwright – I probably should stop referring to her as that until I knew what her name really was – peering into one of the cabinets.

Before acknowledging her, I tapped out a quick message to Robbie:

She's here.

His reply came back quickly.

Ten minutes away – can you keep her talking?

I'll try …

'Good   afternoon,'   I   said,   forcing   a   cheery professionalism into my voice.

She smiled tightly. 'I see you've repaired the shop.'

'Sorry?'

'When I phoned on Friday, you said you'd had a break-in,' she replied, picking up a Danish enamelled brooch and turning it over in her hand.

'Yes, we did. I've been closed for the weekend – today is my first day open.'

As she examined the little brooch, I examined her. She might've taken me by surprise on her last visit, but this time I was prepared and making a mental note of everything from her highlighted hair to the animal print silky blouse and tailored black pants to the tiny bird tattoo peeking out from under her leather watchband.

'You mentioned the letterbox was taken – did you lose much else?' She placed the enamel brooch down and picked up silver sugar tongs.

'Thankfully, no. The police think they were probably startled and grabbed the first things they saw.'

'Hmmm, maybe. Do they have any leads?' she asked, closely examining the tongs.

Somehow I kept a straight face as I said, 'Yes, a few – although they're not saying much to me. You know how detectives like to keep their cards close to their chest.'

She replaced the tongs and turned to face me. 'I imagine there's no hope of recovering the letterbox,' she said.

'I don't imagine so. You must've really liked it.'

'Yes. It reminded me of one my grandmother used to have, but if it's been stolen, well ...' she shrugged. '*C'est la vie.*' She tucked her bobbed hair behind her ears. 'Now, that painting you had to show me …'

'Oh, I'm so sorry,' I began, pressing a hand over my pounding heart.

'Don't tell me you've sold it.' Her eyes narrowed. 'You said you would hold it until I could see it.'

'Actually,' I gently corrected, 'I told you I hadn't had a good chance to look at it, and if I decided to sell, I'd give you first refusal.'

'And have you? Had a good look at it?' she demanded.

'I have,' I said calmly. 'And I won't be selling it until I can have it properly appraised. I would've called you, but you didn't leave your name and number. If you remember,' I added, 'I was keen to save you the trip out here needlessly.'

'Where's the painting now? Can I see it?' Her lips had tightened, making her look older than she'd first appeared, little lines around her thin lips telling me she was at some stage, if not still, a heavy smoker.

'I'm afraid not. I've sent it away to have it authenticated,' I said.

'Sent it where?' The woman's voice rose in pitch. I took a surreptitious look at my watch – nearly fifteen minutes had passed since she came into the stall. Robbie should be here soon.

'I don't think it matters where,' I said, hopefully sounding more assertive than I felt. 'Somewhere safe.'

She huffed in frustration. 'Why didn't you tell me about this the other day? It would've saved me a trip.'

I took a deep breath. 'I told you the other day I needed to look at it properly, and as I said before, I asked you for your details and could've saved you a trip.'

She closed her eyes briefly, and when she opened them, all pretence at politeness had vanished. 'You told me on Friday the painting was locked up here and you couldn't get to it to show me, so when *did* you get a chance to look at it properly?' The words were bitten out.

'I took it home,' I said breezily.

She looked away, her mouth pursed, pulled out her phone and began tapping out a message.

Robbie appeared in the doorway, panting as if he'd run up from the car park. 'Inspector Dawkins,' I said, loud enough for all to hear. 'I thought you'd finished here.' Mrs Wainwright's head jerked up, and her phone went quickly back into her bag. I got the feeling she would've scuttled out except that Robbie had placed himself between her and the exit.

'Just a few more questions, Mrs Barker,' he said, the picture of efficient policing.

'Not a problem, Inspector. I'm always happy to help. Actually,' I said benignly, 'this lady is the one I was telling you about who was very interested in the letterbox the other day.' To Mrs Wainwright, I said, 'I'm sure you don't mind, but the inspector had asked if there was anyone who'd shown specific interest in the items that were stolen.' My smile was sweet in the face of her glare. 'Inspector Dawkins, this is … I'm sorry, I don't know your name …'

Robbie and I looked expectantly at her, but she didn't say a word. Finally, she spat out, 'I don't have time for this. I don't know how you normally do business, Mrs Barker, but if you treat all your clients in this manner, I'm surprised you still have a business.'

She drew herself up to her full height and went to march past Robbie. 'Not so quickly, Madam. I do have a few questions – purely routine, of course. Mrs Barker, is there anywhere we can talk privately?'

'Certainly. I'm due a cup of tea, and I'm ready to close anyway. I'll be in the café if you need me.' I whistled softly for Bally who had no intentions of remaining in the stall with the woman he'd decided he disliked and walked across the corridor to the café.

Ginny had turned her sign to closed and was sweeping the floor.

'Was that our friendly inspector I saw come running in?' she asked with a subtle smile. 'He looked like he'd been running a marathon. Will he want a cuppa?'

'Maybe later,' I said. 'Friday's visitor is back, and they're having a little chat.'

'Interesting,' she pondered, pouring hot water into the teapot. 'I'm not sure what we have left in the cabinet … millionaire's shortbread?' Without waiting for my answer, she placed slices of the caramel and chocolate topped shortbread onto a Shelley plate. It was one of the Art Deco diamond patterns dating back to the late 1920s. Mostly white with red and green diamonds and black geometric accents.

'Yes, please,' I said. 'Although I need to cut back on the sugary treats,' I mused. 'Maybe after Christmas.'

Ginny shook her head pityingly. 'Why do people feel the need to say things like that?'

'Like what?'

'Like what you just said about how you need to cut back. Sometimes I think it's a habit to say it and a habit to feel guilty about eating something like that. So what if you have something yummy when you sit down to enjoy your end-of-work tea? There's certainly nothing to feel guilty about.'

'I suppose –' I began.

'Of course there is a difference between food that makes you feel good and eating to make yourself feel better,' she continued, 'but that's a whole different question. As for you, you're always on the move. I've watched you in here – you barely sit down – and you walk every day. I'm the opposite.'

'Hey,' I said gently, 'where's this coming from? I thought you said your date went well?'

'It did, but I can't help feeling as though I should make more of an effort to lose weight. I look at Bell and –'

'Stop that thought right there, Virginia Wilding. If you're comparing yourself to Bell, forget it – I certainly did years ago. Haven't you noticed she barely eats? If you ask her if she's had lunch, you're likely to get an answer of, "Darling, I haven't eaten lunch since 1995". Food represents nothing more than fuel to Bell, and that's fine. For you and me, it's different – we enjoy it.'

'Too much,' Ginny conceded.

'Perhaps, but what you said before is absolutely right – we shouldn't regard a treat like this magnificent millionaire's shortbread as anything other than a pleasure to be savoured. As for this man of yours, if you're thinking less of yourself because of him, don't see him again. If, however, you want to be healthier for yourself, make those tweaks. I love you just as you are, and if he has any sense, he will too.'

'It's not him,' she said, more downcast than I'd seen her. 'It's me. Richard seems to like me as I am, and as a result, I'm falling into the old habit of wondering what's wrong with him.'

'Oh Ginny.' I reached over and patted her hand. 'That tells me there's something very right with him. Now, drink your tea and tell me all about it.'

It was another thirty minutes when we heard the front door shut, and Robbie came striding into the café.

'Tea, Inspector?' asked Ginny.

'Please call me Robbie, and don't get up. Just point me in the right direction, and I'll make my own.'

When he'd gone, she raised her eyebrows in my direction. 'A man who doesn't expect to be waited on,' she said.

'Don't. Even. Think. It,' I warned, getting an inscrutable smile in return.

'How did you go?' I asked when he was back. 'Or can't

you tell us?'

'I've got nothing firm to hold or charge her with,' he said, 'but I agree with you, Philly; I think she's involved in whatever is going on. She blustered too much not to be, and it took me way too long to get her name.'

'Which is?' I asked.

'Cilla Grey. I put it to her that she'd purported to be a Mrs Wainwright, the long-lost grandchild from Australia at the auction rooms. At first, she denied it, and when I told her I'd requested the CCTV footage from Catherine, she admitted it. She's also admitted to lying to you about decorating a country house. All she's told me is that she's a private investigator and has been hired by someone – she refused to disclose who – to locate certain pieces.'

'The two boxes, the paintings and the books,' I offered.

'Yes. She says she has had nothing to do with any break-ins – her brief is simply to get the pieces on behalf of her client.'

'Did you believe her?' I asked.

'I think some of what she said is true, but I don't believe she had nothing to do with the break-ins. She has an alibi for each of the robberies, though – her partner Tony. She does, however, know that we're onto her and that we're keeping an eye on you, so I suspect you'll be safe,' he said to me. 'I'd like to know who hired her, though.'

'Hiring someone to locate certain pieces isn't a crime,' I said.

'No, but hiring someone to get those pieces by illegal or menacing means is,' he reminded me. 'And that's what I think is happening here.'

'She got quite upset when she found out I'd sent the painting away, and at no time did she ask why it needed authenticating. It wasn't the value of the painting that was important to her; it was the painting itself,' I said.

'Maybe there's something hidden in the painting – the same as in the letterbox,' suggested Ginny.

I couldn't help but look at Robbie, and Ginny didn't miss the exchange. 'You've already found it, haven't you?'

I nodded simply. 'It explains why they're so desperate to get the painting. They have the books, the letterbox, the other painting and the vanity case. We have the birth certificate and photos from the letterbox and the love letters from the painting –'

'Love letters?' exclaimed Ginny. 'This is about a love story?'

'I don't think so,' I said. 'But I adore how you've gone straight to that.'

'I don't think so either. This is about something else, and I suspect it's money,' said Robbie.

'I'm not sure it's just about money,' I countered.

Robbie pulled at his earlobe. 'Maybe. It's been too specific a search which means the old lady has told someone over the years where it's hidden. If they haven't found anything in the other places, they'd have to assume that either it's all in the painting – hence the desperation – or we've already found it.' He turned his eyes on me. 'And if it's the latter, you're still in danger, Philly.'

A chill rushed across my skin, and I swallowed hard. 'If that's the case, we'd better find them before they find me,' I managed.

'We will,' he said, and part of me believed him.

Chapter Sixteen

Robbie's sergeant interviewed Cilla Grey's partner the following day who, as expected, confirmed her alibi. As there were no other witnesses or evidence, Robbie said they were no closer to an arrest. Given that she knew she was being watched, though, I felt much safer than I had done earlier in the week, and Robbie had promised to keep me up to date with any progress.

Also on Wednesday, I attended a small sale over in Harrogate and bought a set of copper jelly moulds, some lovely vintage china trios (for way less than they were worth), a mini collection of Victorian mourning jewellery, the usual assortment of silver-plate, an unusual travelling inkwell in the shape of a globe, and an oak hat block I was seriously contemplating keeping.

On Thursday, the valuer from London authenticated my painting as an early Wilson. While it thrilled me that my instincts had been right, the auction estimate – mid five figures – took my breath away. Although the authenticator expected me to place it in one of the major Sotheby's auctions, I gave Catherine the authority to put it in her next fine art auction on the basis she kept the painting safe until then. Catherine had taught me so much over the years, and it was fitting that she had the opportunity to grow her profile via the knowledge she'd given me.

Simon replaced the captain's chairs (which I'd grown attached to) with a pair of Arts and Crafts oak chairs. I loved their clean lines and the Morris & Co (not original) fabric seat, but I missed the comfort and swivel power of the captain's chairs. Simon was kept busy with a house clearance in Rosedale Abbey, a village in the North York Moors. He'd been out on Thursday for a look and came back very excited.

'There's a Liberty desk I'm keen on,' he said, 'and a lot more besides.'

Bell was off for the rest of the week down in The Cotswolds. Lily, her fashion-mad goddaughter, staffed the stall and kept us guessing with her outlandish outfits. Ambrose and Eugene shook their heads and tut-tutted when she teamed a cut-down op-shop wedding dress with a modified burgundy Edwardian smoking jacket and elderly Doc Martens, but it was clear from their indulgent smiles that she had them wrapped around her little finger. Balthazar adored her – to the extent that whenever she was around, he'd abandon his post beside me to decorate Bell's stall instead.

The Proctors had closed for ten days and were off on

a buying trip in Derbyshire. At least, they called it a buying trip even though the rest of us knew that as keen ramblers, they'd be basing themselves in the Peak district, dusting off their ordinance maps and boots, and fitting in as many walks as they could. This time of the year was quiet for them – people didn't think about their gardens when it was too dark, too cold or too wet to venture into them. They'd be back in time to capture the Christmas gift market and would then take all of January off too.

Ginny was kept busy with the (now) thrice-weekly bus tours leading into Christmas and trying out new recipes – with the rest of us her grateful guinea pigs. A pastry enclosed potato, cheese and onion pie was a hit with us – and Friday's tour group. She also sold several vintage trios for me, so it was as well I had new stock coming in.

On Saturday afternoon, I was at a loose end. The bus tour for the day had left, and outside, the weather gods were thinking seriously about sending us some snow, so customers were few and far between. I didn't blame them – it was raw outside. Ginny had closed early so she could get ready to meet her man, and I ended up wandering into the Ashton's dealership quite simply because I was bored. Balthazar stayed back in my stall in case he ran into Rochester.

'What's this?' I picked up one from a pair of brass vases. 'This isn't your usual thing.'

'It's trench art, lass,' said Ambrose, looking over the rim of his glasses. 'We get them in from time to time – in fact, I sold a rather nice pair to Sir Antony a month back.'

'Which makes it exactly our type of thing,' said Eugene.

I chuckled. 'What are these made from?' I asked.

'These came from shell casings,' said Ambrose. 'And nice examples they are too.'

I prowled around their cabinets. 'Oh, I like this,' I said. 'Tell me about it.'

The item I'd picked comprised a leather case with a flask, a collapsible cup, and a bone-handled (and foldable) knife, fork and spoon.

'This is a campaign set,' said Ambrose. 'Judging by the bone handles and the flask, it would've belonged to an officer – Boer War perhaps. Do you like it?'

'Yes, I do. Very much. I've had something similar in the stall before, but with mother-of-pearl handles and no flask.'

'Yes, that would be right. They became quite popular as travelling sets for picnics and the like,' said Eugene.

I poked around some more. One of my favourite things to do on cold, quiet days was to have a good rummage around in their cabinets – partly to see what was there, but mostly so I could learn more about militaria. The brothers were so knowledgeable in their field – and happy to pass that on.

In one of their cabinets was a round brass plaque. On it was an image of Britannia holding what looked to be oak leaves and acorns, a lion, two dolphins and an inscription that ran around the outside: *He died for freedom and honour.* In a rectangle below the oak leaves (if that's what they were), a name was inscribed. It was a memorial medal of some sort, and it made me sad that it was sitting here in a glass cabinet.

'I know how you feel, lass,' said Eugene softly, coming to stand next to me at the cabinet. 'The idea of selling one of these …' He shook his head, his face sombre.

'What is it?' I asked. 'I've seen them before but have never known.'

'Aye, we get a few in, sometimes with medals as well. It's a memorial death plaque from the First World War – a death penny or a widow's penny, they're called. The next of kin got one of these in the mail.' He grimaced and shook his head slightly. 'A wee bit better and longer lasting than the telegram, I expect.'

The plaque was a cool weight in my hands as I imagined how a widow or a mother would feel receiving one of these. Was it a reminder that their loved one had given their life for their country or a reminder that that was the reason they were having trouble putting food on the table or clothing their children? How do you put a value on a loss like that?

Ambrose took it gently from my hands and placed it back in the cabinet. 'Aye,' he said, 'it gets us like that, too. The only comfort is that the home it will go to next will be respectful of the price that was paid for it to be made.' After a slight cough, he said, 'I'm glad you're here, lass,' said Ambrose. 'Sir Antony wants someone to go up to the hall and have a look at some of his paintings. Most of them have been in the family for years, and he has no idea whether they're worth anything.'

'When he was in the other day, he asked whether any of us were fine art experts, and we immediately thought of you,' added Eugene.

'I'd be happy to,' I said. 'If you like, I'll call him and see if I can't get up there early next week. I need to be in Malton on Monday morning, so I can go after that appointment if it suits him.'

'That would be grand, lass. You've got a good eye and good instincts. We said that to Sir Antony,' said Ambrose.

'Thanks, I appreciate that, and I'll let you know how I go.'

Tom Ainsworth was making good progress and was now home from the hospital. So when I closed up that afternoon, I dropped in on him and Beth.

They both seemed glad to see me; Beth thanking me for supporting her when Robbie was questioning her about the burglary.

'It was so kind of you to drop by that day, Philly, and then to stay while that detective was interviewing me. He had kind eyes, but I was beside myself, I was.'

'It was nothing at all, Beth.'

'It mightn't have been for you, dear, but it meant a lot to me – especially when I knew you had your own problems.'

When Tom asked if I knew whether the police had any

leads, I told him honestly that they did but had no evidence to support their theories.

'It was such a lovely box,' said Tom, his fingers absently touching the bandage on his temple. 'You should've seen it.'

'It sounded beautiful,' I said. 'I wish I had seen it. Let's just hope it's recovered.'

'I hold no hope of that, Philly,' he said. 'It will be long gone by now and is no doubt already in one of those fancy stores in London or the like.'

'Maybe,' I conceded, thinking it was far likely to be somewhere closer by. I only hoped that whoever had it didn't ruin it by looking for a secret compartment that might not be there.

'A funny thing about that box,' he said.

'Oh yes? What was that, Tom?' I forced my voice to remain even as my heart beat faster.

'I'd forgotten all about it until now, but there was something in one of them secret drawers you hear about.'

My ears pricked up. 'A secret drawer?'

'I'd seen it on one of those shows on the telly,' he said. 'Antiques something or other and the bubbly blonde woman – you know the one I'm talking about, pet,' he addressed his wife.

'Christina Trevanion,' Beth and I guessed together.

'She's a bit of alright, that one,' he said, his cheeks tinged pale pink. 'Anyway, she had something similar and was showing how there was a tiny catch under the main drawer that popped out a thin drawer underneath. You wouldn't know it to look at it, Philly, but there it was, wasn't it, pet?'

'It was,' Beth agreed. 'In all the excitement of the robbery, I'd forgotten about that.'

'What was in it?' I asked, excitement creeping into my voice.

'Well, that's the funny thing – there were photos in there. Now, love, where did I put them?' He reached for his glasses which had been sitting on a book on the table beside him. 'I put them in this book, you see.' To me, he added, 'I was up to a particularly good part, so I didn't want to get up to put them away. Now, here we are.' He opened the book to a near-middle page, pulled out the photos and handed them to me.

The first was the same young man from the letterbox. I turned it over and read *Johnny*. The second was of the same man with his arm around another, younger man, a boy really, again the same face from my photo. In the background was part of a structure. I squinted but couldn't make out what it was. Could it be the folly the letters referred to? The inscription on this one was *Johnny and Billy*. The last photo was of the young man sitting on a picnic rug with the young woman from my photos. In the background were the ruins of the abbey and below was the harbour. *Johnny and me. Whitby.*

Who was Johnny?

'Are you alright, Philly?' asked Beth, concern in her voice.

'Sorry? Yes, I'm perfectly fine, it's just that …' I took a breath and decided to trust them both – with at least part of the story. 'I found similar photos in my box before it was stolen.'

'Away with you. Really?' said Tom, sitting up straighter.

'Yes.' I hesitated and then said, 'You've lived in the area your whole life, haven't you?'

'Aye,' said Tom. 'We both have, haven't we love?'

Beth's face brightened as she nodded. 'Why do you ask?'

'I'm interested in the story – in who Peggy and Johnny are, or, rather, were.'

'Peggy?' asked Beth with a frown.

'On the back of one of my photos is the inscription *Billy, Johnny and Peggy*, so I figure Peggy was the owner of my box and yours. The owner of the house where these came from was a Margaret Bishop. Do you know of her?'

'I don't think so,' said Beth. 'Tom?'

Tom was frowning too, his nose wrinkled and his eyes cast to the beams on the ceiling. 'Aye, I reckon I do. But not as Margaret Bishop – we knew her as Peggy. Margarets were often called Peggy.' He scratched behind his head. 'I think her surname might have been Sykes. She lived in the village when I was young. She kept house up at the hall until she married Barry Bishop and moved into Malton.' He put his glasses on and looked closely at the photos. 'Aye, that's her, much younger, but her.'

'How do you remember that?' Beth asked.

He grinned. 'Our mum used to cook for them up at the hall when I was a boy. I met her several times – she was so nice to me. I remember Mum saying Peggy had worked at the hall since she was a girl.' He paused and then added, 'And one day, she wasn't there anymore. That must've been when she got married, I suppose. She seemed old to be getting married, but anything over thirty is old when you're a boy of sixteen, and she must've been in her thirties by then.' He laughed ruefully. 'I wouldn't have thought she was the type to have fancy things like the box I bought, though,' he said.

'What a sad story,' said Beth. 'She must've been in love with this Johnny, and that's why she didn't marry until later.'

'If it's the same person, she got to a good age. She would've been in her nineties,' said Tom.

'Do you recognise either of the young men?' I asked.

He peered at the pictures, frowned and said, 'They both look familiar, but I can't say I know them. Maybe they were in the village when I was a boy.' He squinted at the images again. 'Yes, that would be it.'

'Do you mind if I take the photos with me?' I asked. 'I'd like to see if I can return them to the family if possible.'

'Of course,' said Beth. 'That would be lovely if you could.'

'Well, I'll certainly try.' I gathered the photos and slid

them into my handbag. 'One last question – when you say the hall, did you mean Chipwell Hall?'

'Aye, that's the one,' said Tom.

'Thanks for that. I need to be going, but you take care, eh?'

'Aye, Philly, I will. I think you might be needing that same advice,' he said earnestly.

'Maybe I do,' I said.

'Mind as you go, Philly,' said Beth.

As I walked back to the car, it occurred to me that a lot of people had been telling me to be careful lately. The only way to take their advice, though, was to hand over the photos and the birth certificate and not only was I unsure who I'd hand them over to, with each new piece of information I discovered, I was less of a mind to do just that.

Chapter Seventeen

Sunday was blue and, while still bitterly cold, there was no sign of yesterday's snow, so Balthazar and I took a drive across to Whitby for the day. I'd hoped being there, in the place where they'd picnicked, a place that obviously meant so much to them, might help me feel closer to Peggy and Johnny. I'd hoped it would help me understand a story that felt as though it was only just beyond my grasp, but still it eluded me.

Coming home, the fog was rolling in over the moors, lending it a lonely, almost gothic appearance, and the sun that had been shining bravely this morning was now seriously considering giving up on the day. The drive had, however, given me the space I needed to organise my thoughts.

Back home, I lit the fire, poured a warming merlot and settled down with the photos, the love letters and a blank sheet of paper.

<u>What I knew for sure</u>

- Peggy and Johnny were in love.
- Johnny was attached to someone else.

- Peggy had a baby she named Jonathon Edward Sykes.
- At the time of having her baby, she lived in Malton, and her occupation was as a servant.
- Peggy had hidden her photos and the birth certificate.

<u>What I thought I knew</u>

- Peggy Sykes and Margaret Bishop were the same person
- Peggy appears young in the photos – maybe sixteen to eighteen.
- She originally came from Cornwall.
- Johnny and Billy are of similar appearance and could be brothers.
- Johnny went off to the war and either didn't come back or didn't come back to Peggy.
- Peggy had her baby adopted.
- Peggy worked at Chipwell Hall for the Cunninghams.
- The Cunninghams wouldn't have known anything about the baby, or she probably wouldn't have been employed by them.
- Was she working at the hall when she and Johnny were together?
- Was Johnny also employed at the hall?
- Someone else knows about Peggy and Johnny, and they either know or think they know there was a baby.

I rested my pen on the paper and let the scenarios move

like pieces of a jigsaw puzzle. Who would be interested in the birth certificate of a baby born nearly eighty years ago? And why would it be so important they were prepared to break the law to find it?

I leant back in my chair and bit lightly at my forefinger, my brain racing wildly after the dots that needed to be connected. The only reason anyone would want a birth certificate would be to find information regarding their birth parents, but then again, with the proper identification, you could order a copy of that. No, there had to be more to it.

I'd assumed that it was the birth certificate that was important, but what if it was the photos and the love letters? The birth certificate showed who young Johnny's mother was, but with the photos and the love letters, there was also evidence of who the father could be. These days, with the availability of DNA testing, the rest would be easy to prove.

Would you be prepared to break the law for that, though? I wouldn't have thought so – at least not unless money was involved. And money and parentage added up to inheritance. The question was, was someone trying to prove parentage – or attempting to ensure that all available evidence of parentage was destroyed? Both scenarios assumed there was something worth inheriting – or worth protecting. But what? And why now? The timing couldn't be a coincidence.

I took another sip of wine and studied the photos, willing the answer to present itself. My thoughts kept swirling.

Looking at this from another way, who would want to prove parentage in order to claim or dispute an inheritance? The answer to that question was Jonathon Edward Sykes, or Jonny as Peggy referred to him. Given that Peggy maintained her employment at Chipwell Hall, it was fair to assume she must've given the baby up at birth. However, most children adopted as babies were brought up with names different from those on their birth certificate, and without access to the adoption records, we had no way of finding out what his adoptive parents had named him. Maybe the adoption papers were in the other painting? I was getting ahead of myself and pushed that thought away. Besides, the birth mother rarely had access to that information.

Balthazar interrupted my musing by barking to be let out. I stood and stretched, rolling my shoulders back. I was thinking in circles and going over the same ground but from a different direction. What I needed was someone to look through this with fresh eyes. What I needed was a real detective.

Robbie picked up on the second ring.

'Hiya Philly. All okay?'

'Yes, I was wondering if you were busy tonight?'

'Why? Are you offering to feed me again?' he asked with a hopeful chuckle.

'No, better than that. I was going to shout you dinner at the pub,' I said, smiling in return.

'Sounds good, but I'm buying. I owe you for last weekend.'

The snow was falling again, ever so lightly, the flakes seeming to hang in the streetlights as we walked down to the pub together. I put my hand out to catch some, the warmth dissolving them almost immediately, Robbie smiling indulgently at me. Embarassed to be caught in such a child-like action I wound my striped scarf one more time around my neck for the short walk.

Over the last week, more homes had displayed festive decorations, and the glow from their front windows warmed my heart as the icy wind sliced through my body. I made a mental note to think about putting up my Christmas decorations and adding some cheer to the barn.

The festive markets in York had opened during the week, with their wintry alpine sheds lining the square selling all things seasonal from mulled wine to Christmas sweaters. The city's Christmas lights had also been switched on, and I'd arranged to go into town next weekend with Ryan, Jordan, and the twins to check it all out – the twins being at that age where every part of the season was magical. Their excitement and anticipation took me back to when Ryan and Chloe were that age, and I couldn't wait to experience it again with a new generation.

In The Arms, the tree was decorated and tinsel covered every possible surface around the bar. A fire was blazing in the grate – a motley collection of dogs having taken up residence around it. Balthazar casually wandered across to join them, his tail wagging and nose ready for the inevitable greetings.

Robbie and I found a table in the main bar, and while he went to order us both drinks, I read through the menu which was already offering seasonal specials – and Christmas was still, what, five weeks away? It hit me like this every year; one minute we were preparing for Halloween and Guy Fawkes Night – and then it was a slippery descent into Christmas.

'How's the week been?' Robbie asked when he slid back into his chair, the two of us clinking our glasses together.

'After last week, it's all been weirdly normal for the most part,' I said, the red wine warming my insides. 'And you?'

'Much the same. No more leads on the robberies we're looking at, and as this time of the year is busy, they're likely to pull the resources on the investigation next week. I think you only got the priority you did because of Stewart – but given I don't have any big cases just now, he's happy for me to invest some more time on it.'

'I guess it helps to be the ex-wife of the boss every so often,' I sighed. 'Thanks for letting me know, though – it's what I expected.'

He shrugged and took a mouthful of his beer. 'It's got me thinking, though, how it's all about numbers and resource priorities these days.'

'How long have you been in?' I asked, watching the

light from the fire flicker across his face.

'Forever,' he laughed wryly. 'I'll be sixty-one next year, so that's nearly forty-three years.'

'And you haven't thought of retiring?'

'Audrey and I had plans, of course,' he said, a sad half-smile on his face. 'But since she's been gone, I haven't thought about it – at first because I needed to work, and then because I didn't know what I'd do with myself. I could join an allotment, I suppose, but I've never really had a hobby. I'd see my son in Australia like we'd planned, but it wouldn't be much fun travelling alone, and I'd cramp his style.'

'You don't have to answer this if you don't want,' I said, 'but are you okay pension wise?'

He nodded. 'Yes. I'm well provided for in that regard, and Audrey had some life insurance …'

'So, does that mean you're thinking of it now?'

He shrugged his still-broad shoulders. 'Aye. I get passed over these days for the juicy cases – and I don't blame them for that. I'm part of another time, and modern policing is faster these days with technology being more and more important and the media watching your every move. I still have an edge when it comes to instincts, but I lost what ambition I used to have when Audrey was taken from me.'

What had happened to his wife? Stewart had hinted it was something Robbie didn't speak about; he would, no doubt, tell me when he felt able to. 'I imagine it gives you pause for thought.'

He cleared his throat. 'They're talking about offering packages to officers my age who want to retire and then come back on a casual basis to consult on cold cases. Stewart talked me through it during the week.'

'And you're thinking about it?'

He shrugged in a noncommittal way. 'Aye,' he said simply. He seemed to shake himself and then said, 'Right, what are we eating?'

I acknowledged the rapid change of subject with a little smile. 'I'll go with the pie and chips with mushy peas,' I said. 'It's the right sort of weather for it, and trust me, you haven't had a steak and ale pie until you've had one of these. They even do a real suet crust.'

'With accolades such as that, how can I resist?' He got to his feet. 'I'll be back soon.'

He was a bear of a man but in the nicest possible and slightly rumpled sort of way. Looking at him now, I couldn't imagine he'd ever had the ambition that Stewart had always had. Rather than playing the numbers game, Robbie would've got his completion rate through solid old-fashioned policing and taking the time to develop trust in those he was getting information from. That was clear in the way he'd eased Beth into answering his questions the other day. Even now, up at the bar, Lynn was leaning forward, her generous cleavage on display, a broad and open smile on her face. Robbie wasn't a flirt by any means, but he certainly knew how to draw people in. After all, he'd done it with me – drawn me in, and I was telling him more than I usually would, both about myself and the situation at hand.

We'd only known each other for a short time, but I already knew that if I was ever in trouble, he'd be the one I'd be assured of being able to rely upon. I trusted him completely without really knowing why. Perhaps it was that despite what he'd probably seen and heard over the years, while he was watchful, he didn't seem to be cynical – and I didn't think I could say that about anyone else on the job that I knew. I certainly couldn't say it for Stewart.

Sure, there was that underlying river of sadness under his solid and still exterior and a natural wariness about allowing anyone to get too close to him, but it didn't come across as bitter cynicism, and that was remarkable.

'What are you smiling about?' he asked as he sat back in his chair, placing a fresh wine in front of me.

'You've certainly won a heart in Lynn,' I teased.

'And I suspect it's a gold-plated one at that,' he replied.

'It is. She and Roger have worked hard to be accepted here and to turn this pub around – and they've done a great job of it.'

'You don't need to defend them to me,' he said quietly. That's precisely what I'd been doing.

I nodded slowly. 'You're right, I don't.'

'It's nice how you get defensive of those you care about,' he said, and I hoped that he'd put the blush that had to be in my cheeks down to the warmth of the fire or the red wine rather than anything else.

'So how about you tell me what had you all excited this afternoon,' he urged.

'I've a feeling I know where the boxes and the paintings came from in the first place,' I said, almost falling over my words in a rush to get them out.

He leant forward, his chin resting against the back of his fist. 'Go on.'

'Chipwell Hall. It's the seat of the Cunninghams – a few miles out of town on the road to Whitby,' I said.

'And why do you think the items originally came from there?'

'Because Peggy Sykes worked at the hall for many years. Remember, the name on the birth certificate was Margaret Sykes and the name on the back of those photos is Peggy – and Margaret was often called Peggy.'

'I'm listening,' he encouraged.

'Also, Catherine told me that the deceased estate belonged to Margaret Bishop of Malton, and Margaret Bishop and Peggy Sykes are the same person.'

'What makes you think that?'

'Tom Ainsworth told me that when he was a boy, his mother used to cook for them up at the hall, and he recalls Peggy Sykes from then – and remembers her going away after she got married. He said she married Barry Bishop.'

He frowned, deep furrows etched between his eyes. 'What has Tom got to do with it?'

'That's the other part I forgot to tell you – they found some photos in their box as well and –'

'What did you just say?' Robbie demanded, resting his hands on the table.

'They found some photos in a hidden drawer in their box.' I paused to gauge Robbie's reaction. There was no change, so I continued. 'Tom said he'd been watching an episode of one of the antiques shows on the telly, and the expert was showing how to find the secret compartment in a box like the one he'd bought. There were three photos in there – like those in mine. A couple of young men – Johnny and Billy, who I'm almost positive are brothers – and one young woman, Peggy. One of the photos looks to have been taken on a picnic in Whitby, and another one has a structure in the background I think might be the folly where Johnny and Peggy used to meet. Hang on, I have them here.' I pulled the photos out of my handbag and rummaged around for the envelope in which I'd found the images. 'See? It's the same people, I'd swear it.'

With the pictures all laid on the table side by side, it was apparent the subjects were the same.

'You're right,' he finally said, his shoulders relaxing somewhat. 'Why didn't Beth tell us about this the other day?'

'I asked them that, and Beth apologised. She said it had completely slipped her mind, that she'd been focussed only on what had happened with Tom. Understandable, I suppose. Besides, they weren't to know that I'd found some too – and before you ask, all I've told them is that I found the photos and nothing else.' Robbie nodded his approval. 'I think Tom was a wee bit disappointed that all he found were photos of people he didn't recognise. I suspect he was hoping for a will or an important letter or a winning pools ticket.'

Robbie chuckled. 'Isn't that what everyone hopes for when they discover a secret compartment? After all, photos aren't really worth hiding away.'

'Not usually anyway,' I corrected. 'From the letters, we found it's apparent that Johnny was married or engaged to someone else, but that he also had given her – Margaret or Peggy – assurances he'd come back and marry her. The alarm bells should've been ringing for her then, the poor pet. They never leave their wives,' I added before realising what I'd said. 'Take that back – mine did.' I let out a dramatic sigh and a half shrug to show that I was over it, though.

'I think we can assume from the letters too that she told this Johnny about the baby,' pointed out Robbie.

'True, but the baby must've been given away as Tom didn't mention anything about a baby in his memories, and I'm sure Catherine had said how the solicitor had advised her that the deceased had no direct descendants. If the baby was adopted, though, we'll never be able to find him,' I said, struck suddenly by the magnitude of our search.

I paused as Josie arrived with our pies, and for the next few minutes, we gave our food the attention it deserved.

'I'm going to speak to the solicitor in Malton on Monday,' I said. 'Catherine gave me his details. I have no idea whether they can tell me anything, but I'm going to say that I'm attempting to trace the providence of the painting before it goes to auction.'

'Will that make any difference to the price?' asked Robbie.

'It could do. When people buy an important painting, they tend to be collectors and interested in the story behind the painting, how it came to be acquired. For the really important paintings – your old masters, impressionists and the like – it's quite common to know a lot about when it was painted and who purchased or commissioned it. For artists such as Wilson, who have only become collectible relatively recently, it's the opposite. We know a little about his early life – how he went to work on the harbour when he was young, probably thirteen or fourteen, I guess – but not so much about how he came to have sufficient leisure time to keep himself in food and paint in Staithes and the other coastal towns where he worked. I won't be able to find that out, but I am going to try my luck and see if the solicitor has any records he can help me with.'

I took another mouthful, my knife sliding through the crisp, golden pastry. 'And I have an appointment at Chipwell Hall tomorrow afternoon with Sir Antony Cunningham, the current baronet.'

'Philly …' Robbie warned.

'What? He invited me – he wants me to look at some of his art and let him know if there's anything in there that needs to have the insurance increased, I'd say. I doubt if he's looking to sell any of it – I don't believe the Cunninghams have money troubles – not if the amount he spends with Ambrose and Eugene is any indication. And I won't ask him if he knows Peggy Sykes unless he brings it up. Besides, isn't there that whole above and below stairs thing that they say doesn't exist but still goes on – or at least was still going on when he was a boy?'

'True. It would be most unlikely,' agreed Robbie.

'I refer to him as Sir Antony, but do I address him as that or Your Lordship?' I asked. 'We colonials can never be sure,' I said, trying and failing to keep a straight face.

'The former, I expect,' Robbie said, grinning at my antipodean antipathy for the British class system. 'Sir Antony is a customer of the Ashtons?'

'The brothers have been gradually procuring military antiques for him from the Second World War. In fact, at the last auction at Young and Johnson's, they bought some leather hold-alls that used to be owned by Cunningham senior.'

'That was the same auction you bought your items from?'

As I nodded, I could see from the look on Robbie's face which direction his thoughts were heading in. 'Oh wow,' I said. 'You think they might've come from the same estate?

Catherine didn't mention it.'

He raised his eyebrows. 'It's a question worth asking, don't you think? And if they came from the same deceased estate, why would Margaret Bishop or Peggy Sykes have anything belonging to Sir Antony's father, and why wouldn't Cilla Grey be trying to track that down too?'

I studied the photos of Johnny and Billy again. They were definitely brothers – the resemblance was too strong to be anything else. What had Eugene told me about the Cunninghams? My nail tapped against my teeth as I remembered back to our conversation in the saleroom.

'What is it, Philly?'

'I'm remembering something Eugene told me. He said that Sir Antony's father was named St John – what is with the English upper class that they need to pronounce names so strangely? It's like Colquhoun which is Col-hewn – why bother putting the q in there? And don't get me started on Worcestershire.' Robbie chuckled and shook his head. 'Anyway,' I continued, 'St John was the heir and died in the war, leaving behind a pregnant widow. His brother inherited the estate and the baronetcy and, in the process, got rid of anything that reminded him of St John.

'What had been his name? William. I'm sure it was William. In any case, William soon married widow Cunningham, but as they had no more children, Sir Antony, as the closest male relative, inherited. What if' – I caught my breath – 'John was known as Johnny and William was known as Billy?'

'You're suggesting that St John was Peggy's lover and the father of her child and that Jonathon Sykes could be the heir of Chipwell Hall?'

Is that what I was suggesting? I shrugged. 'Maybe I'm clutching at straws, but it would make sense. And what if William, knowing about Peggy, gave her those things of St John's – not because he couldn't bear to be reminded of his brother, but because he'd promised his brother that he'd see her looked after?'

Robbie rubbed at his chin. 'It fits, but why would a secret kept for nearly eighty years come out now?'

I puffed out a weary sigh, my shoulders slumping. 'I don't know. All of this is only guesswork, and if what we're saying is right, that means that Sir Antony could be behind everything that's been happening. What if, supposing the hold-alls also came from Margaret Bishop's estate, the reason Cilla isn't tracking them down is that she already knows where they are?'

'Okay, let's not jump to conclusions. We need to know more about the baronetcy and whether it can pass to an illegitimate heir. We also need to know where Peggy was living at the end of her life and who she might have confided in. Finally, we should find out who's likely to inherit now as it stands. If an estate like Chipwell is at stake …' Robbie didn't need to go into specifics. I knew what he meant – the future of the baronetcy was worth a little break and enter.

If they knew I held the evidence … A chill ran up my spine.

'Are you sure you should go there tomorrow?' asked Robbie.

I nodded with more confidence than I felt. 'I'll be fine. Sir Antony doesn't know I have the documents, and I'm hardly likely to come straight out and ask him questions.'

'Okay, but be sure to let me know when you finish.' The concern on his face warmed my heart. It had been such a long time since anyone had worried about me – normally, it was the other way around – and it felt … nice.

'Thank you, Robbie Dawkins,' I said. 'For caring.'

His smile lit up his face. 'Anytime, Philly Barker.'

Chapter Eighteen

Before I left the house for the day – Balthazar was not at all happy about being left to his own devices for the second Monday in a row – I made a quick call to Catherine. The bags that had previously belonged to St John Cunningham *had* come from Margaret Bishop's house, and she apologised for leaving them off the list she'd given me. I sent a quick text to Robbie to let him know his supposition was correct. There was probably no way of proving it, but it appeared that Billy had given as many of Johnny's possessions to Peggy as he could.

My first stop for the morning was Margaret Bishop's solicitor in Malton. As I'd half expected, he'd been less than forthcoming with information. While he did confirm that Margaret Bishop was previously Margaret Sykes and helpfully pointed me in the direction of the Probate Registry if I wanted to see a copy of the will, he also added that I'd need to wait until after probate was granted before I could do that. He told me nothing was in the will pertaining to specific items and refused to answer any further questions –

regardless of how nicely I asked them.

After stopping in a café on the high street for a scone (that almost as good as those Ginny produced) and a cup of tea, I was back in Libby for the short drive to Chipwell Hall. While Ambrose and Eugene had visited the hall many times – both on business and for the Cunningham's annual summer garden party – I'd never had the pleasure.

Even though I hadn't expected a house as grand as, say, Castle Howard (which was a few miles up the road), I don't think I'd expected Chipwell Hall to be as elegant as it was – and elegant was the only word I could come up with that would sufficiently do it justice.

Entering the park from a long curving drive through a wood that would probably have bluebells in it in the late spring, the vista opened to display a gracious limestone Georgian manor in the Palladian style – all symmetrical lines with a central portico and sashed windows – rising behind a manicured topiary garden.

I parked in the circular drive and flicked the visor down to sneak a look at my reflection. While Sir Antony had been straight off the farm casual the first time I met him, I suspected that look wouldn't go down well from a business viewpoint so had swapped my jeans for black tailored pants, my Chelsea boots for something with a low stacked heel and topped it with an ink-blue wrap style buttoned shirt. I freshened my lipstick, pinched at my cheeks to bring some colour into them, pushed the wings of hair back behind my ears, took a deep breath and climbed out of the car.

The front door posed my next problem. Did one knock or ring a bell? The decision was taken out of my hands by Sir Antony who must've been watching for my arrival – and who was dressed similarly to how he had been on that first occasion, albeit free of mud.

'Mrs Barker!' he announced. 'It's lovely to see you again.'

He offered his hand, and I shook it lightly. 'Thank you for inviting me, Sir Antony, but please call me Philly.'

'You're doing me a great favour, Philly, and you must call me Tony.'

I smiled and inclined my head slightly in agreement but knew I'd never be able to do it.

Sir Antony motioned with his hand for me to enter the marble-tiled foyer. Grecian pillars flanked a curving mahogany staircase. I tipped my head back to take in the intricately moulded ceiling before casting my gaze around the rest of the space.

A cedar hall stand stood against one panelled wall, a portrait of someone who I assumed, judging by the eighteenth century style of dress, must've been one of the early baronets hanging beside it.

'That's the first George,' said Sir Antony with a wry smile, moving to stand beside me. 'He was the first Baronet of Chipwell. He was also the first in a long line of Georges to hold the title.'

'But you're not a George,' I pointed out the obvious.

'No. My great-grandmother broke that tradition. She was American and brought with her enough money to restore the fortunes of the estate – and is responsible for the electric lighting and some of the other improvements. She argued that gave her the right to "name her son whatever she damned well wanted".' He parodied an American accent, and I couldn't help the laughing.

'My wife, however,' he continued, 'has seen fit to return to the old tradition of Georges,' he said. 'So my son and heir is George, as is his son. I'm afraid, Philly, that Chipwell Hall will again be overrun by Georges. Let's hope they show more prudence with the financial management than the original examples did – although early indications are, unfortunately, to the contrary.' He shot me a quick look, his expression one I couldn't decipher.

'I didn't, however, bring you here to regale you with tales of my ancestor's lack of economy,' he said. 'While I'm not intending on selling any of the works – and the trust prohibits me from doing so – I do need to ensure that my insurance is up to date.'

'Oh, but I –' I began.

'I know you're not a valuer,' he said. 'What I'm after is merely an opinion as to which pieces I should get revalued – I have no intention of paying a valuer to waste my money to tell me that some of my pictures are rubbish when I already know that. I'd prefer to pay to have only the pictures that aren't rubbish revalued.' He peered at me over the top of his glasses. 'You come highly recommended by Ambrose and Eugene. They've told me you have both a good eye and a good instinct, and as I respect their opinion, I'm minded to take their advice.'

'I appreciate that,' I said, wondering whether he'd been told about the Wilson discovery.

'Right,' he said, leading me into what I assumed was the drawing room – a large light-filled south-facing room, the plaster-panelled walls of which were painted Wedgewood blue, the details and cornices – swathed with ribbons and bows – in a contrasting pale cream. The timber floor was covered with the largest Savonnerie-style carpet I'd seen in the wild, and paintings in the impressionist style hung on the walls.

'You have a look around in here while I arrange some tea,' he said.

'Thank you,' I barely whispered, in awe of my surroundings.

To say it was the most beautiful room I'd ever been in was an understatement. Someone with a great deal of taste – and money – had put this room together. Everything, from the sprigged cotton upholstery on the lounges and the curtains to the contrasting colours used on the wing chairs to the chandelier, was both sympathetic to the Georgian theme yet bang up to date. The fireplace was, of course, the focal point of the room. Flanked by classical pillars, the front was ornate, featuring urns and cherubs, while the back was cast iron. The effect was completed with a *trompe l'oeil* fire screen.

The vast windows afforded views out across a great expanse of lawn, bordered by woodland. In the distance, nestled at the fringe of the woods, was an outline of a building. Was it the folly from the letters?

The return of Sir Antony, with a tray holding an Aynsley tea set and a plate of chocolate digestives, interrupted my musings. 'Let's have this first, and then we can get started,' he said, placing the tray on a Georgian walnut occasional table.

He poured the tea and I shook my head when he offered milk and sugar, smiling at the realisation that the tea set matched the colours in the walls and the rugs almost perfectly.

Sir Antony noticed. 'You're wondering which came first – the tea pot or the walls?'

'Something like that,' I admitted, lowering my eyes to the tray in embarrassment. A silver teaspoon caught my eye and I reached forward to lift it from the tray, my heart quickening. 'This is sweet.' I turned it over to check the hallmark. 'Is this a little fox?'

'Yes,' he said. 'These have been in the family for years. This one I'm using has a rabbit on the end. Over the years some have gone missing though; I recall my mother telling me there were other animals too – a stoat, a badger and a hedgehog.'

'I've seen one before,' I said hesitantly, turning the spoon over in my hand. 'In fact, I recently sold one with a stoat on the end.' I replaced the spoon on the tray and lifted my eyes to his. 'I'm almost positive the hallmark was the same.'

He frowned sightly and took a bite from a biscuit. 'How very strange. I wonder if it had originally come from our set – although,' he mused, 'I imagine there must have been several sets made so it could have come from anywhere. Would you like a biscuit? They're not home-made, I'm afraid.' He smiled apologetically and passed me the plate of biscuits.

'No, thank you.'

'I imagine you must purchase much of your stock from auctions?'

I searched his face for a hidden meaning, but finding none, answered him. 'Yes, mostly. Sometimes I'm fortunate and get offered a house clearance – although usually these come via Simon – he's our furniture specialist – and he calls me in to deal with the china, jewellery, silverware, art and other bric-a-brac or small pieces.' I sipped at my tea. 'Is that a folly I can see on the horizon?' I asked, inclining my head towards the window.

'It is indeed, well spotted. My great-grandfather had it built – my great-grandmother liked to take tea in it during the warmer months. It had no other purpose – which was, I suppose, the point. I remember playing in it as a child.' He had a faraway look on his face as if he remembered those days fondly. 'Although as an only child … I did have one particular friend, but my mother didn't like me mixing with the children of the help.' He shook his head slightly. 'How ridiculous it all sounds today. Anyway, if you've finished your tea, I'll show you around.'

As we wandered around the hall, me taking notes as we walked, Sir Antony kept me entertained with stories of his ancestors and the exploits that led to them coming close to losing the estate. The Cunningham men over the years had, it seemed, had a weakness for expensive women and horses.

'It's why we placed the important art in a trust,' he said. 'So it couldn't be sold off to pay debts. Some would say the house and the rest of the estate should've been placed in trust too, but I believe this can be just as detrimental. Like my grandfather before him, my uncle was a prudential manager, a trait I've continued. My son, I'm sorry to say, enjoys the pleasures that the Georges before him enjoyed, so one can only hope he grows out of that before he inherits. His mother, I'm much afraid, indulged him, and he does trade on his great expectations.'

'How old is he now?' I asked, running my hand along the surface of a Victorian mahogany chiffonier.

'Forty-two,' Sir Antony said ruefully. 'And is quite anxious to become the next Sir George – his wife is equally anxious to become the next Lady Cunningham. Sometimes I think she looks at me as if to say, "Hurry along then, old chap."'

I couldn't help but laugh at his expression. 'Does George have any children?'

'Yes, his eldest son George' – he raised his eyes to the ornate ceiling – 'will one day be the fourteenth Cunningham of Chipwell – and his mother is indulging him as much as my wife indulged our son.' He pursed his lips in disapproval. 'We might not have done anything to earn our title and privileges, but we can certainly do much to earn the respect that, especially these days, doesn't automatically come with it. I probably shouldn't say as much, but I hold grave fears for our family's future. The integrity of the family name is everything.'

My pulse quickened. 'Where does your son live now?'

'He and his family have a cottage on the estate but spend much of their time in our London house. George works for one of the financial houses in the city – if you can call what he does work, that is.' As if realising he'd said too much, he smiled tightly, briefly. 'Let's move through to the dining room. Some of my favourite pieces are on those walls.'

Eventually we wound our way through to the library, a room which appeared to have escaped the attentions of the designer who had decorated the rest of the house. Sir Antony must've seen the question in my expression and said, 'This is my domain. My wife has threatened to have her way in here too, but I've stood firm. She wants to paint it all – including the bookcases. Lighten up the room, she says.' He shuddered at the thought.

He leant against the mahogany table that stood in the centre of the library, his arms folded across his chest, and gazed around the room from its rich burgundy walls and heavy cream, gold, and burgundy striped drapes, to the timber floor to ceiling bookcase that stretched the length of one wall. On another wall stood a glass-fronted mahogany display cabinet; it was to that that my attention was drawn.

'This collection is my folly,' said Sir Antony. 'My father died in the war before I was born, and I've devoted many of the years since inheriting this pile and the title to finding out as much as I can about him.' He straightened and walked across to the display cabinet and indicated for me to follow. 'That's one of the few photos I have of him,' he said, pointing at a frame containing a black-and-white photo of a laughing young man on a horse.

'He was very handsome,' I said. He was also Johnny from the photos in my house. 'How old was he when he died?'

'Eighteen and newly married. My parents had a whirlwind courtship and married only a month after meeting.'

'They must've been very much in love,' I said, leaning to get a closer look at the image.

He simply shrugged. 'To quote someone rather famous and royal, "Whatever in love means." It was, to be frank, a business arrangement between my grandfathers. My parents had been promised to each other since they were children –

but when my paternal grandfather became ill and it became obvious my father would enlist as was his duty, they rushed the marriage through. I'm the lucky result of that union, but unlucky in that I never had the privilege of meeting my father.' He picked the photo up and traced the frame with his finger. 'My grandfather passed away two years later, and my Uncle Billy inherited.' My ears picked up at the name. 'The way the story goes, my father had made him promise to look after my mother if anything happened to him, and that's what he did – they were married before I was two.' He placed the frame back down. 'Unfortunately, he also got rid of anything that belonged to my father.' He sucked in a deep breath. 'I've never known whether it was because *he* didn't want any reminders or because he didn't want my mother to have any reminders. It must've been difficult for Uncle Billy to grow up in my father's shadow.'

'You've been trying to track them down ever since,' I said softly.

'Yes.' He nodded sombrely. 'The Ashtons located these bags at auction a couple of weeks ago.' He bent down and lifted the hold-all up for me to see. 'I have a lot of memorabilia from the time' – he waved at the contents of the cabinet – 'but knowing that these were once my father's means so much.' He shook his head as if to move the thoughts along. 'I know he did his duty, but as I'm getting older, I only wish I knew more about what sort of man he was.'

'And your uncle and your mother – were they happy?'

He reached into the cabinet and picked up one of a pair of brass trench ware vases, his thumb moving across the rose embossed on the surface. 'Yes,' he said finally, 'they were. My parents married for a reason as opposed to love – although one likes to hope that love would have followed had my father lived long enough. My uncle had, it seemed, been in love with my mother from the minute he laid eyes on her. The only time my mother ever spoke about it – soon before she passed away – was to tell me that Uncle Billy had been devastated when my parents married.'

'Do you think your grandfather knew?'

He shrugged. 'Who's to say? By all accounts, Grandfather was not a kind man. For him, this estate and the title, family honour and standing came a long way above love in the scheme of things. Our family needed the funds my mother brought to the deal, and her family needed the respectability of our title. It was, as I said, a business arrangement, and marriage to the second son wasn't part of that deal. The irony is that Uncle Billy inherited anyway. It makes one wonder about the wasted effort that was my parent's marriage – except for me, of course.'

'Of course.'

I'm not sure how much more he would've said if we hadn't been interrupted.

'Oh, I'm very sorry,' said the newcomer. 'I didn't realise we still had company.'

'My wife, Lady Cunningham,' said Sir Antony. 'Hilary, this is Philomena Barker from Chipwell Barn Antiques.'

'How lovely to meet you, Mrs Barker.' Lady Cunningham held her hand out in greeting, a brief touch rather than a shake. 'My husband tells me you have quite the eye for art.' Where Sir Antony looked nothing like you'd expect a baronet to look, Lady Cunningham was the exact opposite. Wafer-thin with silver hair cut into a short, disciplined bob, she wore a heather-toned tweed skirt with a lilac wool twinset. Her tone was brittle, and her vowels were as round and polished as the pearls in her ears.

'I do love art,' I said. 'And it was a fine art degree that got me started in the antiques business.'

'Have you ever come across any real bargains?' she asked.

While Lady Cunningham had had a lifetime of making small talk with people like me, there was something in her voice that made my skin prickle. 'Occasionally, yes,' I answered. 'I have, however, also had the opposite – bought something at what I've thought was a good price only for it to gather dust on my shelves and then falter at auction.'

'I see.' The way she said it made me feel as though I'd just told her I was a gambler for a living. Where I'd felt comfortable chatting with Sir Antony, there was something about his wife that put me off balance. I willed my feet to stay still when they would've shuffled and for my gaze to hold firm when it would've slipped.

'What about art? Have you ever found a painting to be more than you've thought it was?'

Did she know about the Wilson? I opted for a version of the truth. 'I have. First comes the feeling that a painting could be more than it purports to be, but then training and education come into play. It's one thing to feel that a piece is special; the challenge is in finding the evidence to prove that it is so.'

'I imagine that sometimes means removing a painting from its frame.' Her pale blue eyes were suddenly beady.

'Sometimes, yes. Thankfully, though, the provenance of your art, Lady Cunningham, is undoubted, so there's no need for any of that.' I shifted my attention to her husband. 'Thank you for showing me your remarkable collection, Sir Antony. I've got what I needed and will email you tomorrow.'

'Jolly good,' he said. 'It's been a pleasure to have your company this afternoon, Philly.' His smile reached all the way to his eyes. Lady Cunningham's did not.

Back in Libby, I sent a quick text to Robbie.

All good and heading home. Will phone to fill you in later.

On the short drive home, I rehashed all I'd learnt this afternoon. While I now knew that Johnny and Billy were St John and William Cunningham and that Johnny didn't come home from the war, I also knew how much Sir Antony would want the photos I had of his father. While we'd been talking, part of me had been screaming inside just to give them back to him, even as I knew I couldn't do that. Yet.

Would he want them badly enough to break the law to get them? I couldn't answer that.

As for his wife, I had the impression she knew more than she was letting on. How much more I didn't know.

Chapter Nineteen

While the Proctors were still away, Bell was back on deck the following morning, her shawl more of a scarf that floated behind her as she moved in a billowing cloud of silvery grey. As we all convened in the café before work (Ginny provided the heavily buttered toasted teacakes), she filled us in on her successful trip to Brookford.

'This is one of the pieces.' She lifted the edge of her scarf, the silver thread glinting as it caught the light. Simon seemed fixated on the item. 'Isn't it gorgeous? I'm calling this, and the matching cocktail dress, Maisie. Can't you see her sailing into a party? Silver shoes, a matching headband with a single feather over her shingled bob. She'd be the silver lady.' From the faraway look on her face, I knew Bell was composing one of her stories. 'The woman who originally wore this would've had plenty of wealthy, handsome suitors that she'd dangle and play with from time to time, never committing herself to any particular one until she was ready to.

'The new owners found it all in the attic in suitcases – five of them. I've taken the lot, of course. The house was lovely too – one of those typical Cotswold stone cottages. Oh, you'd never guess who owns it? Owen and Claire Gallagher!'

'From *Posh or Not* and *Time For Tea*?' squeaked Ginny. 'I would love to meet them. What are they like?'

'Exactly as they are on the telly,' said Bell. 'She's really warm, and he's, well, he's got that brooding, intense, hot chef thing going on, but very friendly too. Claire said they were resurrecting *Time For Tea* next year, and we might see them up here.'

'I hope so,' said Ginny. 'Now that Philly's friendly with the local landed gentry, maybe she can use her influence to get them access to Chipwell Hall to film the episode.' She reached for another teacake, the currants in it gleaming from the melted butter.

'I hardly think Lady Cunningham would agree to that,' I said with a laugh.

Eugene laughed with me. 'Indeed.'

'What have I missed?' asked Bell, her eyes on me.

'Sir Antony invited Philly up to the hall to look at his paintings,' said Ambrose, his chest puffed with the pride of it. Sir Antony had phoned this morning to say how pleased he'd been with the visit and thanked Ambrose for recommending me.

'Is that so?' Bell cocked a quizzical brow in my direction. 'Did he know about the Wilson painting by any chance?'

I shrugged, unsure how much more of the story I

could share. 'He didn't say anything about it.'

'He didn't know before you visited,' said Ambrose, 'but I mentioned it on our call this morning. It's such a coup for you; you should be shouting it from the rooftops.' He paused and gave me one of his serious-teacher looks. 'It's one thing to have a feeling about something, Philly; it's completely another to do the research to get the evidence to prove the instinct right – and that's what you did. You knew Wilson had a habit of signing below the frame line and used that knowledge to verify what you thought to be true. Plenty of others out there could learn a lot from you.'

I was lost for words, not because his praise overwhelmed me – although I was sure that's what he thought – but because Sir Antony now knew that I'd taken the frame off the Whitby painting; there had been no other way of verifying the artist's mark. My heart skipped a beat and then another, and I fought to control my breathing and my expression.

'That's kind of you to say,' I finally managed.

'Kind be damned,' Ambrose said. 'It's praise where it's due, lass. We're all well chuffed you're here with us.'

He mightn't be if it turned out that it was me who brought trouble to our doors.

The conversation moved into a debate regarding the decorating of the barn for Christmas and when we should string decorations. While we all agreed that they probably should've gone up at the same time as the city decorations did, Eugene and Ambrose expressed some concern about their physical ability to hang theirs.

'Don't worry,' I said. 'I'll stay back this afternoon and help you if you like. I need to do mine anyway.'

We decided we'd all put in some time at the end of the day and Christmas-fy the barn. Simon, being the tallest, was to be shared amongst us all for the high work.

As we all stood, ready to open up for the day, Ambrose cleared his throat. 'Ahem, we have one piece of outstanding business,' he said.

'What's that?' asked Simon.

'Next Tuesday is the annual Christmas Trivia Contest at The Chipwell Arms. We usually put in a team – who's available this year?'

He looked around the café, but we were all shuffling our feet or actively trying to avoid his glance.

'Obviously I am,' said Eugene.

'The Proctors will still be away,' said Ambrose, 'and they're usually on board. Simon?'

'Sorry,' he said. 'I have band practice.'

I met his eyes and frowned. Since when was he in a band?

'Since when have you been in a band?' asked Ginny.

'Not long,' said Simon. 'It's a new thing – we play world music – that atmospheric sort of thing.'

'I thought you were into heavy metal or punk,' I said. This morning's T-shirt was Deep Purple.

He shrugged. 'I'm into lots of things,' he said with a

most un-Simon-like grin.

'Bell?' asked Ambrose.

'Sorry, not this year. I have a book club Christmas party,' she said nonchalantly, twirling her filmy scarf.

'I didn't know you were in a book club,' I said.

'It's a recent thing.' She lifted the scarf in her hand and watched it float down. 'We're reading Dickens.'

'What about you, Ginny?' asked Eugene.

'I'll be a maybe,' she said. 'Richard is setting up a drinks night with his friends, so I'll need to let you know.'

'You won't let us down, will you, Philly? No band or book club?' Eugene asked.

'Nope, and no date either, so no excuse – which means I'll be there with bells on,' I said, plastering my best convincing smile on my face.

'Grand.' Ambrose clapped. 'Maybe that nice detective might like to come along too. I'll ask him next time he's in. Okay, that's all I wanted to talk about, so let's get back to work.'

I'd chuckled with the others at the way Ambrose switched so quickly from trivia night to open for business, but the whole time the discussion was going on, I'd been thinking about what it meant that Sir Antony knew I'd taken the back off the Whitby painting. As soon as I was back in my stall, I texted Robbie.

Sir Antony knows I took the painting out of the frame – Ambrose told him.

His reply came through a few minutes later.

Okay, it was bound to come out. Try not to worry – we still don't know that Sir Antony has anything to do with this.

Trying not to worry and actually *not* worrying did, however, seem to be two completely different skill sets, so worry, I did – at first anyway.

Over the next few days, I took care not to be in the barn late on my own or too early in the mornings. I checked and rechecked the locks on my doors each night and arranged for an alarm to be fitted – something Robbie was quietly happy about. Stewart, though, said it was something he'd been telling me to do since the day he left and why it took something like a break-in at the barn for me to see sense he didn't know. Even Bell thought it was a good idea.

'It's not hard to work out where you live, Philly,' she'd said. 'You'd only need to go into the pub, and they'd helpfully direct anyone to your front door. While an alarm will never stop anyone from coming in, it means you won't be surprised by it.'

As the days passed, though, I forgot to wake with a start each time I heard a noise I didn't recognise in the night or jerk to attention when someone surprised me in the stall. I began to think that I'd been wrong, that the involvement of the Cunninghams was purely coincidental and that the entire business had gone away of its own accord.

'In fact,' I said to Ginny on Saturday afternoon, 'I think whoever it was has come to the conclusion there was nothing in any of the items in the first place.'

'Let's hope so,' she said. 'But while you're here, can you try this shortbread for me?'

On Sunday afternoon, Balthazar and I went into York to check out the Christmas markets and the lights with Ryan, Jordan, and the kids. Stewart and Alison brought their children along as well. When I heard they were coming, I almost backed out but decided that doing so would be, as my mother used to say, cutting my nose off to spite my face. I wanted to spend time with Ada and Alfie, and I enjoyed seeing Reuben and Misty. Choosing not to go would hurt me more than it would hurt them.

As it turned out, we had a lovely evening. The night was cold yet clear, and the crowd all seemed to have been drinking from the cup of Christmas cheer and were good-humoured when queueing and patience was required – which was often. The kids and Balthazar were on their best behaviour, although they got (understandably) tetchy as it got later (the children, not Balthazar).

The mulled wine I bought and sipped on as we walked around was the perfect tonic for browsing the market stalls. I bought some dried fruit Christmas decorations to hang in the kitchen to brighten it up. I also chose some woollen wrist warmers to gift to Bell and Ginny, plus some lovely local cheeses, a bottle of sloe gin, some chutneys to take home, and a box of brigadeiros to take into work. I also snuck the kids some bags of handmade lollies, with many giggles from them and some (good-natured) chiding from their parents. What's the point of being a grandparent if you can't bend your own rules?

While the children (besides Reuben who had declared himself too old for such childish pursuits) rode the carousel, I shared the sausage roll and scotch egg I'd bought for my tea with Balthazar and chatted lightly with Alison. Who would have thought it? The spirit of Christmas was alive and well. And when Misty, Ada and Alfie insisted on another ride, but this time with me, I had no issues with handing my purchases and Balthazar's lead to Alison and jumping onto one of the racing steeds.

The children were full of happy and excited chatter (even Reuben) as we walked back to the buses that would take us to the park and ride where we'd left our cars, and the adults all seemed to be feeling the same warm glow inside that I was.

It sounded trite, but as I drove home with Balthazar, I reflected on how lucky I was to have family so close by. It was times like these when I missed Chloe terribly – even though she probably barely gave me a thought outside of her weekly Zoom call – and those Christmases we'd had together before Stewart and the kids left.

As grateful as I was, I couldn't help but feel lonely as I opened the front door and switched the lights on. Our traditions these days were different, with me fitting in with whatever Ryan and Jordan had planned, yet I missed those days when I was the one planning and cooking Christmas dinner. I missed the preparation, the shopping in crowded supermarkets, the 'Are you ready for Christmas?' discussions. These days I only bought presents for the children and shopped for them throughout the year, my Christmas provisions stretching to the ham I'd cook and take to Ryan's and the condiments I'd need in the house for the inevitable leftovers. Maybe it was time to think about a relationship and trusting someone again. An image of Robbie's face floated before me, and I resolutely pushed it away and back into the friend's zone.

On Monday, after cleaning the house and running a few errands, I dropped in to see the Ainsworths, taking some brigadeiros with me. Tom was improving by the day. He asked me if I'd heard anything about the police investigation, and I'd had to reply in the negative.

'It doesn't surprise me,' he said. 'I think they were probably kids.' He shook his head. 'The kids of today…'

'How are your children? You have two, don't you?' I said, seeing no value in the direction the previous conversation had been heading.

'You've got a good memory,' said Beth. 'Our Julie is fifty-two and a grandmother herself now, and Joe is fifty after Christmas. He lives in Leeds.'

'Does he have any children?' I asked.

'Aye, he has three and Julie has four, so by the time you add in husbands and wives and what you youngsters call partners now there's quite the crowd around the table,' said Beth, her beaming smile telling me how she relished having that crowd to manage and cater for.

'If you're going to call me a youngster, I'll have to make sure I visit more often,' I said with a grin.

'You're welcome anytime, Philly,' said Tom. 'You and your dog.' He scratched Bally behind the ears. 'In fact, I'm having a birthday do with Christmas drinks on Sunday evening. We'd love for you to come, wouldn't we, pet? Bring a friend, of course – the more, the merrier.'

'That sounds lovely. Thank you,' I said, feeling genuinely humbled by the invitation.

'Maybe you can bring that nice detective,' said Beth, a twinkle in her eye. 'I saw you two talking that time he was here when Tom was in hospital. I said to Tom that he looked like he had kind eyes and would be good for you.'

'You did, pet,' said Tom. 'Beth always gets things like that right.'

Heat flooded my face. 'Thank you, I might. But don't go getting any ideas; he's just a friend.'

'Of course he is,' said Beth with a definite cheeky twinkle in her eye.

Tuesday evening and the trivia contest came around quickly. Ambrose had cornered Robbie late last week when he'd dropped into the barn on his way back from somewhere or another.

'Just the person I was hoping to see. Did Philly mention we need you on our trivia team on Tuesday night?'

'No, she didn't.' Robbie raised his eyebrows at me, and I shrugged in response.

'You're not busy, are you?' asked Ambrose.

'Well, no, but –'

'Good, we'll see you there. Seven pm at The Arms.'

'I'm not good at trivia,' Robbie said once Ambrose had gone back to his stall.

'It's Christmas trivia, so I don't think it matters,' I said. 'We put in a team every year – and usually do very badly, but everyone is busy this year.'

'I can't imagine why.'

Robbie and I had arranged that he'd pick me up and we'd walk down and have a bite to eat before the trivia began. 'It's one of the only ways we can be guaranteed a table,' I'd said, but in truth, I enjoyed sharing a meal with him.

While we were waiting for our meals to arrive, I told Robbie about the Ainsworth's invitation.

'They suggested you might like to come along too,' I said, knowing my cheeks were bright pink.

'What about you?' asked Robbie hesitantly. 'Would you like me to come?'

'Yes.' My smile was fast and genuine. 'I would love you to come along – if you want to, that is.'

'Then I'll come,' he replied with the utmost certainty.

Josie chose that moment to place our meals in front of us. 'Fish and chips for you Philly, and toad in the hole for you Inspector,' she said, adding with a sideways glance, 'You're becoming quite the regular around here now.'

'Thanks, Josie,' I said pointedly. As she left, not before she cast me another knowing smile, I said, 'I'm sorry, Robbie.'

'What for?' he asked.

'The … you know …'

'The innuendos you mean?' He seemed to enjoy my discomfort. 'I find it quite flattering that they think I'd be good enough for you,' he said with a look that made my face flame again.

We'd no sooner finished our meals than the plates were whisked away and replaced with the trivia sheets. Ambrose and Eugene wandered through from the other side of the bar and joined us. 'We've got high hopes for you, Inspector,' said Ambrose.

'Call me Robbie, please.'

'Well, Robbie, we have high hopes.'

The strains of Wham's 'Last Christmas' were played, and half the room groaned.

'What's that about, lass?' asked Eugene.

'They've just been Whammed,' I said. When all three men looked back at me blankly, I explained. 'There's a competition called Whamageddon where you're still "in" if you haven't heard "Last Christmas", the original, of course, in full.'

Robbie chuckled. 'What do you get if you win?'

'No idea,' I said. 'I've never bothered to learn the details.'

Robbie laughed, that rumbly belly laugh I looked forward to hearing.

He laughed even harder when Roger, dressed as Santa and acting as quizmaster (ably assisted by Josie dressed for the occasion as Mariah Carey in 'All I Want for Christmas') asked, 'What's happened to you if you've been Whammed?'

When the half-time interval rolled around, we were quietly confident. The Ashton's had a good knowledge of old movies, literature and the inevitable wartime Christmas questions, and Robbie and I were surprisingly good on the more contemporary subjects.

'What did LadBaby build their city on to snag the Christmas number one spot in 2018?' asked Roger.

'Sausage rolls,' said Robbie quickly. I raised my eyebrows and wrote it on the sheet as Ambrose and Eugene were open-mouthed in amazement.

'What did they love in 2019 to snag the Christmas number one spot?' Roger asked, enjoying his pun so much he used it a second time.

'Let me guess – sausage rolls?' I drawled. Robbie's grin was answer enough.

We waited for the rush to die down before venturing

to the bar at interval and were waiting for Josie to pour our drinks when Lynn said, 'Florrie Miller! I haven't seen you in here since last year's Christmas trivia. What have you been doing to yourself?'

Robbie's eyes met mine, and he swivelled in his chair to regard the woman standing – or rather balancing on a crutch – beside him.

'I got broken into,' said Florrie, 'and fell down the stairs when I went to go after the buggers. It was lucky it was just the last stair I missed.'

'There's a bit of that going around,' said Lynn. 'Philly here works up at Chipwell Barn Antiques, and they had a break-in too.'

'So did the Ainsworths,' added Roger from his position behind the bar. 'You're lucky you didn't hurt yourself badly. What was stolen?'

'Just a painting,' she said. 'I've no doubt I scared them off before they could take more. The worst of it is I bought the painting only the day before. It was my friend Peggy's, you see, and I wanted something of hers to remind me, and now it's gone. I always loved that painting. Peggy always said she'd leave it to me, but she forgot to write it down. "I'm too young to be bothering with a will," she used to say.'

'Was that Peggy Bishop you're talking about?' I leant over and asked. 'Sorry,' I said in response to her questioning look. 'I couldn't help overhearing. I'm Philly Barker, and this is my friend Robbie Dawkins.'

'Florrie Miller,' she replied. 'And aye, she passed a while back.'

'She must have been a good age?'

'Ninety-four,' said Florrie, 'and she still had all her faculties too. Proper sharp Peggy was.' She narrowed her eyes at me. 'Did you know her?'

'No,' I said. Robbie picked up our drinks from the bar, and we shifted away to allow the next patron space. 'But I bought some things of hers too, and that was what they stole in my break-in.'

Before Florrie could say anything to that, I added, 'You're not going to manage those crutches and your pint glass in this crush. If you lead the way, I'll bring your drink to the table.'

'That would be much appreciated.' Before she set off, she asked, 'I think I saw you bidding at the auction. You bought the letterbox, didn't you?'

'I did, and the painting of Whitby, plus a few other things. I was wondering if I could chat with you about Peggy. Maybe after trivia?' I placed the glass of beer on the table she was sitting at, her friends too busy arguing over a disputed answer to notice.

She nodded slowly, 'Aye. I'll come and find you.'

I touched her arm briefly. 'Thank you. I appreciate that.'

Chapter Twenty

Our team ended up coming a respectable second in the trivia competition. Given that the team from Chipwell Barn Antiques were usually way down the leader board, Ambrose and Eugene were beside themselves.

'Proper chuffed I am,' said Ambrose, scrounging around in the box of chocolates we'd won for second place to pick out his favourite.

'You'll have to be on our team every year, Robbie,' said Eugene.

We didn't have to wait long after they left for Florrie to find us. 'Mind I don't have long,' she said. 'I don't want my lift leaving without me.'

'You certainly don't,' said Robbie. 'Can I get you another beer?'

'Don't mind if I do,' she said, waiting for Robbie to pull the chair out from under the table.

As she sat down and made herself comfortable, I took the chance to take in her appearance. Her age I put at somewhere north of seventy, and she had the ruddy complexion of a woman who'd spent plenty of time outdoors in all weather. The lines in her face, however, were lines from smiles and laughter, memories largely, I assumed, of good times, not bad.

'I'm so sorry you lost your painting,' I said. 'It must've meant a lot to you.'

'Aye,' she said simply. 'It's been hanging in Peggy's front room for as long as I can remember. That and the one you bought – the Whitby one.'

'They must hold bitter-sweet memories for you. You knew Peggy for a while?'

'Ta.' Florrie acknowledged the pint Robbie placed on the table in front of her. 'Peggy married my Uncle Barry, and I used to stay with them on the holidays. After my uncle passed away – about twenty years ago now – I'd still visit Peggy as often as I could. She used to say those paintings and the boxes – your letterbox and another fancy one – were given to her by someone she loved very much. I always thought it was my uncle, but in the last few years, I realised it probably wasn't.'

'Did she talk much about the boxes?' I asked.

'Aye. Towards the end. Your letterbox was where she and her lover – Johnny, she called him – left messages for each other. "They still hold my secrets," she'd said once. "Them and my paintings."' Florrie smiled wistfully. 'I always wondered what secrets she was talking about – presumed it was the name of her lover.' She turned her gaze on me.

'Why are you asking these questions?'

I glanced across at Robbie who nodded slightly. 'Because I found some photos in my letterbox before it was stolen – and another document. The person who broke into my stall and the Ainsworth's house – and yours too, I think – were looking for them.'

'I see,' she said slowly. 'So it's the bairn you'd be wanting to know about, then?'

I let out the breath I'd been holding. 'Yes. Did Peggy tell you about the baby?'

'Only in the last few months or so before she died. She'd been trying to find him, you see. The bairn, that is. She said it was the only regret she had in her life, that she'd had to let him go. She was, she said, a slip of a thing back then and hid her pregnancy for months. When she couldn't hide it anymore, she went away to have the bairn and then, a few weeks later, came back to work.'

'She was from Cornwall originally, wasn't she?' I asked.

'She was. How did you know that?'

'One of the books I bought was from Cornwall, and the inscription implied it was home,' I explained.

'Yes. When war broke out, she came up here – her parents were worried about keeping her safe. The housekeeper at Chipwell Hall was an aunt and took her in. When she was old enough, she went to work at the hall too,' said Florrie. 'Even though Sir Antony was only sixteen when she left to marry my uncle, he always made sure she received a Christmas card from the hall, and he came to visit her from time to time – even when she was in the nursing home.'

Robbie's head jerked up, and my breath quickened, but I fought to keep the surprise from showing on my face. 'That's nice of him. Where was she living?'

Florrie named an aged care home on the outskirts of York.

'Did Peggy go to Cornwall to have the baby?' I asked, bringing the subject back on track.

She shook her head. 'No, I don't believe any of her family knew anything about the baby, although she said she'd told them up at the hall that she was taking a trip to see her family.'

'She was fortunate they kept her job open for her,' I mused.

'Oh, they didn't,' said Florrie with vehemence. 'Sir Antony's grandfather was a mean old bugger. But when she came back, one of the girls had just gone off to get married, so Peggy took her job.'

'You say she was looking for the baby,' said Robbie, who'd been quietly taking notes until now.

'Yes. I have the impression she found him, too – not that she had the chance to say as much to me. She'd done one of those DNA test things, and it had brought up a match – not a son, mind you, but a close relative.'

'She must've been sharp if she could work her way around the websites for those things,' said Robbie. 'I know

I'd have problems with it.'

'Our Janet bought me one for my birthday, and when I told Peggy about how it brought up a cousin I hadn't heard from in years, Peggy asked me if I'd help her do it. She hoped that maybe her boy had done a test, hoping to find her. So we did one. She said someone at the home was helping her with the emails and the like – she'd asked me, but I can't make head nor tail of things like that.' Florrie shook her head and made a face. 'Our Janet managed my test for me.'

'Did you know she had some photos of Johnny and baby Jonny hidden in the boxes?' I asked.

'I knew they were hidden somewhere. She showed me the photos and the birth certificate before she went into the home, but I didn't see where she'd got them from. Do you think there was something hidden in my painting too?'

'Possibly. Would Peggy have told anyone else about where they were?'

'I wouldn't have thought so,' said Florrie. 'But if someone at the home was helping her find her son, she might have told them.'

'And you say you think she found him?' Robbie asked.

Florrie drained the last of her pint. 'I think so. The last time I spoke to her, she said she had big news for me. She sounded like she had a new lease on life, something to live for, but then … then the next morning, I received the call to say that she'd passed away suddenly in her sleep.' She dabbed at her eyes with a tissue she pulled from under her bra strap. 'I still miss the old girl.'

I squeezed her hand. 'I'm sorry we've brought it up again for you.'

'Don't you go worrying about that. It's grand to talk to someone who's interested in her. She was lonely over those last few years – outlived everyone, you see. And when she had to go into the home …' Florrie shook her head miserably. 'We didn't have the room, or we would've had her with us. My Frank helped her sell her home, and all the furniture went into storage until she passed and it could be sold too. He was going to get it sold earlier, but she wouldn't agree to it in case she recovered from whatever ailed her. I told her, "Peggy, there's no cure for old age," but she wouldn't be hearing of it.'

Robbie's eyes met mine – so that was why the break-ins happened now. With everything in storage until it went to the saleroom, there would've been no way of accessing the items.

Florrie bent down and reached for her bag. 'I'll have to be going,' she said. 'But if you want to talk to me again about Peggy, here's my number.' She pulled out a pen and wrote her number on the back of a drink coaster.

'Thank you, Florrie. We appreciate everything you've told us,' I said, standing to help her with her crutches. 'Here's my card; call me any time if you think of anything else.'

'One last question, Florrie, if I may,' said Robbie, also standing. 'Who inherits her estate?'

'It's split between her son and me – if her son can be located within twelve months of her passing. Otherwise, it comes to me. Not that it's worth a lot – and Frank and I have no need for it now. But if you can help find him, it would make her dearest wish come true.' She patted my cheek. 'I'll have to come and have a look at your stall, Philly.'

'I'll put the kettle on for you if you do,' I said, taking her elbow to steady her.

As Robbie helped manoeuvre her through the crowd and back to where her party was waiting, I considered what we'd learnt.

'I know it's late,' I said when Robbie made his way back to me, 'but did you want to come for a cuppa before you drive home?'

'Aye.' He rubbed at his chin with his thumb and forefinger. 'Florrie's filled in plenty of gaps, but I have more questions now.'

We collected jackets and made our way out into the night. The drizzle was light, but it was obvious from the wet footpath it had been raining. I slipped on a fallen leaf, Robbie grabbing at my arm to steady me and dropping his hand only as we got to my house. As we opened the gate, an engine started, and a car parked across the road drove off, the headlights disappearing around the bend in the street.

'Did you see anyone get into that car?' Robbie asked, his gaze darting up and down the now-empty street. I shook my head as goosebumps tickled my shoulders. 'No, nor did

I.' When I glanced at him, his mouth was in a tight, straight line. He watched me for a moment before his mouth curved into a reassuring smile. 'Whoever it was has gone now.'

Balthazar greeted us as if we'd been gone for days rather than a few hours and bounded around the kitchen like a puppy, jumping on first me and then Robbie, making sure we didn't have the scent of any other dogs on us, that we hadn't been unfaithful to him while he'd been languishing here on his own.

As the kettle boiled, I pulled two mugs down from the cupboard; Robbie summed up his thoughts.

'I think we can discount Florrie from having anything to do with this,' he said.

'I agree. The solicitor wouldn't need the photos or love letters. They'd be able to order the birth certificate and get the adoption court records unlocked to tell them who the baby was adopted by and under what name. The rest is a matter of locating where he is now.' I popped a couple of brigadeiros onto a side plate – they were yet to make it into work – and turned to face Robbie. 'No, this has to do with proving paternity. I still think it's about Chipwell Hall.'

'So do I.' He nodded, laying his notebook on the bench and flicking it open to a page full of scrawl. 'Everything is pointing towards Sir Antony.'

'Yet, when I met him, I would've thought he'd be the last person to be involved in something like this.' I paused in thought, a tea bag dangling from my hand. 'Paternity is only an issue if Jonny is older than Sir Antony, isn't it? And the title isn't in dispute – the research I've done shows it can usually only be passed to a legitimate male relative, so this has to be about the estate.'

'And that can be separated from the title when it comes to inheritance,' added Robbie. 'If someone thinks they have a claim to it.'

'Surely there's a limited amount of time within which to make a claim, and I'd suggest almost eighty years is long past that.' I poured hot water into the cups and pushed one in Robbie's direction.

'There's no time limit on scandal and family honour, though, and from what you've said, Sir Antony has made it clear that the family name and honour is very important to him.'

'True. You just need to see the money he's spent over the years in tracking down information about his father. How would he feel if he found out that the father he idolised had fathered another child?' I leant against the kitchen bench and cradled my tea mug. 'It's also a coincidence that Peggy died the day after hinting to Florrie that she'd found her son.'

'Yes,' said Robbie grimly. 'Tomorrow, I'm going to pay a visit to the aged care home. I want to know if anyone else visited Peggy in the final day or so – and I want to know what the cause of death was. I'd also like to understand if anyone on staff was helping her with her search.'

'There's nothing I can do, is there?' My shoulders

slumped as I sighed.

Robbie drained his tea and grinned. 'Nowt.' He put his empty mug in the dishwasher. 'I'll be off then. I'll let you know how I go.'

He kissed my cheek, grabbed a brigadeiros and left, holding up a hand in farewell as he walked in the drizzle towards his car. As he pulled out and drove away, I double-checked the doors were locked and armed the security system. From behind the curtain, I peered out into the darkness to see if the car from earlier was back. It wasn't, but even so, Balthazar could sleep on my bed.

Just after midnight, I thought I heard the front gate squeak open and sat upright, my eyes taking a few seconds to become used to the dark and my ears straining for any other noise. Balthazar bolted downstairs barking, so I switched the lights on in my bedroom. Shortly after, the gate squeaked again, and when I peered out of the window, a car was driving away. I couldn't be a hundred percent sure, but I was certain it was the same car that had been outside when we returned from the pub.

Chapter Twenty-One

After a night of tossing and turning and a strong coffee, I called Robbie and told him about my late-night visitor. He was silent for a few seconds and then told me not to worry – which was difficult to do given he sounded concerned too.

'You'll be fine at the barn today, but I'll call by for you this evening, okay?'

I nodded, and then I remembered he couldn't see me nodding, so I said, 'Thanks. I know I'm being a trouble, but I do appreciate it.'

'It's no trouble at all,' he assured me.

I was at work and sharing a cuppa and some marmite and cheese scones – another (successful) experiment of Ginny's – with the team when Stewart phoned.

'Dawkins tells me there's been some trouble at your place,' he said by way of greeting. 'What exactly have you got yourself involved in, Philly?'

I sighed heavily. 'I haven't gotten myself involved in anything, but thanks for your vote of confidence.'

'Well, something is going on. Dawkins told me you had

an intruder last night, and he thought someone had been waiting for you to come home but had scarpered when they saw him.' He paused and then added, 'You seem to be spending a lot of time with him – not that it's any of my business.'

'Balthazar scared whoever it was away,' I said, standing and walking away from the others and back to my stall. 'And no, my friendship with Robbie is none of your business. As for what's going on, I haven't become involved in anything, but I've become *part* of it accidentally. What exactly did Robbie tell you?'

'That he thinks it's to do with some old photos, letters and a birth certificate you found. I said the other week I trust your instincts, Philly, but we've had no solid evidence to follow. The best I can do is have someone do a drive-by a few times during the evening. Dawkins said he's got some leads he's following up today, but I need to know that you're safe.'

'Aww, Stewart, I didn't know you still cared,' I said cynically, pressing the laptop on button harder than necessary.

'Was that necessary? Of course I care!' He puffed out a frustrated sigh. 'Okay, you know the drill – if you feel as though anyone is watching you, change your routine. Don't go into the barn until other people are there, and make sure you're not there on your own in the evenings. Dawkins said he'll see you home.' He paused and then said in a gruff but endearing voice, 'I mean it, Philly – just because we're no longer together doesn't mean I stopped loving you.'

My eyes filled, and I blinked madly to stop the tears from overflowing. I was trying to put a brave face on it, but I'd barely slept last night.

'Thanks, Stewart.'

'Just be safe – and do what Dawkins tells you.'

It was a tour bus day, and even though the weather was closing in outside – with snow forecast for later – we all did steady business.

The pineapple bookends I'd bought the other week sold, as did the jelly moulds from the Harrogate auction, a silver-plated embossed bachelor's tea set that had been on my shelf for almost a month, and the Clarice Cliff teapot and sugar sifter I'd shown Robbie that first day we'd met. That wasn't counting the assorted silver, jewellery and vintage china that went out the door. It was, indeed, a good day.

Bell (who today had resembled a flamboyance of flamingos with a pink feathered stole) had a steady stream of people through her stall all day and collapsed into this week's chair (a wing-backed Edwardian number) with a groan when we finally closed the doors. She flung her long legs over the burgundy arms of the chair and groaned again – in case I hadn't heard her the first time. 'I'm completely jiggered,' she said. 'But' – her smile was self-satisfied – 'that was the best sales day ever. Whoever came up with the idea of contacting the bus tours needs a medal.'

'That would be Ginny,' I said, looking up from my own balancing.

'Well, we should all be thanking her. How did you go?'

'If it isn't a record day, it's certainly close to it,' I said. 'I'm going to need to restock these cabinets before the next tour on Friday, that's for sure.'

Simon wandered in (today's T-shirt was an oldie – Sex Pistols) and looked pointedly at Bell's legs. 'My feet aren't on the upholstery,' she said defensively.

'How attached are you to that chair, Philly?' he asked.

I grinned. 'Sold?'

'Uh-huh. I'll swap it over in the morning. What a day, hey? Anyway, I'm off.'

He didn't quite look at Bell as he said it, but she jumped to her feet and said, 'I may as well go too. See you tomorrow.'

Well! I wasn't sure what was going on there, but something definitely was.

Ginny came in as they left, her eyes following them out. 'What's going on there?' she asked.

'I have no idea.'

'I'm so glad he finally was brave enough to ask her out,' she said. 'He's had a crush on her for years. I'm happy for them.'

'Yeah,' I said, hoping I didn't sound as wistful as I suddenly felt. 'So am I. How's your new man going?'

Pink flushed across her face, matching the colour of

the Christmas jumper she was wearing. 'Really well. In fact' – her cheeks were now fluorescent – 'I spent the weekend with him.'

Impulsively, I stood and hugged her. 'I'm so happy for you, Ginny. When are we going to meet him?'

'I thought I might bring Richard to the Christmas drinks … if that's okay?' she asked hesitantly.

'Of course it's okay.'

'How are you going? Ambrose was telling me how Robbie starred at the trivia contest last night.'

'Yes, he did. I don't think he'll ever get off the team now.'

'And that other business? Is it sorted yet?' Her face grew serious, and I turned away from her and fiddled with the remaining silver in the cabinet.

'Not yet,' I said. 'But Robbie's following up a couple of leads today.'

'Well, let's hope it's over soon.' When I turned back she was glancing at her watch. 'I'd better finish up – we're going for some drinks with Richard's friends tonight.'

'Wow, you are making progress!'

She giggled nervously. 'I just hope they like me.'

'Don't start on with that business again, Virginia Wilding. They'll love you.' I hugged her again. 'You go have yourself a lovely night.' As she turned to leave, I said, 'Have you seen the brothers this afternoon?'

'I looked in on them a while ago. They still had two

customers with them,' she said. Then frowning, she added, 'Come to think on it, I haven't seen them leave, so they might still be there.'

'Hmmm. I might go down and give whoever it is the hurry up.'

'Good idea. I'll see you in the morning.'

Balthazar was snoring loudly on his mat, so I left him to sleep while I popped next door.

The brothers did indeed have customers with them – a man and a woman – and when the woman turned at my entry, my heart fluttered in my chest. It was Cilla Grey.

She smiled, and the action did nothing to calm my nerves. It was a stiff smile, and it chilled me to the bone. Her partner, who had been sitting at Ambrose's desk, stood and held his hand out. 'I don't believe we've met,' he said. 'George Cunningham. Although you've met my … Cilla.' My eyes flew to Ambrose's. He was nodding as if nothing was wrong, as if he'd been expecting me to be overcome with the delight that had to be associated with meeting Sir Antony's son.

I ignored George's hand. 'Presumably, Cilla's partner Tony?'

He shrugged. 'Not strictly a lie – Antony is, after all, my middle name.'

Eugene looked pleased. 'I didn't realise you'd met before,' he said. 'Was that when you were at the hall on Monday?'

I shook my head. 'No. I've never met George before, but they' – I summoned my most benign expression – 'have been very interested in acquiring the items I purchased from the auction the other week.'

'I bet they were,' said Ambrose innocently. 'That Whitby painting was quite the find. I was telling them how you had the presence of mind to remove the frame to check for the signature of the artist.'

Eugene was frowning, picking up on the vibes in the space.

'Very clever indeed,' said George. 'In fact, I think you found something that belongs to me in that frame.'

'And what would that be?' I asked, my mouth dry, my breath coming faster.

He took a step towards me. My breath came faster, but I willed myself to hold my ground. 'You know what it is,' he hissed, eyes narrowing on me. 'And I want it back – and the painting, if it's worth as much as the old man says it is.'

'Given that it – if, indeed, there was something in the back of the painting – never belonged to you in the first place, I don't think you're in a position to ask for it now.' I planted a hand on my hip and forced my eyes to meet and hold his. 'Besides, I bought the painting fairly – it, and its contents, belong to me.'

He was silent for a few seconds, so quiet I swear I could hear my heart beating. 'I don't think you understand.' He looked across at Cilla who had moved between me and the door. 'I want what you have, and I generally get what I want, don't I, honey?'

'You do,' she agreed.

Ambrose's sharp intake of breath cut through the hush. 'I thought this woman was your secretary. Are you saying there's something else going on?'

I almost laughed out loud. Poor Ambrose was more upset at the thought of Sir Antony's son having an extramarital affair than he was of whatever else was going on in the room.

'I know you found the photos and the birth certificate in that piece of old wood we took from here. And I know you found the letters in the back of the painting. And I want you to hand them all to me.'

'Or what?' I asked, standing my ground.

'Your father would be horrified if he knew what you were doing,' blustered Ambrose. 'I'm calling the police.'

Without taking his eyes from me, George said to Ambrose, 'You don't want to do that. Get over there with your brother where I can keep an eye on you.' George waved him across the room with the duelling pistol I hadn't noticed he was holding. It looked like one of the pair displayed in the cabinet closest to Eugene. If it was, what had Eugene told me about it?

Ambrose struggled to his feet and hurried across the room to stand beside Eugene, both casting worried looks in my direction. I swallowed again and wondered how long it would be before Robbie came to pick me up.

George spoke to Ambrose. 'My father would be proud of what I'm doing,' he said. 'I'm protecting the honour of this family.'

'What? By breaking and entering, thumping an old man, robbery with intent?' I counted the offences off on my fingers. 'Yes, I see your point; he'd be so proud.'

In a split second, Cilla came from behind me and slapped my cheek. 'You know nothing,' she hissed.

Horrified, my hand flew to my face, cradling my cheek as if that could make the pain go away. Ambrose and Eugene gasped in unison. I took a deep breath and said, 'I know George is trying to obliterate any evidence of his grandfather's other son – the son who might just be able to contest for a portion of his estate. I also know that the police have spent today looking into the sudden death of one Peggy Bishop – who used to work at Chipwell Hall when she was a girl. I also know that those investigations include checking on the records of anyone who visited Peggy in the last months of her life.' Cilla's eyes flicked from mine to her lover's. 'And I know your name will appear on that list.' That last one came to me in an instant, but I could tell from the way Cilla's spine stiffened that I'd hit the jackpot.

Cilla's hand swept up again. Whack! I rocked back on my feet. This time I tasted the saltiness of blood on my tongue. 'Shut. Up!' she shouted. 'You know nothing!'

I stumbled back and doubled over, my face in my hands,

trying to breathe through the searing pain in my cheek, jaw and chin. Slowly, with clouded vision and sucking in another deep breath, I straightened my back and concentrated my stare at George. 'I know Peggy gave birth to a son – your uncle, your father's half-brother in December 1944. His name was Jonathon Edward, but Peggy called him Jonny, and he was your grandfather's first son; some might say the true heir to the estate. His name was as close to St John's as it could be without naming him as the baby's father.'

I used the back of my finger to wipe some blood from my nose. 'I also know your father prizes family integrity above nearly everything and would be mortified if he knew what you'd done to damage it.' I flung the words at George.

In the corner of the room, Eugene inconspicuously shuffled forward.

George noticed too, swinging his arm and pointing the gun. 'Stay where you are.' When Eugene slunk back, George came closer to me, the gun now hanging in his left hand, and poked his finger into my chest. I took an involuntary step back. What had Eugene told me about that gun? 'And you do as Cilla said and shut up. My father would be proud, you hear? Proud because I'm protecting the family honour.'

'Answer me this,' I said as a drop of blood from my nose landed on my top. 'How did you find out about Jonny?'

He screwed up his nose and flicked a glance at Cilla. 'I don't suppose there's any harm in telling you,' he said. 'I received an email from someone who'd done one of those

DNA tests. It matched with a test I did. My wife bought it for me for a laugh on my last birthday. This person said they thought my father might be their uncle and I could be their cousin. Both of my parents were only children, and I knew I didn't have any cousins, so I ignored it – until they wrote again and said they'd had a match for a possible grandmother and did I know a Margaret Bishop.

'I didn't know the name but mentioned it to my mother, and she remembered my father always sends a Christmas card to a Margaret Bishop who used to work at the hall when he was a boy. She said she'd heard rumours that my grandfather had been friendly with one of the hired help before he went to war, but nothing had ever been proven, and my father refused to hear talk of it. So when she asked me to contact this person and see what I could find out, I agreed.' He shrugged and smiled smugly. 'It was easy to get to know the old lady.'

'Is that where you met Cilla? At the aged care home?' It had been a guess. I was right by the way Cilla's head jerked up.

'Sure was! She was a carer there, and I needed someone on the inside,' he replied with a smarmy grin.

'And before too long, she was happy to do anything you asked?' I didn't wait for an answer. 'What did you tell her – that you'd leave your wife for her? That she'd be the next Lady Cunningham? Imagine that, someone like Cilla Grey in Chipwell Hall.' I dragged a derisive laugh into my voice. To Cilla, I said, 'It was never going to happen, you know. They never leave their wives.'

She went to slap me for the third time. Ambrose and Eugene yelled 'no'. At the same time, George grabbed Cilla's wrist before it connected. 'Don't listen to her, honey; she's trying to rile you up.'

I lifted a shoulder, a 'whatever' look on my face. 'I suppose Peggy wanted to talk about the old days at the hall with you?'

'Constantly.' He rolled his eyes. 'She was going on and on about her dear Johnny. When she told me she had some photos of my grandfather, I told her my father would love to see them some time, and if she told me where they were, I'd see they were given to him. Then she told me about the boy – and I promised her I'd help her look for him.' He paused and smirked at his cleverness. 'Of course I had no intentions of doing either.'

'But she found her son – that must've disrupted your plans,' I threw back at him. George fixed his attention on me – and Cilla's was on him – allowing Eugene to sidle closer to the cabinet that held the other pistol. 'How did that happen?'

'I had to go away for business, and Peggy asked one of the nurses to access the email account Cilla had been monitoring. The person who'd contacted me had sent a message through to her that we hadn't been able to intercept.'

'What I don't understand is why you'd go to such

lengths to get the photos back? What does it matter if your father has a half-brother?'

He waved the gun at me, a weird, almost surprised, look on his face. 'Don't you get it? This half-brother is older than my father, making him the rightful baronet and his son the heir. He might have a claim on the Chipwell estate.' He shook his head in disgust. 'What would happen to my reputation if word got out? I have deals riding on the fact that I'm the next Sir George of Chipwell – I can't afford our family name to be dragged through the mud. Family name is everything to my father – his father's integrity is everything to my father. I need to get rid of anything that can prove otherwise.'

'I thought the baronetcy could only pass to legitimate heirs – so this person might have no claim.'

'You don't know that!' he yelled, spittle catching on his lips.

I took another involuntary step backwards, as if I'd been slapped again. 'What I do know is that in doing this today, you've done far more damage to your family name. All your grandfather did was fall in love. You might've gotten away with the break and enters, but you won't get away with this. What do you intend to do with us? You can't get rid of us.'

'You don't think?' he said, his mouth twisted into a sneer.

'For a few photos and love letters? Hardly.'

For a second, he turned away, seemingly unsure.

'Don't listen to her, honey,' said Cilla. 'Just get what we came for, and let's get out of here.'

George glanced across at her, half acknowledging what she'd said, and then shook his head, his gaze narrowing on me. 'That's enough talking now. It's time to hand over the letters and the photos.' He pointed the gun at my chest, and I remembered what Eugene had told me about the pistols. To have them on display, they had to have been decommissioned. George wasn't to know that though - and nor did I know if he had anything else at his disposal. But the brothers had looked so worried when they saw it ... What if I'd got it wrong?

'Where are they?' he barked – the gun wavered.

My heart pounded as furiously as my head, but George didn't need to know my fear. I shrugged and held open my palms. 'Obviously not on me.'

His eyes slid up and down my body. I took another step backwards and came up against Ambrose's desk. With the gun still aimed at me, George demanded, 'Cilla, check her bag. They'll be in her handbag.'

Balthazar. Oh god. My throat closed at the image of Bally waking to find that woman going through my things. I swallowed hard and attempted to control my breathing and thoughts. Bally barked, and then there was a yelp followed by a thud. The distressing sound distracted George's attention for enough of a split second, allowing me to reach behind for the letter opener that always sat on the desk, accidentally kicking Rochester's cushion in the process. As I stabbed George in the thigh with the letter opener, Rochester leapt up to dig his claws into the other thigh – Rochester's claws being more effective than the tool I'd used. George dropped the gun and screamed, 'You little bitch!' and grabbed for me.

Eugene and Ambrose were on him then and wrestled him to the ground, virtually sitting on him to make sure he couldn't move. Rochester, stretched luxuriantly, sauntered over to where his masters had immobilised George, nonchalantly stretched out a claw, and slid it down George's arm, causing him to scream again. 'Bloody cat!' Rochester looked at him dismissively and retired to his cushion to lick his paws.

I stumbled back and sat heavily on the edge of the desk for the briefest of seconds before rushing into my stall to find Bally – who was sitting obediently beside Ginny, the pair of them guarding Cilla who was cowering in the corner. Ginny had a rolling pin in her hand that she shook at Cilla from time to time.

Bally jumped all over me in grateful welcome. I hugged him hard and ran my fingers across his coat to check for any injury. 'If you've hurt my dog …' I shook my finger at Cilla.

'He's okay,' said Ginny. 'She kicked him, but not hard.' She blanched as she saw the blood on my face. 'Did she do that to you?'

I nodded.

'And the other one?'

'Ambrose is sitting on him,' I said. 'He's not moving far. Rochester got him too.' And then we both laughed because we couldn't help it.

Cilla looked as though she was going to make a run for it, but Ginny waved her rolling pin at her again. 'Don't even think about it.'

Sirens sounded, and within a minute, Robbie burst through my stall door, out of breath. Taking one look at my face, he swore. 'God, Philly!'

'It's okay,' I said, dabbing at the blood with the back of my hand. 'But I hope you have back-up on the way.'

'They've just pulled up,' he said. 'Ginny phoned.'

'I thought you'd left,' I said to her.

'I had, and then I realised I'd forgotten to turn the light off in the kitchen so came back in – and that's when I heard raised voices. I peeked around the corner and saw what was going on so called the police.'

'I'm glad you did,' I said, hugging her quickly.

'I was already on my way here when the call came through,' said Robbie. 'I'd been to the aged care home and found out who'd been visiting Peggy Bishop.'

'George Cunningham,' I said.

'Yes. How did you know?'

'Because he's next door, and Ambrose is sitting on him while Ginny got his lover under control.'

'His lover?'

'Cilla Grey. He told her she'd be the next Lady Cunningham.'

'Of course he did.' Robbie smiled then. It was a smile that said without words how glad he was that I was okay. I nodded once to let him know I understood. 'And you say Ambrose is sitting on George?'

'Uh-huh. Although Eugene might've taken over by now. And Rochester got involved too.'

He hugged me briefly. 'Okay, let's get this mess cleaned up, and you can tell me all about what happened here this afternoon. Ginny, can you grab some ice for Philly's face?'

'Sergeant?' he called to one of his colleagues. 'You can take this one away.'

As the officer walked a handcuffed Cilla out, her head bowed, the fight all out of her, I glanced across at Ginny. 'Oh my god, Ginny – you'll be late for your date.'

'It's okay,' she said. 'I rang and told Richard what was happening, and he's coming here to meet me instead.'

As she said the words, the front door flew open again, and a tall man came tearing through and bundled her into his arms. 'My brave darling,' he crooned and kissed her thoroughly.

When they came up for air, Ginny nestled into his chest, his chin on the top of her head. He said, 'You must be Philly Barker. I'm Richard Harrison, and I've heard so much about you.'

'I'm pleased to meet you too.' And then a delayed

reaction hit me, and suddenly I was light-headed and queasy. I staggered to Simon's wing-back chair, collapsing into it, hanging my head between my knees.

'Philly!' Ginny tore herself from Richard's arms and knelt beside me. 'What can I get you?'

'Ummm, some tea would be lovely, and some ice, but do you mind passing me a tissue first? Simon's sold this chair, and if I get blood on it, he'll kill me.'

Chapter Twenty-Two

Things moved quickly after that. Cilla and George were bundled into police vehicles, and Robbie and his sergeant – a lovely fresh-faced man named Lewis Stanley (yes, I know!) took our statements. Stewart came down to check on proceedings too, and presumably me, and somewhere between it all, I got cleaned up as much as possible.

My blouse had drops of blood I feared wouldn't come out in the wash, and when I leant closer to the mirror, the marks from Cilla's palm were visible. I dabbed some concealer into my red skin and worked some tinted moisturiser across it, and by the time I emerged from the bathroom, even though my cheek still stung like blazes, I looked a lot less damaged.

Balthazar was feeling so brave and important he walked past Rochester with his head and tail in the air, only sidestepping into me when the cat moved his tail menacingly. He seemed unscathed from Cilla's boot to his tummy.

The duelling pistol was bagged as evidence even though Ambrose and Eugene insisted it wouldn't have been able to harm any of us. 'I was more concerned he would use it to hit you, lass,' Ambrose said, pulling me into a comforting hug.

I didn't say that I'd been afraid of that too.

'You should've seen Philly,' Eugene said to Robbie. 'She stood up to him, and yet she must've been terrified, but you wouldn't have known it.'

I shrugged as though I had the situation under control and said to Robbie, 'I knew you were coming to pick me up, so figured I needed to keep him talking until you got here.'

I might've downplayed it for my audience, but I think Robbie knew it was all an act.

'I can't believe it was Sir Antony's son,' said Ambrose. 'And to think I recommended you to him.'

I rubbed comfortingly at his tweed sleeve. 'If it makes you feel better, I don't think Sir Antony had anything to do with it.'

Once Robbie and Lewis left, Ambrose, Eugene and Rochester went home, and Ginny, Richard, Balthazar and I went to the pub. I'd hit the proverbial wall at some point, but adrenaline was still pounding through my veins, and I needed a red wine (or two) to bring me down.

By the time we got there, news of the goings-on at the barn was all everyone was talking about, and when Lynn handed us our drinks, she said, 'This one's on me.'

Robbie joined us at around nine, at which point the other two made their excuses. They left, wrapped around each other with smitten grins. It was lovely to see Ginny so happy, and Richard appeared to be besotted with her.

At the bar, Robbie was speaking to Lynn and Roger while he waited for his pint. The bags under his eyes were more prominent tonight, as were the lines on his forehead. He managed a tired smile for me when he sat down, though. 'It appears you're now a minor celebrity around here,' he said.

'By this time tomorrow, they'll be saying I single-handedly brought them both down,' I chuckled at the craziness of it all.

His smile slipping, he said, 'You did good, Philly. You held firm and kept your head. It could've ended very differently otherwise.'

I shuddered at the thought of the alternative outcome he was referring to. 'It's funny, but when I was in the middle of it, my training came back to me.'

'I'm glad it did,' he said and filled me in on what had happened after the arrests.

Cilla, once she realised George had been using her for his own purposes, soon confessed everything, and after some early lambasting about who he was, and didn't they know who his father was, George, upon finding out that Cilla had thrown him under the proverbial bus, also came clean. A search was underway at Cilla's flat in York, and Robbie was confident they'd find the stolen goods there. 'So even without the confession,' he said, 'we'll have enough to charge them with break and enter, robbery and assault.'

Robbie drank deeply from his pint, wiping his mouth with the back of his hand. 'George was truly worried that Jonathon would have a claim on the estate when his father died – even though the likelihood of that was small. At the crux, though, was family integrity. The deals George was making in the city were on the back of a baronetcy that had seen little scandal – and none in the last couple of hundred years. Even if he had no rights to the title, George didn't want the appearance of an illegitimate son making noise or making a claim that ended up being a costly court case. He lives an expensive lifestyle – most of it funded on debt – and couldn't risk that being compromised.'

'What about Peggy? Did he have anything to do with her death?'

'No. She had a massive stroke in her sleep.'

For some reason, that comforted me. 'Do we know who Jonathon is?' I asked.

'We do. I've been speaking with the solicitor, and he's confirmed it.' He leant in closer to whisper the name, and I choked on my wine.

Robbie insisted on walking me home and checking the house. 'Just in case they'd come here before heading up to the barn,' he said.

While I was waiting for Balthazar to finish his nightly ablutions, I caught Robbie in the middle of a massive yawn. 'Okay, that does it,' I said. 'You're staying here tonight. The guest bed is made up; I'll grab you a towel, and you can make yourself comfortable.'

'But –' he started.

'No arguments, Robbie. I'm about ready to drop, and I'm sure you are too, so I'll show you to your room and see you in the morning.'

I didn't know whether it was the events of the day, the knowledge that everything was resolved quite satisfactorily or that Robbie was a few yards down the hall, but I slept better than I'd done in weeks, only waking when Balthazar decided it was well and truly time that I was up.

When I came downstairs in my dressing gown, Robbie was already showered and dressed and had made tea and toast. 'I hope you don't mind,' he said awkwardly, 'but I helped myself.'

'I'm glad you did,' I said, pouring a cup. 'Did you sleep okay?'

'Out like a light,' he said. 'You?'

'The same.'

Then there was a brief silence, and he said, 'Philly,' and I said, 'Robbie,' and we both laughed.

'This shouldn't be awkward,' I said, leaning back against the counter and blowing on my tea.

'I know.' The tips of his ears were pink. 'Now that this is over …'

'Can we still see each other?' I finished.

He nodded, and that smile I'd come to appreciate

spread across his face.

'I'd like that,' I said.

'So would I.'

We gazed at each other a little stupidly. Then he chuckled and said, 'I'd better be off.'

I leant in and pressed a kiss to his unshaven cheek and thanked him for staying.

He replied with a gentle kissed my cheek and said, 'See you soon, Philly Barker.'

'Be sure that you do Inspector Dawkins.'

When I arrived at work the following morning, Eugene and Ambrose were regaling the others of our exploits the previous evening.

Bell (in a faux fur capelet) and Simon (wearing Black Sabbath) couldn't believe they'd missed out on all the action – although Ginny did mutter something about whether they'd missed out on *all* the action and Simon's face and neck tinged pink. Bell simply shrugged.

It felt almost anticlimactic to open the doors and attend to the business of selling antiques, but that's what we did. The surprise of the day, however, came when Sir Antony strode into my stall just before closing time.

I'd been restocking the cabinet with a couple of Pokerware frames and some pressed glassware goblets and bowls when someone cleared their throat. I turned, the usual smile of greeting on my face, but when Sir Antony stepped forward, my smile fell, and my heart rate increased. As I would've taken a step backwards, he held up a hand in conciliation.

'Please, Philly, I don't blame you for being wary.' When I pinched my lips together and said nothing, he continued. 'I'm here to apologise on behalf of my son even though I know what he did was unforgivable. If it means anything, I want you to know I had no idea what was going on. My wife confirmed to me only this morning that George had spoken to her about it, and she'd asked him to investigate the veracity of the claims.'

'I see,' I murmured, not sure what else I could say.

'She wasn't aware George had taken the actions he did and is as appalled by that as I am.' I kept my doubts about the truth of that comment to myself. He continued, 'As for my daughter-in-law, she's staying in the London house for the time being, but I imagine she'll take him back – he has no money of his own, you see, to make it worth her while to seek a divorce. And that, Philly, is the future of this baronetcy.'

His voice trembled on the last sentence, and he seemed to visibly shrink into his well-worn clothes.

He took a deep breath to collect himself and then said, 'The inspector I was dealing with this morning told me this came about because of some photos of my father and a child Peggy had.'

I nodded and took a few more steadying breaths.

'I know I'm asking a lot and understand they belong to you, but I'm wondering if I might see them.' Hope flared in his pale eyes, even as he appeared to be expecting rejection.

'I tell you what,' I said, reaching out to touch his arm lightly. 'Why don't you sit down, and I'll get a cup of tea and one of Ginny's scones – it's Stilton and blueberry today, and you mightn't think it would work in a scone, but it does.'

'Thank you, dear,' He smiled gratefully and sat in the Victorian mahogany grandfather chair Simon had brought around this morning, looking frail against the buttoned blue and gold upholstery.

When I came back from the kitchen with a tray of tea things and a plate of Ginny's scones, he was still slumped in the chair in the same position I'd left him in, a man who looked as though the wind had been knocked out of him.

I poured tea, and he accepted the milk and sugar with a faint smile. 'Okay,' I said, 'some of these photos are on loan to me, so I can't allow you to have them, but I'm happy for you to look at them and to have them copied.'

'Thank you, Philly,' he said. 'That's kind of you.'

I laid the photos on the desk, and at first, he simply gazed at them. Finally, his hand shaking, he picked up the one of his father and uncle, lightly tracing his father's face with his finger.

'He was very handsome,' I said. 'I can see his likeness in your face too.'

He reached for the one of Peggy and Johnny. 'It's

strange to think of her as a girl.'

'I understand you were very kind to her after she left the hall, and especially after her husband died,' I said.

'It was the right thing after all her years of service to us,' he said simply. 'My grandfather, you see, wasn't a kind man and treated the staff badly. If I'd known then what I know now though …'

'You wouldn't have been so kind?' I suggested, hoping I was wrong.

'No. I would have done so much more for her. She must've felt so alone.' His tone was regretful, and I believed he would've done all he could to make things easier for her.

'I think your uncle helped her as much as he could,' I said. 'The suitcase and hold-all you bought the other week came from Peggy as well.' I paused and said gently, 'Your uncle wasn't trying to have all memories of your father removed; he was simply giving them to someone who missed your father as much as he did.'

He peered at the picture, the ruins of Whitby Abbey in the background. 'They look so happy, don't they? I'm glad he had some happiness – given what happened so soon after these photos were taken.'

'They do. I think they were very much in love. In fact, I have some letters you might like to read.'

He looked up at me, a sheen of moisture across his eyes. 'Thank you, Philly. After George has behaved so badly towards you, I don't deserve your kindness.'

'You're not your son, Sir Antony, and as a grown man, he's responsible for his actions.' I hesitated and then said, 'And what of your half-brother? Have you been told about him?'

His eyes lit up. 'Yes, I have. It's ironic to think that I'd always wanted a brother and didn't know I had one – and him living so close. We played together when we were boys, you know.'

'Here,' I said, handing him the love letters. 'You take these, read them, and your brother might want to read them too.'

He reached across and patted my hand. 'Thank you.'

'You're very welcome. Now I'm going to duck in next door and see if Ambrose and Eugene would like to join us.' When a cloud came over Sir Antony's face, I added, 'Don't worry, they don't hold you responsible for George's actions either.'

He nodded, and I left to find the brothers.

On Sunday evening, Robbie and I attended Tom Ainsworth's birthday and Christmas drinks party.

It was the first time I'd seen Robbie since Thursday morning in my kitchen, and part of me felt more awkward about it than the occasion warranted. After all, we were still friends.

When Robbie arrived to pick me up, he waited longer on the step than he had done previously and looked at his shoes instead of me when I invited him in.

I sighed and decided that one of us needed to break the ice, or this could go on all evening. 'Hey, I didn't miss something and this is a date, did I?'

'What? No, of course not.' His gaze flicked to mine and then away again.

'Phew, you seem so nervous you had me wondering there for a minute,' I said with an exaggerated shake of the head.

His expression lightened when he saw my smile, and he laughed, still somewhat nervously, though.

'How many more times do you think we'll need to have this conversation?' I teased.

'Oh, I'd say until both of us are ready to turn one of these non-dates into an actual date,' he said. A lopsided grin settled on his lips.

'That's what I thought,' I chuckled, and just like that, we were back to what was quickly becoming normal for us.

'Is this an event Balthazar will be attending?' he asked after giving Bally the attention that was his due.

'Well, he was invited, but no. This is one Bally can sit out, and I have the perfect bone to keep him company.'

Beth met us at the door, took our coats and offerings of wine, and said, beaming, 'So much has happened since you were last here.' She took my hand and beckoned us to follow her to where Tom was chatting animatedly with Sir Antony. I greeted each of them with a kiss on the cheek, and both men shook hands with Robbie.

'It's good to see you looking so healthy, Tom. And you too Sir Antony.'

'Tony, please,' insisted Sir Antony.

'Okay, Tony it is.'

'I'll just duck off and get you both a drink,' said Beth, 'and let Tom tell you the good news.'

'I think you both know my brother, Tony,' said Tom, beaming.

'I don't think it's much of a surprise to these two,' said Tony, watching mine and Robbie's expressions carefully.

'Perhaps not,' said Robbie.

'But good news it is nevertheless,' I said, giving them each another kiss. 'Now I see you together, I can see the family resemblance. Did you ever have any idea, Tom?'

'Nowt,' he said. 'Don't get me wrong, I've always known I was adopted; I just didn't know my birth details. I could've but had never worried about it.'

'But didn't you …'

'Know about the DNA match? No. That was all on this one here.' He grabbed the arm of a tawny-haired man who was standing nearby. 'Philly, Robbie, meet my son Joe. He was the one who'd done the test, and when a match came up for a potential cousin – George –'

'I contacted him,' said Joe. 'I thought it would be a surprise to Dad to find out more about his birth family before it was too late. I couldn't believe it when George came up as a match – although he was using an anonymous user ID – and then when Margaret came up as a potential grandparent, well …' he shrugged his shoulders.

'You visited Peggy, or Margaret, didn't you?' asked Robbie. 'Just before she died.'

'I did. She told me her story and about Johnny and the baby, well, Dad, I suppose. She said she had a birth certificate and some photos hidden away that she was unable to access but that she'd see what she could do. I was about to tell Dad, but she died, and I thought I'd better wait.'

'But then the solicitor tracked you down,' Robbie said to Tom.

'And I reached out straight away to Tony,' added Tom.

'Even though it was my son who'd almost killed him,' said Tony.

'To think I knew my mother all those years,' said Tom with a wistful expression on his face. 'And my brother.' He shook his head ruefully. 'At least we've got a chance to get to know each other properly now.'

'I'll drink to that,' said Tony, raising his glass to Tom's.

Chapter Twenty-Three

The following Saturday afternoon, we closed early, and the traders of Chipwell Barn Antiques held our annual Christmas drinks party.

Ginny and I were responsible for the food and had laid it out on the trestle tables that were set up along the centre corridor: tiny cheese and onion scones, the Stilton and blueberry scones that had been such a hit lately, Ginny's famous mini sausage rolls, and Welsh rarebit toasties that I was sure would be a favourite on the lunch menu for the rest of winter. There were pinwheels with cheese and prosciutto, cocktail sausages glazed with cranberry and soy, and potato scones with smoked salmon and crème fraîche.

For those who wanted something sweet, we had plates piled high with chocolate brownies dusted with a sprinkling of icing sugar snow and jewelled with pomegranate seeds, three different shortbreads – one dusted with clove sugar, an orange and cardamom-scented version, and a spicy cheese and sesame biscuit – and some Christmas rocky road.

Bell (in a red faux-fur-lined Santa cape) was on drinks

duty and had pots of mulled wine and a selection of Christmassy coloured cocktails served in martini glasses, as well as some fun mocktails for the drivers and the children. Simon (in a Wizzard T-shirt with a Santa hat) was dealing with the Christmas playlist.

The Proctors (who were back from their buying trip and still amazed at all that had happened while they were gone) had been responsible for the decorations, and in addition to the massive tree that now stood at the end of the barn between their and Simon's stall, they'd strewn the space with tinsel and stars and filled the long trestle tables with different sized jars holding tea lights and candles. The whole effect was of a fairy-light-filled wood.

The Ashtons, both dressed in their best auction-day tweed ensembles, dealt with the invitations and directed operations.

As well as our regular customers, the Ainsworths had come along, Sir Antony and Lady Cunningham were there – the latter unbending by the minute after one of Bell's suspiciously scarlet cocktails – as well as Florrie Miller and her husband. Ginny's Richard was happily helping her to pass around trays of canapés, and as well as Robbie, I'd invited Stewart, Alison, Ryan, Jordan, and their children.

It was later in the afternoon when I brought Balthazar outside – ably assisted by Misty and Ada – to do his doggy business when an old lady wheeling a squeaky pram approached us.

'I'm so sorry to interrupt, dear; it sounds like there's a party going on in there,' she said. 'I was hoping to speak with one of the dealers.'

'I'm sorry,' I said, 'but we're closed this afternoon. We'll be open for business again on Tuesday morning, though.'

'I didn't want to buy anything, dear,' she said. 'I was cleaning out my attic, you see, and found this box of old pottery up there. I have no idea whether it's any good, and I have no use for it, and you have such a reputation for quality goods … Would you like to take a look?'

There was something in the older woman's faded blue eyes that put me on guard. 'Sure,' I said.

With that, she removed the cover from the pram and turned down the blanket to reveal a pair of Clarice Cliff vases and a teapot, all from the Bizarre range.

'Do you mind?' I asked, trying to contain my excitement as I inclined my head towards the pram.

'Of course, dear,' she said, beaming.

I lifted the teapot out by the (hollow) handle and weighed it in my hand. 'These are lovely,' I said. 'Are you sure you want to sell them?'

She shook her head regretfully. 'No, but I'm about to move into an aged care home, and I can't take them with me, can I? So I said to myself, May, why don't you see if you can't get a little money for them?'

'And you said they came from your attic?'

'Aye, they've been up there for years. I have more

besides.'

I smiled at her and laid the teapot beside the vases. To Misty, I said, 'Sweetie, can you get Robbie for me?'

Recipes

It would be remiss of me to end this novel without sharing a few of Philly's and Ginny's recipes. You can, of course, find more from this – and my other novels – at my website brookfordkitchendiaries.wordpress.com.

Parkin

Parkin, sometimes known as Ginger Parkin or Yorkshire Parkin, is a sticky ginger cake – although it's also sold in some parts of the county as a biscuit or cookie.

The recipe differs in colour depending on where in the county you are and whether the recipe is made with golden syrup and caster sugar or a combo of treacle and golden syrup and brown sugar. The latter is a little more crumbly, at least in the first few days after baking, but both versions are lovely. I must confess to being partial to the dark, sticky, treacly version, but I love them all, and this is the one my husband prefers.

It's an absolute doddle to make – pretty much melt and mix. The hardest part is not cutting it on day one – it's one of those cakes that becomes more sticky and less crumbly as it sits and is best if left for a few days (if you can) after baking.

My husband has, however, gotten around this problem by slicing a square in half lengthwise and buttering it to have it with his coffee. Needs must and all that.

Ingredients
- 225 g self-raising flour
- 110 g caster sugar
- 2-3 teaspoons ground ginger (we like it really gingery)
- 1 teaspoon bicarb soda
- 25 g porridge oats or oatmeal (not the quick oats type)
- 1 egg
- 200 ml milk (preferably full cream)
- 55 g butter
- 110 g golden syrup
- 22 cm square cake tin, greased and lined with parchment/baking paper

Method
Preheat the oven to 150°C/300°F/Gas 2.

Sift the flour, ginger and bicarb into a large bowl and stir in the oats and sugar.

In a small pan over low-medium heat, gently melt the butter and syrup, but don't allow it to boil. Set it aside for a minute to cool slightly.

Beat the egg into the milk and set it aside.

Gradually pour the butter and syrup into the flour and stir it through. The mixture will be thick and clumpy and smell like Anzac biscuits. Pour in the eggy milk and stir until the batter is smooth. Don't worry if the batter is looser than you're used to cake batters being. Pour into the lined tin.

Bake for about an hour or until a skewer inserted into the centre of the cake comes out clean and your kitchen smells of Christmas. Depending on your oven, start checking for doneness at around the 45 minute mark.

Spiced Cheese And Sesame Shortbread

These are very moreish and perfect with a drink ... or at any time, really.

The recipe is simple: 100 g each of flour, butter and cheese, toss in a few spices and pulse it in the food processor. Sure, you then need to pop the dough in the fridge for a bit to chill before baking, but that's time you can use to get on with other things.

Ingredients

- 100 g chilled unsalted butter, cubed
- 100 g plain flour
- 1/4 teaspoon cayenne pepper
- a good grating of fresh nutmeg
- 1/2 teaspoon caraway seeds
- 50 g grated cheddar cheese
- 50 g grated parmesan cheese
- 1 teaspoon sesame seeds
- You'll also need a large baking sheet, lined with baking parchment

Method

Put all the ingredients (other than the sesame seeds) into a food processor and pulse until it comes together to form a dough.

Scoop it out onto some baking paper and form it into a log shape, the diameter the size you want your biscuits. I prefer smaller bite-sized biscuits.

Sprinkle over the sesame seeds and roll the log through them until it's coated with the seeds. Wrap in the baking paper and chill in the fridge for an hour. (If you want, you can freeze it for later at this point).

Heat the oven to 180°C (160°C fan).

Remove the log from the fridge and cut it into slices about 8 mm thick. Arrange on the baking tray, leaving about 2 cm between each biscuit, and cook for 10-12 minutes or until golden. If you want to serve these warm with drinks, grate over a sprinkling of fresh parmesan, otherwise allow them to cool and crisp up.

Self-saucing chocolate pudding

This is a simple self-saucing chocolate pudding, one I've been making since I was a kid. I've even made this pudding in a cast-iron Dutch oven in a campfire, and it's tasted amazing.

Ingredients

What you need for the cake
- 1 cup self-raising flour
- 2 tablespoons cocoa powder
- ¾ cup caster sugar
- 80 g butter
- ½ cup milk
- I teaspoon vanilla extract
- 1 egg, lightly beaten

What you need for the sauce
- ¾ cup brown sugar
- 1 tablespoon cocoa powder
- 2 cups boiling water

What you do with it

Preheat the oven to 180°C (160°C fan) and grease a small (1.5 litre) ovenproof dish. I use a small Pyrex.

In a small saucepan, heat butter in milk until melted. Add the vanilla and set it aside to cool a tad.

Sift flour and cocoa into a large bowl, stir in the sugar. Combine the egg, milk, vanilla and cooled butter in a jug and slowly add to the dry ingredients, mixing until well combined and smooth. Spoon into prepared dish.

To make the sauce, sprinkle combined sugar and cocoa over the pudding and carefully pour over the boiling water.

Bake for 40-45 minutes and enjoy it warm with custard or ice cream.

Before you go

If you enjoyed *Philly Barker Investigates* I'd love it if you left a review in the usual places. If you'd like to stay up to date with what Philly gets up to next, you can sign up for my newsletter at my website: https://joannetracey.com

You can also drop by and see me – virtually speaking, of course – here:

My blog: https://andanyways.com
Facebook: https://facebook.com/joannetraceywriter
Instagram: https://instagram.com/jotracey

Acknowledgements

Sometimes I think this part – the writing of the thank yous part – is the hardest stage of the process. Yes, even harder than editing, but not harder than writing the back cover blurb (that *really* is the hardest). So, with a deep breath, here goes.

The usual thanks go to my fabulous editors – Nicola O'Shea and Jo Speirs – for making my words read so much better than they did when I first wrote them. To Nicola, I can't believe this is the ninth (is that right?) book we've worked on together. Here's to many more. To Jo, I apologise for my commas. Thanks also to Keith Stevenson for turning my manuscript into a real book.

The feedback and support from my early reading team is invaluable, so thank you from the bottom of my heart to Pieta, Sue, Deb, Donna and Deborah.

I couldn't do what I do without Grant and Sarah, and this time Grant even helped me with the action scene towards the end – although I had to remind him on numerous occasions that Jason Statham didn't have a starring role,

Philly had no access to an arsenal of weaponry, and there would be no spectacular car chases through the streets of Chipwell. Heavy sighs.

This book, however, wouldn't exist if it weren't for my mother. Mum has always had an interest in antiques, vintage china, and family history, and she's passed that on to me. So this book, more than any other, is – with all my love and thanks – for her.

About the author

Joanne Tracey lives on the Sunshine Coast in Queensland Australia with her husband and a cocker spaniel who takes her role as resident flop-dog and guardian of Jo's office very seriously. An unapologetic daydreamer, eternal optimist, and confirmed morning person, Jo writes contemporary romance, romantic comedy, women's fiction and cosy crime. When she isn't writing or day jobbing, Jo loves baking, reading, long walks along the beach, posting way too many photos of sunrises on Instagram and dreaming of the next destination and the next story.

Jo's life goals (apart from being a world-famous author) are to be an extra on *Midsomer Murders* and to cook her way through Nigella's books.